CLASS NOTES

CLASS NOTES

A Novel by
KATE STIMPSON

Times
BOOKS

Published by TIMES BOOKS, a division of Quadrangle/
The New York Times Book Co., Inc. Three Park Avenue,
New York, N.Y. 10016.

Published simultaneously in Canada by Fitzhenry & White-
side, Ltd., Toronto.

Library of Congress Cataloging in Publication Data

Stimpson, Kate.
  Class notes.
  I. Title.
PZ4.S859Cl   [PS3569.T483]   813'.5'4   78-58172
ISBN 0-8129-0794-9

Manufactured in the United States of America.

For Sue Larson and
Mary Mothersill

CLASS NOTES

1959:
Class Reporter
Susan Crawford Neall
(Mrs. Martin G.)
2901 Locust Avenue
McLean, Virginia

Our Class President, Serena Bell, *reports that people are still talking about our last year's reunion. We showed that 1959 is taking on the world with even more than the usual Harwyn spirit. Serena has changed jobs and is now the subsidiary rights manager for Denton Press. She has the same apartment, though, in the New York building where Edna St. Vincent Millay once lived. Serena also sends news of* Fran Coltron. *Fran has given up her job in Washington where she was an administrative aide in the Justice Department, and has gone on a two-month walking trip through France and Spain.*

Muffy Gallagher Kelly *writes that Tom has been sent on a dream assignment to Southeast Asia for A.I.D. Muffy will be following him soon. "We just want to get Lucinda out of diapers,"* Muffy *says. "She's very bright and lively, a potential Harwyn daughter. Adam loves his little sister and wonders if they'll look 'different' from the other children in Saigon." Muffy tells us that* Cissie Chase *recently married Tom Poston (Branford '57) in a garden wedding at her parents' place in the Berkshires. Tim is doing well with Shearman and Sterling, the New York lawyers. Muffy and* Martha Woodbright, *who is working for her Ph.D. in archaeology at the University of Pennsylvania, attended their old* suite mate. Muffy adds that "Adam got to be the page boy, which made him feel very grown-up."

Another marriage: Naomi Weissburg, *to Benjamin Werner, in her home town of Montevideo. Naomi and Ben will live in Larchmont, while he commutes to his job on Wall Street.*

Rhoda Rendowitz Siegal *sends word that John loves his residency in surgery at Beth Israel Hospital in Chicago. Rhoda has given up her job as a fashion coordinator for Milano's, the Midwest retail store chain. "It's more important for Joshua to have a full-time mother during these early years," she explains. She plans to become active in her neighborhood Citizens for a Better Schools Committee. 1959 seems to care about education.* Amarillo Reich Jacobs *reports that she has been elected to the Kindergarten Council in Lakeville, Texas.*

Important message: Not that much other news has floated in from you out there. I want to hear from you, especially those of you who seem to have disappeared from the face of the earth since graduation. Have you been gold-digging in Alaska? Or raising kids? Or doing important volunteer jobs? Give us a minute and your Class Reporter a line.

Harriet Elizabeth Springer, B.A. '59, has been for five years one of the silent. I have not known what to say, without shame. I am not married, and my job is hardly distinguished, particularly for a graduate of a college that trains people, if they are to have careers, to write scholarly monographs. I help to write a syndicated advice column, "Idealistic Beauty." This still seems odd, because I doubt my physical allure, my sex appeal, my natural being. My hair is like a black hedge; my eyebrows like thick branches snapped from the hedge; my eyes like anxious birds hiding inside. My nose has a ridgebone as big as a thumb, but my mouth is as narrow as the flare of my nostrils. A jaw drops like a plumb line from the junction of earlobes and skull. The body does matter. As one of the competitors of "Idealistic Beauty" told her readers:

> It has been said that beauty is only skin deep,
> but judging from the number of letters in which
> the big Problem is beauty (or lack of it)
> I would say that skin deep is deep enough.

Now, though, may be the time to speak. Boasting is bad, and people resent it. If I were doing "Idealistic Beauty," I would have said, "Bragging is a no-no. People who toot their own horn play sour notes." But I have some achievements to send in to Susan Crawford Neall. "Idealistic Beauty" does not go out under my name, but it earns enough money to buy a share in a summer home on the Hudson River and an American Express card. I have been having an affair with an older, obscurely famous Mexican surrealist. The Mexican finds my job silly enough to be obscurely interesting and my body more gratifying than I might know.

My fable may lack the flare of an apocalyptic fire; the charred whiff of a holocaust; the scent of the golden apples of the sun; the glint of the silver apples of the moon. If it were carved, it would be a plain frieze, without much relief. Yet, it would also show someone who has tried to be successful, and sensual, and good. I have my story, too, and with it, to Susan Crawford Neall, I will send a small contribution to the Alumnae Fund. There are many ways to put on a full-court vanity press.

PART 1

I grew up in the West. People assume that means California, but it was Northville, a lumber and fishing town of twenty thousand built around a bay in the Pacific Northwest. I lived in a brown-shingled house constructed on the side of a hill with a view of the water. On three sides were terraced gardens, a lily pond, rows of evergreens and fruit trees. The two-storied house was comfortable but simple. Nature, not culture, gave the Northwest its primary aesthetics. A mile away, in the five-block downtown business district, was the bank my grandfather Springer had helped to found.

Nearly everyone in Northville was pleased to have settled there for life. I clamored to get out, to a place where people read books before the Reader's Digest *condensed them. My mother and I were sure that education was the way. We were unsure what traits college admissions officers preferred, but we assumed that the more impeccable I was, the better. Only superb grades, high college board scores, extracurricular activities, and a fine character would permit me to enter a liberal arts college that respected the life of the mind, especially that of women. To fumble was an existential folly. I willed the translation of our assumptions into palpable achievements.*

Harriet worried throughout Sophomore World History. Miss Hughes wanted to speak to her after class. What could she have done wrong? Her last assignment, a graph of the iron laws of military history, had gotten an A plus. On the chart were five cannons. Each signified a recent European war. Written on the

3

shells leaving their mouths were the effects of the war that were to become the causes of the next. On the shell of World War II was a black "?."

When the others left, Harriet stood before Margaret Hubbard Hughes. A small woman, her skin was worn and gray, her thinning hair set in rows of rolls the size of tiny hot dogs.

"Harriet," her teeth clicked as she talked, "have you ever done any public speaking?"

"I've done debates and oral reports, and I've read the lesson in Sunday school."

"Did you like it?"

"I thought it was interesting." A white lie. Debate scared her. The risk of loss was too immediate.

"As you may know," Miss Hughes caressed her blotter, "I am in charge of debate at Northville High, and of our public speaking contests. Each year the state system sponsors an important competition. The person who wins the school contest goes to the Nookagillish County contest, then to the Northwest region contest, then to the Washington State contest. Northville, I must add, has never won a county contest, though Northville is our county seat." She sounded desolate. Her fingers clasped together.

"That's too bad."

"Exactly. However, I think this year we have a golden opportunity. I want you to enter. An intelligent girl from a family like yours ought to do well."

"But I've never done any formal public speaking."

"I think you have the capacity to learn. This year the subject is to be 'The Pacific Northwest and Its Trees.' The Continental Lumber Company has donated the prizes. Each speech will last fifteen minutes. I already talked to your mother earlier this morning to urge you to enter. She thought it was a splendid idea."

"I can try," Harriet said. She saw her obedient self, in blue-and-green plaid imitation kilt, reflected in Miss Hughes' tinted rimless glasses.

"I am sure you will. Now you must hurry along to algebra."

That weekend Harriet went to the library. Reluctantly, she returned Tallulah Bankhead's autobiography. She had read it three times. Tallulah Bankhead was less beautiful than Elizabeth Taylor, but, more brilliant and urbane. Every Sunday afternoon Harriet listened on her radio to *The Big Show*. "Dahling," Tallulah, mistress of ceremonies, would growl deeply to Ethel Barrymore, "Dahling, you're so mahvelous. Did you know that I had three faucets on my bathtub? Hot, cold, and gin." Oh, New York sophistication. Now, soberly, Harriet looked up trees, forests, lumber products, and Washington State in the card catalog of the Northville Town Library. She learned:

> True, in the past, men, overwhelmed by the bounty of nature, cut trees and did not replace them. But modern methods of conservation, which the timber industry has pioneered, have replaced the unfortunate, but understandable, practices of the past.

The Northville High School speech competition was in November. If it had been a football game, a pep rally would have preceded it. The school would have gathered in the gym. The Rally Club Drill Squad would have pounded in formation on the varnished floor. The principal, coach, and cheerleaders would have led one thousand students in the school hymn.

> Good old Northville, dear old Northville,
> We want to see you win,
> You're our school, beloved school,
> As close as any kin,
> Rah, rah, rah.

But it was a public speaking contest. Scattered throughout the school auditorium were the judges: the principal, a Methodist minister, and a language arts teacher from Seattle.

The last contestant to speak, Harriet waited in the first row. She wore the costume she and her mother had planned: pink wool cardigan sweater; gray flared flannel skirt; pink wool stockings; clean saddle shoes; a pink-and-gray silk scarf, ends pointing toward each of her small, discreet breasts. In her mind the transcript of her speech unrolled. Then, her turn. All five feet seven inches erect, she walked to the podium. She faced the dark air of the auditorium, hers to enrich and vivify, with dignity, and began:

Ladies and Gentlemen:

I stand before you as someone who will inherit the future. I care about the political and economic and spiritual health of my

5

state and of my fellow citizens. I also care about beauty, about the waters, the mountains, and the forests of the Pacific Northwest. What symbolizes the political freedom, the economic vitality, the spiritual wonder, and the natural beauty of our state? Ladies and gentlemen, the tree.

Done, she thanked her auditors. She walked past the American flag, down the steps at stage left. Miss Hughes patted the seat next to her. "Sit here, dear," she whispered. "I hope you win." Harriet, unable to watch the judges huddling in the orchestra pit, began to murmur her speech to herself again. She had finished only the introduction when the dark, thick, balding principal mounted the stage. "I am pleased to announce," he said to the space before him, "that the Northville winner of the Washington State High School System Speaking Contest for this year is," he paused dramatically, "Harriet Elizabeth Springer, Class of '55."

"Oh," gasped Miss Hughes, "I'm so glad," as Harriet, conscious of her obligations, arose to shake the judges' hands.

Harriet was, in general, conscious of her obligations. In her world, people attended to their duties, even if it ruptured their desires and their games. In 1942, when Harriet was five, Big George Springer, her banker father, put country before family and went to war. His three children dressed up for his farewell dinner. Georgie, the oldest, in his suit. Harriet, the middle, in a dress, hair brushed into long, plump sausage curls. Anne, the youngest, in a dress like Harriet's, the family's pretty darling.

Before dinner, Big George and his reserved, unswerving father sat in tweed-upholstered chairs at the end of the living room that overlooked Northville Bay.

"I'll keep things going in the bank, son," Grandfather Springer promised. "I'll see to it that your seat is warm when you get back."

"I've got to go. You know that, Dad."

"I know."

Harriet crawled through the dining room to the kitchen. Her mother, stirring gravy, was talking to her mother, Grandmother Yates. "What if he doesn't come home? What if he doesn't come back? How am I supposed to bring up a boy and two little girls

6

alone?" Eleanor Springer's voice frightened Harriet. She loved her father. She took showers with him, watched him shave, stirred his lather, wore his ties, and longed to be like him and open the doors of the bank's steel vault.

"You'll do what you must," said her Grandmother Yates. "You always have."

After dinner, without tears, the family lined up on the sidewalk to wave as the car taking Big George to the Army base U-turned down the hill. Harriet saluted with one hand and hung on to her Grandfather Springer with the other. That night she saw her mother through the half-opened door of her parents' half-empty bedroom. Her mother, in a nightgown, was at the window, twisting her wedding ring, crying. Harriet wanted to escape, to find the latest copy of *Life,* to read news from the war zones. Her mother saw her. "Come here," she called. "Come here. I need you. There's only us now. Stay close to me." Harriet and her mother had clung together, the mother's tears matting the child's hair, while the child, initially reluctant because the mother seemed so fierce, closed in, to protect and to possess the fierceness for herself.

During the war her mother grew until she defined the contours of her children's world. She led them in burnishing their father's memory. Each morning they put a fresh flower in front of the picture of him in dress uniform. Each night she wrote to him. Each Sunday she supervised the children's weekly V-mail letter to him. In his absence she never betrayed him, but in that absence she became the children's presence. Dutiful and dramatic, she cared for and entertained them. Despite her irresistibility, the war, for the children, was still a trauma that was not a physical blow; a pain that was not bodily anguish. Harriet had to learn her great images of heroism and beauty from its suffering and blood.

In 1943, a year after her father left, her Uncle Charles spent a day of leave at home. Her mother's younger brother, he was an officer in the Naval Air Corps. Harriet hoped he would fly P-38's, her favorite plane. She waited for him in the kitchen, standing at attention, the butt of her wooden rifle at parade rest on the linoleum floor. Then the swinging door between the dining room and the kitchen opened. First, her soft, silvery Grandmother Yates. After her, a strange woman entered the stream

7

of northwestern light that flowed through the kitchen windows and transformed it. Glossier than Eleanor Springer's, her hair hung to her tanned shoulders. She wore makeup, but she was not cheap, though Eleanor said that people who put on cosmetics tended to be. She dressed like a gypsy: gold hoop earrings; white blouse with puffed sleeves; a flaring, dark blue skirt; white sandals. But her exotic loveliness transcended gypsy garlic, the creak of wagons, the muck of tea leaves. Finally, his hand on her back, her uncle, taller than her father, tanned, too; dressed in a white uniform with gold epaulets.

"Sis, I want you to meet Vivian Clare." Her uncle's voice was bold, tender, proud. Harriet was introduced. Miss Clare spoke to her. "Your uncle says that you can read whole chapters of *Little Women* already, and you're only in the third grade. I bet Jo is your favorite, isn't she?" Thrilled at being known, Harriet dropped her rifle; shook her head, first in negation, then in assent, and buried it in her hands.

Miss Clare sat on the white, metal kitchen stool. A dark rose among the vegetables. "I'm glad Charles wanted to bring me to Northville," she said. "I've heard so much about you."

"We only have forty-eight more hours before my leave is up," Charles said.

They had iced tea and Kool-Aid in the side yard. Charles and Miss Clare sat next to each other in canvas lawn chairs. Sun, filtering through the large leaves of the grape arbor, touched, but did not burn off, the silky gauze of secrets, of eros and of sacrifice, that hung around them. Harriet wanted to have them both: Charles, the cool strong flesh of the just warrior; Miss Clare, the warm charitable flesh of beauty. A god and goddess, within their world, before their departure for private rooms and public battle-fronts.

The next week Grandfather Springer and Aunt Agnes brought an Agnes relative to tea. Priscilla, from Bend, Oregon, her beige hair in soft cylinders. Demure pink lipstick to match her suit. "I'm going to work as a secretary in an insurance office," she said. Harriet picked up a stick from the ground and hit her. Her mother screamed at her to apologize. She would not and was sent to her room. Endurable punishment for punishing a woman who was not Vivian Clare but sat in her chair.

The glamour of Charles, of Mars, was fixed the next year.

Eleanor Springer made one exception to her brain-stitching rule and allowed Harriet to go to a movie. With her Grandmother Yates she walked through a carpeted lobby, up red stairs, to balcony seats in the Patriot Theater. As the ushers, high school boys and older women, walked up and down concrete aisles, their feet crunched on popcorn, gum wrappers, and candy apple sticks. But Harriet sat as regally as brave Princess Elizabeth or Princess Margaret Rose of England reviewing troops under wartime hardship.

She knew several shades of darkness: the night outside of a car; the interior of caves; the cavity inside tree stumps; the bathtub in which she sat, curtains drawn, after the family was asleep, spraying water between her legs. However, the darkness of the theater was hazy, beckoning, and new. Then Harriet heard the music of ecstasy, the trumpets and drums of the Navy hymn. On the screen a painted scroll unrolled. In the first dark days of war gallant men fought bravely against the onslaught of the Oriental enemy. She knew about the Japs. In waterfront parks around Northville foxholes were dug among the roots of the reddish, peeling madrona trees. She sat in them, with her wooden gun, scanning the glittering blue inlets and bays of Puget Sound; watching for the thin, snaky head of a submarine periscope that would signal their invasion. Beasts, eyes aglint with glee behind round, gold-rimmed glasses. Madmen, who used swords to behead civilians and to rape wives and nurses.

Now Gary Cooper, a Navy doctor, as tall as her Uncle Charles, led wounded American boys through hordes of Japs, over fields of pain, to safety. Good men died, teeth clenched, so their buddies could be free. Gary Cooper lived, to salute his superiors. Medals for Gary Cooper. Harriet left, as reluctantly as a polio victim might an iron lung. At dinner she was quiet.

"Cat got your tongue?" her brother asked.

She glowered at her blue-and-white china plate. He would never be as valiant as Uncle Charles, or Gary Cooper.

The family celebrated the end of the war with people at the bank. Grandfather Springer held out bags of confetti for the employees as if they were communion cups. They prayed, too, at church at a special thanksgiving service. Eleanor Springer erased the blackboard on which she had kept count of the war dead, Americans and their allies. Then the family drove to

9

Union Station in Seattle to greet Captain George Baxter Springer. The living were coming home. The architecture of the depot imitated ancient temples, but its builders had mastered tools the ancient gods had never seen: wooden ties, steel rails, rights-of-way through thousands of miles of grasses, gullies, trees, and stone. In his dress uniform Big George walked through a metal gate. "I'm back," he said. They surrounded him, like water glittering on the body of a leaping dolphin. They swept through the terminal to the car. "Will you drive?" his wife asked. Holding out the keys. "Not tonight," he said, "We can wait until tomorrow to get things back to normal."

He climbed into the back seat of the Buick, the children rolling about him. "I've been in Texas, Virginia, and England," he said. "I almost got shipped to Germany. But nothing, nothing, is as good as the Pacific Northwest. It's God's country."

"It's time you got home, son," Grandfather Springer said from the front seat.

"The worst thing that happened to me in the war," Big George continued, as if he were looking at a skull, "the worst thing was when some damn fool broke open my footlocker and stole the pictures of my wife and kids. He could have taken my razor, or my wallet, or some of my extra food, or some of the presents from home, but he took the pictures of my wife and kids."

Harriet, on his lap, looked up at the flesh of his jaw and neck. A tremor of dislike divided her. Other men had been killed; felt shrapnel explode in their arms and hearts; run from foxhole to foxhole across asphalt fields in Sicily or along sandy beaches on Pacific islands so hot that their boots rotted overnight. Heroic chaplains, crosses dangling from their sweaty necks, had helped to shoot down enemy planes as their own mortally wounded bombers plunged through flak and searchlights to a foreign grave. But this man, to whom she had written a V-letter every Sunday night, for whom she had bought stamps for war bonds every Wednesday at school, this man, a staff officer, had hardly been under fire. The worst thing that had happened to him was to have his pictures stolen. Where were his medals? His scars?

Then a quake of guilt for her disloyalty broke her. She pushed against his large, warm body. Her hand rubbed his cheek, outlined his mouth, pulled at his lower lip. As if she were not there, he talked on, "I don't know, Dad, how I escaped having to put

10

more time in with the Occupation Forces in Germany. Maybe a foul-up was on my side this time." Her hand left him. She crawled off his lap, over her brother, to seek, bereft, her Grandmother Yates. After they parked in their garage, George Springer toured his home. His wife and mother-in-law put roast beef, salads, Parker House rolls, fresh pie on the table. During the feast, Harriet knelt with her plate beneath the end table in the living room where she hoarded her presents at Christmas. Nothing was filling the space between her and the dark-haired, jovial man who was eating, ravishing the food, laughing.

Then Grandfather Springer and his second wife, Aunt Agnes, went to their own house; Grandmother Yates to the guest room on the first floor next to the playroom; Georgie and Anne upstairs to bed. Harriet, prowling, pushed open the swinging door between dining room and kitchen. There, as if they wanted to devour each other, her parents were kissing. Her father bent over her mother, her mother arched back and yet against him. Her mother, the power and boundary of the child's world, was being overwhelmed, submitting, yearning. Harriet let the door swing shut. In pajamas, she stood in the dining room. The gold oak table and chairs, the gold oak sideboard, the gold rugs—these objects were as familiar as her tongue. But a weapon, as sharp as a bayonet, had separated her from her parents, and a barrier, as tough as a bunker, was between her and her mother tonight.

Two weeks after Harriet's triumph in the high school speaking contest, her mother chauffeured her and Miss Hughes thirty miles to Mountainview Consolidated High for the Nookagillish County round. Harriet warily inspected the home economics classroom in which the competition was slated. Next to a temporary podium was a baby bathinette, a naked rubber doll and a pile of diapers sprawled on its covers. Her opponents seemed gawky: two boys in white shirts; two girls in skirts and sweaters of materials harsher than her own.

She was the fourth to speak. Before she began, she patted the bathinette with public confidence. "Maybe the baby here is only a doll," she said, "but it's good to see that people care about the future." A judge made a note in the poise column. Gladdened, she straightened her shoulders.

11

Ladies and Gentlemen:

I stand before you as someone who will inherit the future. I care about the political and economic and spiritual health of my state and of my fellow citizens. I also care about beauty, about the waters, the mountains, and the forests of the Pacific Northwest. What symbolizes the political freedom, the economic vitality, the spiritual wonder, and the natural beauty of our state? Ladies and gentlemen, the tree.

Once more, she won. She ticked it off. In the car Miss Hughes was jubilant. "The regionals are next," she said. "I've never been able to attend the regionals with one of my students before. What a glorious opportunity; for you, too, Harriet."

Because she was a county champion, men's clubs invited Harriet to speak. The Lions met Wednesday, each wearing a blue overseas cap, in Spot's American Restaurant. "Here she is," the Chief Lion announced, "the little lady who has won this year's Nookagillish County High School Speaking Championship. Let's give the little lady one of our biggest roars. Let's show her how glad we are to have her in our den."

The dullness of the animal cry was a warning. With sinking jauntiness Harriet clasped the lectern. "Gentlemen," she improvised, "I am glad to be the only lady here today. I suppose I will never get to be a Lion, but I still want to stand here before you as someone who will inherit the future." The men tipped their chairs back, pulled their caps down, and nodded. To arouse them, slack, bored, and soggy as they were, she compelled her reserves of audacious earnestness:

Thus it is our pleasure to keep the Pacific Northwest green. The careless cigarette in a shaded forest will bring ashes and charred stumps. We will be unhappy. It is also our life to keep the Pacific Northwest green. To replenish our forests, after they have given us our paper and our pulp, is our sacred duty, a sacred duty to the wonderful trees and to ourselves. When we cut them, they give us shelter and income. They make us special among the people of America. They give us life. When we cut a tree, we can count the rings of its life in the stump. But do we count the rings of our life? Gentlemen of the Lions Club of Northville, we should. Keep the Pacific Northwest green.

12

"Keep it green, team," a Lion shouted. She stood, taking in the leftover applause; below her on the table was half a portion of apple pie a la mode a la Spot's.

The next Tuesday, Harriet was to appear before Rotary. Her father's club, Rotarians were a cut above the Lions: optha-malogists, not opticians; store owners, not managers; mayors, not assistant comptrollers; pulp mill president, not personnel director. On Monday night Harriet sat with her mother on her parents' bed. Four posters, like young tree trunks stripped of branches and stained, guarded them.

"What if they don't like me?" Harriet worried.

"Now, darling, you just perform as well as you can. Daddy's friends will be there, so you do your best."

The next day, she took the bus to the Hapsburg Hotel. The cleaner had delivered the gray skirt and scarf; her mother had washed the pink sweater; she had polished the saddle shoes. Her father, thumbs in vest pocket, was waiting for her at the news-paper and cigar stand. He put his arm around her. "Eddie," he said expansively to the man with him, "I'd like you to meet my oldest girl. Harriet, shake hands with Mr. Rivers. He's in charge of this shindig today."

"You're a sweetheart to come to talk to us," Mr. Rivers said. His badge said LUMBER MANUFACTURER. "We old men need a pretty girl to lift us out of the doldrums." A pretty girl. She quivered with shy, nervous pleasure. He escorted her to the head table, pulled out her chair, rearranged the bowls of flowers so that one was in front of her. "We old men really do need you," he repeated. "A breath of fresh air."

"I don't think you're so old."

"You're a sweetheart to say so, but we are. We get stodgier and stodgier, while the world goes by, and other people get to go out and raise hell."

His blond hair, receding, had left fuzz, as a wave deposits spume on sand. His body was soft. However, his face was mobile, good-humored. If easily bored, easily gratified. He dressed more sportily than other men at the head table—his jacket and pants did not match. "It would be fun to have a drink," he said to Harriet.

"My parents don't believe in it, particularly for us kids."

"I'll have to be careful, I'll lead you astray." He winked. "Ready to do your turn? I know you'll do just fine. Pretty girls never let me down."

She sat suspended in tension while President Hal opened the meeting; read greetings from Northville's sister club in Canada; led the singing of "Happy Birthday" for all members born in November; and, finally, intoned: "Today we have a real treat in store for us. Our banker's girl, our own George Springer's oldest gal, has just won the Nookagillish County High School Speaking Championship. She's the best of all the Nookagillish students for the year, but then we wouldn't expect anything less from George and his consort, Eleanor." The president looked at his notes. "Her subject is 'The Pacific Northwest and Its Trees.' She's a lovely young lady. I'll bet that George and Eleanor are real proud of her. Fellow Rotarians, here she is, Harriet Elizabeth Springer, a Rotary child."

Applause ascended and steadied her. "Mr. President, Mr. Program Chairman, Gentlemen of the Rotary Club, and Daddy." They laughed at her joke. As she spoke, their interest supported and exalted her, until she felt like a warrior, defending them, their state, their nature. Hand raised, as if it held an invisible sword toward the chandelier, she rang out:

Trees, trees make us special among the peoples of America. They give us life. When we cut a tree, we can count the rings of its life in the stump. But do we count the rings of our life? Gentlemen of the Rotary, we should. Gentlemen of the Rotary, we must. Gentlemen of the Rotary, we will. Keep the Pacific Northwest green. I beg you, keep the Pacific Northwest green.

Richly, gratifyingly, three hundred palms beat against each other. "That was a real inspiration," President Hal said. "How did Big George get a girl like you?" "Pretty girls never let me down," Eddie Rivers said. Big George even took her to the bus back to school. He walked confidently, part of the mortar of the town. Now she was a daughter worthy of him. In journalism class Mr. Durksteiner sat on her table. He plunged the brush in and out of a bottle of rubber cement. "Darn it, Harriet," he sighed, "the boys around here are crazy. If I were a kid again, I'd be chasing after you all the time." Then he lumbered back to his desk. Harriet knew it was wrong to gloat over her victories, over her performance, over the attention of men, but relishing them she was very happy.

When Harriet was nine, Eleanor Springer was relieved when Master George and Miss Harriet were invited to the first North-ville Young People's Subscription Dance. Her children were clearly marked to float securely above the Nookagillish Indians on their reservation twenty miles away; above the quarrelsome Forrests, who lived across the street on County Assistance; even above her own childhood. Big George Springer might have been included in a Young People's Subscription Dance but not an Eleanor Yates.

Big George, a year back from the Army, drove his two oldest to the Hapsburg Hotel. "Got your invitation, honey?" He looked down at the little girl next to him on the front seat. She was in her best coat, white gloves, black patent leather Mary Janes, short white socks. She was hefty. Going through an ugly duckling stage. Too bad.

"Mommy said we didn't have to bring them. Mommy said our names would be at the door."

"Okay, if that's what Mommy says." He disliked the fact that his older daughter used his wife's words to correct him. Being henpecked was one thing, being chickpecked was another. However, he was reluctant to take his older daughter on. Other things were easier. He left Georgie and Harriet at the hotel ballroom. Crystal chandeliers, with flame-shaped electric bulbs, hung stiffly from the ceiling. At the far end was a red velvet backdrop and a wooden platform. There stood a woman in an evening gown. A man in evening dress was at a grand piano.

"Look how dressed up everyone is," Olivia Kasper whispered to Harriet. Olivia, one of Harriet's best friends, was the popular beauty of her class.

"This is fancier than I expected," Harriet said, in some awe.

"Good evening, boys and girls," the woman in the evening gown spoke with impressive aplomb. "I am Madame Hastings."

The parents who were that evening's chaperones nodded at each other. Madame Hastings had been hired from the most reputable and expensive dance academy in Seattle.

"Tonight, at our first subscription dance, we are going to learn

15

how gentlemen ask ladies for a dance and how ladies accept their invitation. Boys, when Mr. Ralph begins to play, you will get up. You will walk slowly across the room. Go up to the girl with whom you wish to dance. Then bow, like this. Then say, 'May I have the honor of this dance?' Now, boys, repeat after me, 'May I have the honor of this dance?' "

The boys mumbled shyly.

"Now, boys, keep trying. You ought to be able to do better than that. Girls, when a boy asks you to dance, say, 'Thank you.' Stand up and take his arm. He will crook his arm so you can take it. Then, the both of you will walk onto the dance floor. The boys will be gallant. The girls will be graceful."

"Thank you, thank you, thank you," murmured Harriet. She liked to learn, even when it was not a form of compensation.

Impassively, Mr. Ralph threw before them a loud version of "The Danube Is Blue." The boys struggled up, but then, as if caught in the music's currents, stopped. "Boys, you can't be afraid of the girls, can you?" Madame Hastings taunted. They resumed their forced crossing. Ten feet from the girls, they clotted and swerved toward Olivia. Bobby Green, whose father was the lawyer for the Springers' bank, broke away and reached her first. Defeated, the rest spread out and dribbled toward other girls. Hands clamped to the side of her chair, lips ironed into a smile, Harriet waited until she was the only one left on the side. Then shambling before her was her brother. "Come on, Hairy, Mom said I had to dance with you if nobody else would." Her glove fastened to his sleeve. "Thank you," she said. He sullen, she humbled, they moved across the parquet floor, loathsome partners for the evening.

Later, safe in bed, she took refuge in her radio. A rebroadcast of a state investigative hearing about corruption was baffling but enthralling.

"How could you tell," a legislator asked, "what the man looked like?"

"Because," a witness answered, "I saw his face in the red light over the door."

Why did people laugh?

"I can hear your radio," Anne, her brother's favorite, suddenly whined meanly from her bed next door. "I can hear your radio. How can I sleep if it's so loud?"

16

"You can*not* hear it," Harriet yelled. She jammed the box beneath her pillow.

"I can, too. I can't go to sleep. I'm going to tell Mommy on you."

Harriet leaped up. She pushed open the door between her room and Anne's. Pulling the startled child out of bed, she twisted her legs around the smaller body and began to pound her head against the floor, thumbs against her throat.

"You can*not* hear it, you can't," she whispered viciously.

Anne gagged. In the fuzzy gleam of the night-light, Harriet saw spit drooling from her mouth. "I've killed her," Harriet thought. Dread drove out exultation. She fled back into her room to huddle under her covers and listen for the death rattle.

"I can too hear it," Anne croaked.

"I hate you," Harriet screamed in relief. "I hate you," as the sheets and blankets in her mouth stopped the sound.

During the year of lessons, she hoped that things would change when she got older. She tested her ambition four years later. The Gobbler was a school dance to which girls invited boys, after some strategic planning. With other girls Harriet went after school to the Youth Club, a grimy room between the Fair-Vue Tavern and Mac's Mobile Station. There they danced together to a jukebox until the boys arrived after turnout for sports.

"I think I'll ask Johnny Black to the Gobbler," Darlene LeSueur confessed to Harriet. She was the pudgy, self-assured daughter of a discount drugstore owner. The Springer family did not socialize with the LeSueur family, but Harriet did with Darlene. A wheel, Darlene had power at school.

"I hope Johnny says yes," Harriet encouraged her. She was concentrating on making her crepe-soled saddle shoes synchronize with Darlene's inside a rectangle of dusty light.

"Don't lead so hard," Darlene said perfunctorily. "Are you asking anyone?"

Harriet risked trusting Darlene. "I was thinking of Jake Jablonski."

"Gee, I don't know. He's hard to get."

"Do you think I shouldn't?"

"I didn't say that."

On the bus home Harriet brooded about Jake: taller than she, but stooped; dark, shaggy hair, like hers; mature enough to shave;

and tragic. Though Jake was as good as she in algebra, his father brutally demanded that his son not get too big for his pants: Jake was to stay away from college and toil on the family fishing boat. After dinner she called the Jablonski home before nerve collapsed. "Hi, this is Harriet, Harriet Springer, from school."

"Yeah?"

"Jake, do you know about the Gobbler?"

"Yeah."

"It's only a month away. I was wondering if you would like to go with me. I mean, I think it would be fun if you would go with me."

"No."

"Are you sure?"

"Yes, thanks anyway."

"Well, I just thought I'd ask."

"I guess so."

"Well, I guess I'll see you around school."

"Guess so."

"Well, I guess it's time to say good-bye."

"Guess so."

Harriet stayed home the night of the Gobbler and listened to the cast albums of Broadway musicals. Her mother told her that when she was older the theater would matter more to her than school dances.

One memory—though a guilty, secret one—succored her through such promises and such defeats. When Harriet was a tall, gawky twelve, Olivia Kasper's parents organized a hayride, a class treat. Even Joanne, who was adopted and had B.O., got to go. Olivia was the fourth child, the first daughter, of a passionate marriage. She looked like her mother: tawny hair; high forehead; hooded, gray-green eyes; cheekbones that curved up toward the arc of her eyes. Grown men sought her out to dance at the Country Club on Sunday nights. Despite their friendship, she disturbed Harriet. On Saturday, when they played croquet on a Springer side lawn, Harriet would trap herself staring at Olivia's elegant, bare feet.

In the school parking lot the class regarded each other with a sick, prophetic anguish. For all of them, "hayride" flashed luridly among the signs of their ordinary speech, inseparable from sex.

Yet less than half the boys had had nocturnal emissions. Harriet did not even know the term. Less than half the girls had begun to menstruate. Harriet had not, but her mother had explained it to her some months before. Eleanor had sat at the kitchen table, hands cramped together. She had stared out over Harriet's head. "I have to tell you about something that's going to happen to you soon," she had said grimly, seriously. "You mustn't worry about it. It's very normal. It's called the curse." Harriet had listened carefully to her mother's clinical narrative of the traveling egg, the waiting uterus, their mutual fall, unless she were pregnant, as monthly blood. She realized this would happen to her. Yet, as she often did, she tried to detach herself from her flesh. She had begun to do this as a defense during those painful times when her body seemed unwanted, but she had learned that it helped whenever she thought that any experience of her body could or should not be wholly hers.

"Peewee," Greg Brown yelled at Chuck Wertner, "I heard about your sister Mona. Jerry Andrews blew her up on a hayride with a stick of TNT."

Chuck slugged Greg in the face.

When they climbed in over the steel tail gate of a truck, girls sat on the left, boys on the right. Fresh, thick hay covered the floor. Harriet was next to her friend Betsy Metcalfe. "I wish I were home," Betsy said. Harriet pulled at the cuffs of her blue denim pedal pushers. Rude to tell the truth and agree.

After an hour's ride the truck parked in the clearing at the end of a pitted track at Cedar Bay. Plenty of cover, Harriet thought, if I have to go to the bathroom. A fire was burning on the beach. Hot dogs and buns, mustard and relish, potato salad and carrots, marshmallows and pop, were set out on driftwood planks. Fifty feet away salt water lapped at dark mounds of seaweed, stones, and sand.

Betsy and Harriet ate together. The tines of their wooden forks furrowed the paper plates.

Glenn Davis is younger than Bill Pauley, Jr.," Harriet said firmly.

"How do you know? Your mom only let you go to the movies once in your life."

"I read *Time* and *Life*." No need to mention forbidden *Photoplay* and *Modern Screen*.

"Glenn Davis only looks younger," Betsy said. "He has been to West Point, and in the Army."

"But he is younger. Bill Pauley, Jr., is much older, and all he's ever done is to help his father run a bus business in Florida. That's why Elizabeth Taylor broke her engagement to him and started going steady with Glenn Davis. Last year Elizabeth Taylor got 1,065 invitations to college proms, and she could have married Bill Pauley, Jr., but Glenn Davis is younger, and more famous, and he's done more things himself."

"This is a dumb conversation," Betsy said, "about a dumb subject."

"Star light, star bright, first star I see tonight," Harriet chanted to the darkening air and brightening sky, to deny that she was hurt. Feet crumbling in smokewood, she slipped off the log, to burn her plate in the fire.

She had worshiped Elizabeth Taylor since 1944. She had read about *National Velvet* in *Life* and begged to see it. Her mother's law against movies remained. Frustration only inflamed Harriet's ambition. She would meet the star in person. She took up a vigil in front of the house to watch for cars with California license plates. A talent scout might be driving one. She stayed on the sidewalk until sunsets to the west, over the islands on the mouth of the bay, slashed the sky crimson, purple, pink, orange, and gold. If she were to see a messenger from Hollywood, she would leap high—right arm and left leg extended—and begin to sing. The car would stop. The talent scout would stop. He would ask her to come to Hollywood for a screen test.

"Will I meet Elizabeth Taylor?" She would be as courageous and calm as Elizabeth had been when she took her horse over big jumps in *National Velvet*.

"Anything."

Harriet's test would dazzle M-G-M as Elizabeth Taylor's once had. Then she and Elizabeth would mount black horses and visit the homes of other stars—creatures of pure light and radiant color.

On her way home from school she furtively searched for stories about Elizabeth Taylor in tabooed movie magazines. Then, in an interview in a *Photoplay* on a tin rack in a gloomy grocery, Elizabeth said how grateful she was for fan mail. She read the letters that inundated M-G-M between homework assignments at the

M-G-M school. In perfect cursive, Harriet wrote the British-American beauty who was only a little older than she:

Dear Elizabeth Taylor:

    I have never sent a letter to a movie star before. However, I admire your career very much, and I am sure *National Velvet* is a masterpiece. I would appreciate it if you would write to me and tell me how I might come to California. I would like to talk to you.

                        Sincerely,
                        Harriet Elizabeth Springer

She was sure that Elizabeth would notice the similarity of their names. She mailed the request to M-G-M, Hollywood, California. Her research had turned up neither Elizabeth's home address nor that of the art gallery her father owned.

Two weeks later the postman gave her a brown envelope with a California postmark. She was too excited to open it until she found her mother in the basement. Between two pieces of cardboard, like the filling of a store-bought sandwich, was a glossy $3'' \times 5''$ head shot. Across the lower-right-hand corner was "Best wishes to Harriet from Elizabeth."

"Mommy," close to tears, "there's no letter, just a picture."

Her mother left the canning jars. "But Harriet," she said, as if discovering a miracle, "your name is on it. It was sent to you."

Harriet taped the photograph to the mirror of her dresser. She stared into two faces in the mirror: her swarthy skin, messy hair, big nose, crumpled mouth; Elizabeth Taylor's creamy skin, tossing ringlets, delicate nose, smiling mouth. Aspiring Harriet. Successful Elizabeth.

She supposed that Elizabeth Taylor had never been on a hayride. "Watch out." Terry Neilsen, carrying a board piled with sand, was staggering toward her. In a rush of inertia he threw the sand on the fire, wobbled, and stopped next to her.

"I never thought I'd make it. Old Man Kasper really piled a load on my board."

Terry stuffed his hands into the side pockets of an athlete's leather-and-wool jacket. He was the shortest boy in the class, in the lowest group in reading and arithmetic. He was, though, on

21

the baseball and track teams. "I sure ate a lot, too," he mused. "Seven hot dogs." He spat proudly at the fire struggling against the suffocating sand. Then, to her astonishment, he asked if she wanted to sit next to him on the way home. Voice more casual than her body's lapse into gratitude might suggest, she said yes.

"Let's get into the truck," he said. They climbed over shingle and beach rose and log. In a corner of the truck was Olivia, with smirking, happy Bobby Green. Scattered against the walls were other couples. In the center were singles: Joanne; Jan, the boy with the girl's name; fat Henry, who had wet his pants until fifth grade. Terry led Harriet over the tail gate to a place against the left wall. Sharp ends of hay jabbed into the exposed calf skin between pedal pushers and socks. The discomfort was as trivial as mosquitoes to explorers in a mangrove swamp who think they hear the splashing of the Fountain of Youth behind the next tangled clump of trees.

Mr. Kasper checked to see that everyone was in. "Okay, troops," he shouted, "here we go."

Before they were on the concrete highway, Terry leaned over Harriet. He put his hands on her shoulders and started to push her down. She was stiff, her body a stone tablet of forbidding sexual law. The glum figures in the middle of the truck obscured her vision of Betsy against the wall opposite her with Chuck Wertner. But she saw Olivia and Bobby slide down. If Olivia could do it, the law must be suspended. Holding her jacket so that the hay would not get inside, she cracked the granite of her flesh, and sank down. Terry's tight mouth struck hers, retracted, struck again. She put her left arm around his shoulders. Gradually, his kiss became wetter, more open. She shut her eyes and pressed her fingers against his neckbones.

She was murkily aware that Chuck Wertner was swinging a flashlight around the truck. Then she felt the light on her, as implacable as Terry's body. "That's not nice," she thought, more worried that Terry might stop and not return. Their noses scrunched together, their breathing synchronized, mind and body swerved toward each other.

"Seventy-four, seventy-five, seventy-six," Chuck was counting, "seventy-seven, seventy-eight, seventy-nine. Seventy-nine. Terry and Harriet have just set the record for the longest kiss."

They sat up. "We're pretty good," Terry said proudly for them both. "We're the best." He put his arm around her. To accommodate him, she huddled down. They leaned triumphantly against the corrugated metal wall. Terry even walked her home. She could not tell her mother, who would disapprove of public exhibits of sexuality, but she still knew that she had more than measured up, this once, to the baffling imperatives of femininity.

Still, when the Springer family had dances in the living room, playing records on the phonograph, Big George asked his wife first, then his younger daughter, and, finally, Harriet. By then, her legs were wilting. She was there but last; last but there. One summer morning after the hayride, she was practicing the piano in the living room. Her mother and Grandmother Yates were talking about her in the kitchen. "She's not popular at dances or with boys, but when Mr. Warren took the last set of family pictures, he said he wished the camera could show how good-looking she really is," her mother said. Harriet could not decipher her grandmother's response. Then her mother added: "It doesn't seem to bother her. She's strong. Besides, she's so good at school and at doing things. I want her to get the best education she can. That's the important thing for a girl like her."

To reward her mother for her loyalty, Harriet practiced even louder octave scales, their assault upon the dullish, but demanding, world.

On the day of the Northwest Regional High School Speaking Contest, Miss Hughes lay crying on a cot in the darkened teachers' lounge. Harriet, in her speech costume, sat beside her on a tin chair. "I so much wanted to come." Miss Hughes took off her glasses to wipe her eyes. "I have never had a student go before. But I can't, I can't go with this headache."

"I wish you could." Two-faced Harriet.

"You will do well, won't you?" Miss Hughes took Harriet's right hand. "You must do well for us."

"I hope so." Harriet shoved her left hand under her leg.

"You'd better go now. Your father is waiting. You are a lucky girl, aren't you, to have a father who will leave his job to drive his daughter to her contest."

"I am," Harriet said. But she knew her father was coming only because her mother wanted to be near to Grandmother Yates.

Grandmother Yates was sick, cancer and the swarming infirmities of age. First she was in the hospital, then in the Springer spare bedroom, then in her own brass bed. Special nurses watching her. As her gaze became as filmy as the gauze curtains on the window overlooking the backyard trees, an old war between her daughter, Eleanor, and her son, Charles, became more vicious. Though close to her mother, Harriet received only random reports about the battle. The closer the struggle, the more Eleanor sought to conceal it.

Harriet had first discerned the trouble a little after Charles had left the Navy and returned to Northville. Crouching on the stairs, eating toothpaste, she and Anne had heard their mother fighting with her brother, even though she had always told them that fighting within families was bad.

"I won't do it." Their mother sounded like she might cry, too. "I won't turn that power of attorney over to you."

"I'm her son. I'm the logical one to have it. I came home from the war to take care of her."

"You came home from the war to have a place to live and a free ride at the bank and to try to get at her capital."

"I'll take you to court and prove you're wasting the assets of her estate."

"I've handled that estate since 1932 when Daddy died. I educated you with that estate. I've tripled its value. I won't have you walk in and take it away."

"Children, children, please." Their grandmother was sitting on the sofa. Her voice as futile as a bird's trying to save its nest from a combine roaring through a field of grain.

"You may wear the pants in this house, Eleanor, but you can't run my mother's life anymore."

"Bastard. Sanctimonious bastard."

Charles had walked out, leather gloves whacking against his palm, long legs scything through the door.

"Quick, Anne, come with me." Harriet had led them to their parents' bedroom. It was still serene, in order: their mother's silver comb and brush, a picture of her dead father on her glass-topped dressing table; their father's turtle-shell comb and brush, his picture of his dead mother on his bureau; their mother's Gesell book on child development and the recent *Saturday Review of Literature* on her bedside table; their father's *Time* and *American Legion Monthly* on his bedside table.

"Anne," Harriet said, "are you my ally?"

"I guess so," Anne said.

"You really have to be my ally. You have to sign a treaty." Harriet printed on a sheet of paper:

MUTUAL DEFENSE TREATY

I, Anne Josephine Springer, pledge my allegiance to my sister, Harriet Elizabeth Springer. I will be loyal to her in peace and war. I will defend her against her enemies. This treaty is to be good for the entire future.

Signed this day of November 18, 1947,
Northville, Nookagillish County, Washington
State, United States of America, a Free Land.

She helped Anne block out her signature and told her she would die if she broke treaties.

Then, three years later, the Springer family was hunting for a Christmas tree on some woodland Big George owned. Hefting the ax, he lined his children up to march down a rutted logging track. "You're in the Army now, you're not behind a plow, Hup two three four," they chanted in military unison. Harriet hoped a tree would fall on them all and leave her alive. Her picture would be in the papers all over the world. Elizabeth Taylor would notice and send for her because Harriet was so poignantly lonely and wonderfully brave.

However, the woods and the sharp, suffusing air were porous enough to absorb even her disgruntlement. They walked across a plank bridge over a brown, frothy stream. Broad-leaved skunk cabbages lined its banks. On either side of them were masses of alder and evergreen; fragile eruptions of bracken fern.

"Rub them on you if you get stung by nettles," Charles had once told Harriet.

The afternoon was collapsing into evening. To the west the sky was a purple mass into which giant girders of cloud were riven. To the east the foothills of the Cascade Mountains were blurring into dark and tender shapes.

"Charles called this morning," Eleanor announced when they were back in the car. The eight-foot tree was tied to the roof. "He wants to bring Alice Henderson to Christmas dinner at one o'clock at our house. Then he wants to take Grammy to Christmas dinner at Alice's house at six. I think that's too long a day for Grammy. She's not feeling that strong."

Harriet sucked on the edge of a graham cracker. "Is Charles going to marry Alice?" she asked.

"She'd be a fool if she did, but neither of them need my permission to make a mistake."

"Why would Alice be a fool?" asked Anne.

"Because he only wants her money."

"Now, Mommy," Big George said, "she's got a yen for him, too. Henderson was talking to me at Rotary the other day. He says that Alice has had her eye on Charlie since they were in high school."

"But it wouldn't be nice, would it," Anne went on, "to marry someone if you didn't love them?"

"Your uncle seems to think he can set his own rules."

"Mommy," Harriet unwrapped a question she had hoarded for years, "why didn't Charles marry Miss Clare who came to see us during the war?"

"Because he discovered that she had a Jewish grandmother."

The children were scandalized. Jews drove too fast and talked too loud and sold old clothes, but people were supposed to ignore other people's race and religion. Their mother insisted on that.

Now, in the car, Harriet could not ask her father about her mother and uncle. She was too busy typing out her speech in her mind, reminding herself that she knew the words. Big George managed his car as if it were an obedient ship under sail, the steering wheel a placid tiller. He drove as if his child were as calm as he. The school in which the Regional Contest was scheduled looked like Northville High: a three-story stucco building built in the 1930s; a stone frieze of fruits and grain over the entrance; a new brick wing to the right; athletic field to the left. A vice principal greeted them at the auditorium door. He gave Big George an aisle seat and put Harriet in the front row. She spied out the competition.

One boy was like the ones she had beaten in the county contest. His dark suit was too big; white shirt too shiny; cowlick too busy; lips too fleshy; nails too bitten. She bit her nails, too, but she at least put on a Band-Aid if she drew blood. One girl was the color of oatmeal. However, a second girl was adultly elegant. She might

26

have been a college graduate, or a model in *Seventeen* or *Mademoiselle*. She wore a black, fitted suit; stockings; leather heels. Harriet was suddenly clumpy in her saddle shoes. She had on lipstick and a discreet swath of eye shadow. Harriet's skin was natural, dingy. She had lacquered her fingernails. They flashed a message to Harriet as if they were ten premonitory signal fires.

The typewriter in Harriet's mind clattered enough to permit her to ignore the speeches of the hick boy and the oatmeal girl. Then the second girl walked up the five scruffed wooden steps to the stage. She stood at the podium, American flags flanking her, as if she both respected and transcended such mere criteria of judgment as "poise," "dignity," and "physical bearing." She lifted her head and raised her arms. A priestess who forgave the crowd the shabbiness of her temporary altar, she invited the devotees to conjure up another, more opulent temple. "God once gave man," she began, "a magnificent garden in which to live. In the cool of the evening he strolled there among his creatures, birds and beasts and man."

The keys of Harriet's typewriter jammed.

"Yet, our ancestors, unworthy citizens of God's empire, disobeyed him. Adam and Eve broke his just and generous laws. God banished them from the Garden. However, God sent Jesus Christ, his son and our Redeemer, to the blighted earth. God was merciful, a mercy beyond our human reckoning and ken. He sent his only begotten son, Jesus Christ, to earth. He gave us a chance to build another garden, not of flowers but of cedar and of fir; a garden for men brave enough to march over mountains, to drive wagons over plains, to ford raging rivers, to wade through mountain-cooled streams finally to reach, ax and heart in hand, God's new paradise on earth, our Pacific Northwest."

Harriet's typewriter was moving again, but the phrases fell out like lead. She gaped at the gray field of her skirt. "Let us be God's creatures again," the priestess said. As she passed from eloquence to silence, Harriet heard more fervor than fifteen people ought normally to produce. Will demanding a sturdy tread, she climbed to the stage. The other girl, waiting near the podium, touched her shoulder. "Good luck," she said sweetly and clearly. The audience applauded again. As Harriet arranged her outwitted self, she felt as if she were a dry-mouthed, thick-fleshed animal stumbling inside a gunnysack. Her hands grasped the sides of the podium as if it were a chair against the wall of the Hapsburg Hotel Ballroom.

"Ladies and Gentlemen, I stand before you as someone who will inherit the future. I care about the political and economic health of my state and of my fellow citizens." Her right hand touched her left breast, as if she were pledging allegiance to the flag. "I care about beauty. I care about nature." Empty auditorium seats regarded her. Her father crossed his legs and stroked the brim of his hat. "I care about the waters, the mountains, and the forests of our Pacific Northwest." She begged the audience to give her any response, even the most fleeting. Her hands shook, shook at the podium. "When we cut a tree, we can count the rings of its life in the stump." Only the animal inside the gunnysack hoisted her up. "Keep the Pacific Northwest green." She heard applause so scanty that silence would have been preferable.

Slumped in her seat, she watched the judge bounce up to the stage. A plump man in a gray suit, white socks, black shoes. "Well, folks," he began cheerily, "every regional contest that I have been privileged to attend has been a lollapalooza. This one has been no exception. But, after a long, hard huddle, we have voted unanimously to award First Prize for the Second Region in the Washington State High School Public Speaking Contest to Miss Shirley LaVerne Wentworth of Placid High School. Her reward is a $100 United States Savings Bond and a trip to the state contest in Spokane. Come on up, Shirley, and get your reward."

Shirley LaVerne arose. Harriet sat, chin jutting from her neck. If she were not first, it hardly mattered if she were second, third, or fourth. Going home, in the crisp winter night, she wanted to cry. She had failed. Her father had watched her fail. She looked down at the prize in her lap: a bulky ski jacket, shirtlike collar, snap-in buckle, as purple as a dying bruise.

"That seems practical," her father said.

"But it's a boy's jacket."

"Don't let that bother you."

She wanted to ask him if the defeat would hurt her college applications, but the distance between them was too great for her easily to reveal her needs. She wanted him to touch her, but he had the steering wheel, the clutch, the light dimmer switch. They were both glad to get home. He was hungry, and she could finally confess to her mother that she had lost, to hear her mother console her and say, "Too bad, but you're good enough to do better next time."

A few weeks after the speaking contest, Grandmother Yates was dead. Her small estate had to become the field for the war between her son and daughter. Her body could no longer do. The day after the funeral, Harriet went with her mother to Grandmother Yates' house. Metal folding chairs from the service had to be stacked; lilies had to be thrown away. "My grandmother is dead," Harriet told herself. Gnawing at grief, she bit empty air. Strange to be so numb, because she had loved her grandmother and hidden, when necessary, among the welcoming caves of her benevolence.

Outside, the damp rawness of February grayed mountains and the bay; blackened evergreens. As they were leaving, Charles approached. With him was Billy Reinhardt, a real estate man. Harriet wanted to kiss her uncle, but her mother commandeered the ground between them.

"You're not letting any grass grow under your feet, are you?" she asked.

"Eleanor, we're the only ones left. We should try to make the most of what we've got."

But her mother stared at him contemptuously. Then, pulling Harriet, she ran off the porch to her car. Her husband and father-in-law were at home reading the *Northville News*.

"Charles was there, with Reinhardt," Eleanor greeted them.

"Not much you can do about it, Mommy," Big George said. "If Charles got the house, Charles got the house. A will's a sacred trust."

"But he's only selling it to spite me."

"He's probably selling it to meet the first interest payment on his Cedar Bay property," Big George said reasonably. "He's carrying a $500,000 mortgage."

"At least I kept the bank out of the financing on that one," Eleanor said. "But he's got his wife's money now."

"What's he going to do with that land?" Grandfather Springer asked. His measured, unaccented voice rarely changed pitch. "He's not planning to farm it."

"It's one beautiful piece of beach," Big George was at once wistful and professional, "and it could be one beautiful deepwater port. Shell or Texaco could build a refinery there."

His wife was no longer listening. She was upstairs, lying on her bed, hands smashing against her face, sobbing, "Damn him, damn him, damn him."

After Grandmother Yates' death, Eleanor Springer became even more conscientious and energetic. She lived as if through the act of mothering she could honor her own mother's ghost. She sent her son George east to a prestigious college, to Yale. He was to get a fine education and make contacts that would be valuable when he returned to Northville to become the third Springer in the bank. He went, pretending not to be scared but having stomachaches. Eleanor wrote every other day and sent food. She decided that Harriet should do something about her looks. Sulky, morose, Harriet found herself driving to Seattle with her mother. Rain drizzled from a gray, lowering northwest sky.

"What's this woman going to do to me?" she asked.

"I don't know exactly, dear, but you're so handsome that it's a shame not to make the most of it."

"Handsome, what kind of an ideal is that, handsome? I thought you said it didn't matter if I wasn't invited to the Junior Prom and things like that?"

"It'll be worth it to you someday." Eleanor Springer drove cautiously, as if rambunctious children were still in the back seat. You just can't slop around in old clothes with your hair messy for the rest of your life. You've got to be well rounded. You've got to be well groomed as well as being smart. I won't have my daughter grow up to be a brute."

A brute? What more did her mother want? She played the cello in the school orchestra. She was on the staff of the newspaper and the yearbook. She had been elected to the Rally Club. The lowest grade she had ever gotten was an A minus, in First Aid. She turned out for girls' sports. She had been appointed to the Traffic Squad and helped patrol the halls at lunchtime. "I'm not a brute," she said. She stared out of the window at the red buildings and gray silos of a dairy farm.

"I never said you were. I only said you mustn't be."

"How did Daddy get the name of this woman, anyway?"

"He talked to Doctor Cliff at Rotary."

Harriet gloomily imagined what her father must have said. "Burt, I'd appreciate a little advice. My daughter has this moustache. It's not much of a problem, but her mother's been after me to get something done about it. Got any ideas about where she can go?"

"You know, Harriet, that Daddy and I want what's best for you. We don't want you to have to use depilatories. We want something done permanently.

"Darlene LeSueur uses NAIR." Darlene's upper lip, if scalded, was flawless and bald. "Her father gives it to her."

"That may be all right for Darlene, but it's not good enough for you."

"Okay, okay." Irascibly.

They drove on to Seattle, the overbuilt hills, the profitable lakes. Myrna McCoy Associates was in a suite in the Pine Professional Building. In the waiting room, studying a *Reader's Digest,* was a man. Harriet wanted to ask her mother why a man would worry about facial hair, about tufts blossoming in the warm soil of the nostril, along the lips, over the eyes. But because it was wrong to talk about people in front of them, she sat quietly until the receptionist took her and her mother into an inner office. There, between teak desk and Venetian blinds, was a plump, sleek, middle-aged woman. Her hair shone with a discreet henna dye. Framed certificates on her walls were lit from above, like paintings.

"How old is your child?" she asked Eleanor.

"Seventeen."

"That's young. Mother Nature is a hard worker. She plants new crops of hair until we're well past adolescence."

"But you can do something now, can't you?" Eleanor asked firmly.

"Of course, but I want to be honest about what I can and cannot do with Mother Nature. Do you want her eyebrows done, too, or only the moustache and the little chin whiskers?"

"Heavens, no," Eleanor recoiled. "I don't want her to be artificial."

"A little touch-up never hurts," Myrna McCoy said. "But you're her mother, not me." Then she took Harriet, alone, into the treatment room and helped her to lie down on a leather table. "Thank you," Harriet said. Her arms were at her side, her saddle shoes touching neatly. On her right was a squat metal box with dials. A thin pole rose from it, topped with a ring over which a dozen cords were looped.

"Now dear," Myrna McCoy said, "I'm going to put this mask over your eyes so the light won't hurt them. If you feel anything, you lie very still and it will all go away." Harriet was tied into darkness. Myrna McCoy's hands and bending body urged her to abandon her wariness. Then her upper lip was pricked. The flesh went taut, like the chain of a leaping dog.

"Relax, dear, just relax, Everything will be just fine," Myrna McCoy soothed. Five more pricks, a sound at once whoosh and hum, and her upper lip fell apart in strips of pain. She cried out.

"Now, dear," she heard, above, to her right, "it's all over. It didn't hurt, did it? We can do it again, can't we? We're brave, aren't we?" A cool swab passed over the lip. "That's only a little alcohol, to make you feel better. You can be a brave young lady now, can't you?"

Harriet wanted to pull off the mask, tear the needles out of her face, and run away. But what would her mother, one corridor and two walls away, say? What would Myrna McCoy think? Better to have her eyeballs turn to stone and her tears silently erode them than to be cowardly and discourteous. "Let's go," she said. Prick. A new needle. She willed her hands to unbunch out of fists. Prick. The next needle. She willed her hands, her body, to lie flat.

When it was over, her body was staggering. Her mother took her to lunch at an elegant department store. They shopped for a new crinoline skirt. "Darling," her mother said, when they were back in the car on Highway 99, "we only do these things so that you can have a good life, so that you can have a better life than I had, so that you can go away to college and be happy."

Harriet wondered if the windshield wipers could make her eyes cross against her will. It was raining again.

"You do understand, don't you?" her mother urged, "You do know how much it matters, don't you?"

"Why didn't you go to an eastern girl's school? Didn't you want to?"

"I didn't know about them, but I did want to go to college in California."

"Why didn't you?"

32

"Because the school had a quota about women. They only let a few in. I didn't make it. Besides, my father didn't want me to go so far away from home."

"How did your father die?"

"I've told you before. He was hurt in an accident during the Depression. That's why I had to leave the state college before I could graduate and go to support Grammy and Charles. And that's why it was so hard for me when Charles came back from the war and wanted to take over Grammy's life. I had worked so hard to see that they were safe. I know you love your uncle, and it's been hard to have us quarrel so, but I want you to understand me, too."

The rain blurred the windows even as the wipers cleared them. Harriet felt the threat of her own tears. Her mother was the bravest person she knew, a victim who came through against all odds to improve a hostile world. And now her mother's voice seemed to be reaching down into some deep, previously hidden, vessel of memory. "Darling, would you promise me something? Will you always take care of yourself? You're almost everything to me."

Harriet would have given her anything.

"After Daddy and I got married, I kept on working until Georgie was born. I wanted there to be enough money for Charlie's education. He kept dropping in and out of graduate schools before he went into the Navy."

"I didn't know that."

"Daddy and I have tried to protect you children. Whenever he came home for vacations, he wouldn't work. He wouldn't help. He did whatever he wanted, no matter how much it cost, no matter how much it took from Grammy and me. Then he started seeing a woman who was a waitress in the Hapsburg Hotel. She was older than he was and had a little girl, but Charlie said she gave him something nobody in his family could. I guess we couldn't give him sex.

"We told him to stop seeing her. We said it wasn't fair to her, it wasn't good for him. But he always was a selfish man, and he went on doing what he wanted. When he went back to college, we all breathed a sigh of relief. Then, one Sunday afternoon, Daddy and I were in the backyard. I was pregnant with Georgie. The doorbell rang. She was at the door. I'll never forget it. She was all dressed up, as if she were going to church. It was Indian summer, and we all sat in lawn chairs under the grape arbor. She said that she was pregnant, and what were we going to do about it?"

"Charles was the father?" Harriet felt as repelled as she had the afternoon after her triumph at the Rotary Club. She had come home, and after her mother's joyful welcome Harriet had said that she had liked Eddie Rivers. Her mother had told her Eddie Rivers was abhorrent: a lustful, exploitative man who slept with his secretaries; a man who, as a boy, had slept with the family maids. Harriet shrank from and disowned her attraction to him.

"That's what she said. She said that if we didn't help her, she was going to let everybody in town know. She knew that the Yates weren't rich enough to have it matter, but that the Springers were. Then she looked at me and said that I could have a baby and be safe, but she couldn't and that it wasn't fair, and she was going to do what she had to do to get by."

"What happened?"

"Daddy gave her some money and sent her away. Then we arranged to get her more money, and told her to get an abortion." Her mother sounded as if there were a sudden gag at the mouth of memory. "We never saw her again. Daddy told Charles what we had done, but he never thanked us. He never did anything to acknowledge what we had done." Her mother paused, to swallow down the gag. "You must promise me, darling, you must promise me, that you'll take care of yourself. You won't let yourself get dragged down in the mud."

"I'll be all right," Harriet said. "I promise, Mom, I really do." She feared what she was doing. It seemed as endless as her mother's grief and need and courage. Yet she no more wanted to resist this initiation into her mother's world than she wanted to amputate her love at its source.

Her mother let her go to the rest of the six electrolysis treatments alone. At the last one, as if it were a graduation present, Myrna became confidential, friendly. "I work hard," she said, wiping a needle with alcohol-soaked cotton. "I've got to have the concentration of a brain surgeon, but I sure don't get the glory. You'd be surprised at who comes in here for treatment. It's not like working at the studio, but I get my share of local bigwigs."

"You worked in a movie studio?" Harriet had never before been so physically close to Hollywood glamour.

"At M-G-M. I moved here when my husband got a job at Boeing's, but my girl friend is still there."

"Did you work on any of the stars?"

"Some of the biggest. You're not the only person in the world with a few hairs too many. Some of those people who look so wonderful when you're watching them, they're King Kongs before we take care of them." Nostalgia sweetening her, she told Harriet to come back when she was done with school and about to marry, so that they could finish what they had begun.

"I'm not going to get married until I finish college. I want to go to an eastern school, to Harwyn."

"That's fine, but don't forget about that M.R.S. degree, too."

Harriet wanted to ask about Elizabeth Taylor. Why had she divorced Nicky Hilton? *Photoplay* had said that at the time of the wedding they were dreaming of satin blankets and lacy robes for their first baby. Then, mysteriously, trouble. Ground diamonds in the wedding cake. Used condoms in the champagne punch. But Myrna had a new client waiting.

Muscles still feeling as if they had been wound on ratchets, Harriet ate some strawberry waffles at a restaurant near the bus station. She declined a free toothpick at the cash register. Her mother frequently admonished her children about things that other people might have touched first. "You can pick a nickel up off the street and then put your fingers in your mouth, but how do you know that someone with dog manure on his shoes didn't step on it just before you touched it?"

The smell of exhaust in the depot threatened to veer Harriet's body out of control. She got a window seat on the Northville bus, but she could not read her book, a novel by a French author, André Malraux. The bus roared and jerked too much. Her fingers browsed at the hairs Myrna McCoy had left for later. At the next station, a man sat next to her. His face a series of blunt-edged bones that shoved against the stubble and craters of his skin. He folded a black coat over his lap. As the bus ground on, he seemed to bump into her. She glanced at him, but he was resting in his seat, eyes half closed, mouth hanging open.

When her thigh stung, she looked at him again. He appeared the same. She scrunched into her corner, smiling uncertainly, to apologize if she had been rude. Then the book was hit out of her hands. The man was laughing. His left arm was holding his coat as if it were a curtain between the aisle and his lap. In front of it a huge, smooth, purplish-pink thing was climbing from the stage of his pants. His right hand was making it bow to her. Georgie's penis was much smaller; her father's, in the shower, had dangled from a mass of hair; the one in a book her mother had also used to teach her sex was a bunch of arcs and lines. This, this was growing, rancorous, alive. The man's right hand moved toward her to wrench her hands from her lap to put them on him. "I can't," she thought, panicked, "I can't." She pulled herself up and tried to push out into the aisle. His hand went under her coat, against the back of her legs. In the aisle, she fell against the back of the seats in front of her. "Please, dear God, please, dear God," she prayed, "make people think it's the bus."

"Want the next stop?" the driver asked.

"Yes, please." Her throat and mouth were congealing.

The engine exhaust of the bus left a dark film on her legs when she got off. Across the road were pasture, fence, ditch, Burma Shave signs. She waited for the next bus, pretending a car was coming for her. She reached Northville enough on schedule not to call attention to herself. She could not tell her mother what had happened to her. She had no language for the thing, the fear. At dinner she sat isolated from her parents and her sister until her father said something about Chinese politics.

"I suppose you got that idea from *Time*," she taunted him, to cling to speech again. "Why do you read that stupid magazine?"

"It's a good magazine." He tucked his napkin into his vest, tugged at his crotch. "Good dinner, Mommy." He forked up some mashed potato.

"It's a stupid magazine," she said. "A good magazine for stupid people. A really good magazine for really stupid people."

She watched him kick back his chair, lunge around the table. As he yanked her out of her chair, she kicked out, but as the slaps came at her blistered face she held her head toward them before her mother shouted and her father let her go. That night she dreamt that she was on a bus near a beach. A bald man in a yellow Hawaiian shirt was near the rear exit. He smiled, put his

36

hand between her thighs. Then he disappeared. Her body was left like a jet of water. On the beach were a group of ragged men in battle dress. One, missing a leg, waved a stump at her. Then she was in bed, her legs open, Gary Cooper next to her, his right leg between hers, as her liquid body flowed into his.

Harriet had not wanted to take this written examination. Her mother insisted that she do it. The Northville High School student body had elected her as its candidate. "I won't," Harriet had rebelled, "I don't believe in the DAR. How can I take their crummy good-citizen test if they wouldn't let Marian Anderson sing in Washington, D.C., just because she was a Negro?" Her mother had reminded her again of her duty, not only to abstract principles of racial justice but to the concrete human beings with whom she took physical education and shared a cafeteria. "Besides, darling," her mother had said, "it will be an achievement on your college record."

So she sat, Northville's candidate for the Washington State Good Citizenship Award of the Daughters of the American Revolution, in an otherwise empty social studies and hygiene classroom. Except for the Latin section of College Boards, an exam had never stumped her. But these questions were about American colonial history and the Revolutionary War. Her breakfast orange juice, milk, hot Ralston, and cod liver oil threatened to overwhelm her body. Her mind was sputtering. Then the stubbornness that had driven Yates and Springers across the Atlantic Ocean and the North American continent to Northville stiffened her. An article in the *Northville News*, "Tips for Taking Tests Triumphantly," returned to her. She breathed deeply. She stomped on demon panic. Of course, she knew what the Bill of Rights guaranteed; what three differences were between Benjamin Franklin and George Washington. When her mind balked on the name of the thirteenth colony, she reminded herself not to spend too much time on one problem. She passed on to the essay question, "The United Nations Today."

She warned herself that the essay might be an ambush. The horrid DAR opposed the hallowed U.N. If she supported the U.N., she might be marked down. However, she thought of Tom Paine and Florence Nightingale and Sergeant York and Eleanor

Roosevelt, heroic figures who stood up for their beliefs when it mattered. She would not buckle under to bigotry and prejudice. Flushed with moral resolve, she wrote:

> America was created in order to give all people access to the principles of the Declaration of Independence in 1776: life, liberty, and the pursuit of happiness. The role of the United Nations is to permit all people to share in the principles of America in the 1950s. The United Nations is to expand the American dream, just as it has expanded America's name. The job of America is to help the United Nations to become a global United States.

When the ardent five hundred words were done, the name of the thirteenth colony still hung inaccessible in memory. On the shelves of the room was the district's American history textbook: *America, Promise and Power*. It stared at her. "I can't cheat," she said. "It's wrong." Her incomplete answer also stared at her, a burning empty space. "I can't cheat," she said again. "I've never done anything like that in my life." Her body, as if it were not listening, walked to the book and located a chapter on the colonies. Her hand wrote in, "New Jersey." When the principal came into the room to collect the paper to send to the DAR State Committee, she was checking for spelling errors on the U.N. essay. None discernible.

Harriet repressed the memory of the morning. She also distracted herself with a new worry. A few days later Clive McGee was waiting for her in the middle of the high school's back corridor. She joined him there. If they had stood next to the wall, they would have signaled the world that they liked each other. Clive and David Patterson were the two smartest boys in her class; they were friends, but David, because he played basketball and spoke with a less affected accent, was more socially acceptable. A year ago Harriet had thought David might take her to the junior prom. They had met in the public library. She had asked what he was reading. "Nothing much. It's supposed to be the hardest book in the world." Stamped on the spine was *Kant: The Critique of Pure Reason*.

"That's supposed to be good." She had read the Kant entry in her family's *Encyclopedia Brittanica*.

"Yeah, I'm giving it a try."

"I'm reading *For Whom the Bell Tolls*. Hemingway got the title from the poet John Donne."

"Is that so?"

A deep gaze over the checkout counter. Enough to arouse hope. Not enough to get an invitation to the prom.

"I've got news for you," Clive now said. "The fellows on my locker corridor have been talking about you."

She was startled. Neither desired nor despised, neither dating nor sleeping around, she was hardly fodder for their gossip.

"They say they nominated you for Queen Sweetheart when we balloted for Valentine Sweethearts yesterday."

"I don't believe it." She did not. She was a Good Citizen in the school, not a Queen of Hearts.

"That's what the fellows on the corridor say." He shifted his books. "Did you finish writing up the physics experiment?"

"Last night." She was the only girl in physics. "Why are the guys doing it?"

"Why should I presume to explain? I've got to go to trig." Clive's ambition was to get into Cal. Tech.

She had Senior Home Economics. Aproned, she stood with Betsy Metcalfe in their kitchen unit, waiting for Miss Griese to inspect their recipe books. "Betsy," words against her will, "have you heard anything about some guys nominating me for Queen Sweetheart?"

"Not a thing."

"Clive McGee told me they had, but I thought he might be kidding."

"At least you might win something. And you've already been Princess Intelligence twice. I've never won anything." Passionate unhappiness.

"It's all dumb. It won't matter when we get out of here," Harriet said. Loyal to her friend who shared Harriet's disdain for required home ec and mandatory Rally Club attendance at Friday night football, where they sat waving crepe-paper pompons that melted in the rain until the colors ran down their hands and wrists, as if they had slashed their veins and held the wounds up to the sky.

At the end of the day, Harriet saw Darlene LeSueur alone in the row they shared on Girls' Locker Corridor. "Darlene," she said, "do you know anything about some guys nominating me for Valentine Queen Sweetheart?"

Darlene twisted the key in her locker padlock, chewed her gum. "I haven't heard anything," she finally said. "I wouldn't worry if I were you."

But she did. What if the boys had sat around in shop, or in the Boys' Corridor, and said to each other that Harriet Springer would be a great Queen Valentine Sweetheart? The idea of traveling in the alien land of beauty shyly tickled her flesh. But what if they had voted for her only to laugh as she stumbled out on the stage, to be crowned with their mockery? During the day, she hid from her suspicions in her work; late at night, in a war novel she was rereading. Each time a character said the mysterious word "Fug" her legs trembled. On Valentine's Day itself, because there was going to be a school assembly, she put on her Rally Club outfit. She breakfasted, opened her Valentine present from her mother, packed lunch, caught the bus to school. At eleven o'clock, she sat with other seniors in the front rows of the auditorium. The school orchestra was tuning up, sounds plopping from the instruments like milk from a frozen bottle. Mr. Troutman, the principal, walked on stage, with a floor mike. He had earned the Northville school system's most prestigious honor: a master's degree from Teachers College at Columbia University in New York City.

Pledge of Allegiance and National Anthem led, he nodded at the school. "Northville is the best school in Nookagillish County," he said. Student cheers. "Nookagillish County is the best county in Washington State as well as being the most northwesterly. Washington State is the best state in the United States. The United States is the best nation in the world. Therefore," he halted before reaching his logical apogee, "Northville is the best school in the world, and our Valentine Sweethearts the best sweethearts in the world."

Harriet sat, as apprehensive as she had been before the College Board exams were passed out. Mr. Troutman waved a sheet of paper. "Last night Mr. Klasp, your assistant principal, and I counted the votes for your nominees for the 1955 Valentine Sweetheart contest. Let me say that your king is kingly, your queen is queenly, your sweethearts sweet. Now, let's end this suspense. I'm going to read the names of the following boys. Will they go

40

to the boys' stage door. I'm going to read the names of the following girls. Will they go to the girls' stage door. And, as I read the names, will the orchestra please favor us with a little appropriate background melody?"

"Let Me Call You Sweetheart" bounded out. Then Harriet's name intruded into the jumble of lyrics decomposing in her mind. She crowded her way between the knees of her classmates and the backs of the seats toward her destiny. Backstage the football coach was lining up the boys, the drama coach the girls. Slowly, behind Mr. Troutman, the stage crew was lowering a ten-foot-high heart constructed from paper, wood, and velvet. "King and Queen Sweetheart" was printed on it in gilt. The school began to sing with the orchestra.

When the heart was secure, the manager of the lights crew hit it with three strong spots. "Gee, Harriet," said Olivia Kasper, "what do you suppose we've won?" Harriet's muscles clenched involuntarily.

"Boys and girls," Mr. Troutman exclaimed, "here they are at last, your sweethearts. Students of Northville High, Your Sweethearts for Courtesy—Princess Gail McGale and Prince Ernie Partree." The president of the Girls' Council and the manager of the basketball team shyly approached stage center.

Mr. Troutman gave Gale a red paper heart, on which "Courtesy" was white-inked. She pinned it on Ernie. Mr. Troutman gave Ernie a heart for Gale. The school watched, simmering, wondering if the tips of his hand would slip and graze, in public, on the forbidden hillocks of her breasts? Fastidiously, Ernie fastened the heart on Gale's collar.

"Now," Mr. Troutman glanced at his list, "Your Sweethearts for Intelligence, Princess Harriet Springer and Prince David Patterson. Come on, brains, take your bow." A blow of sad relief cleansed Harriet. She walked toward David. He stared over her head. She fixed his heart to his V-necked sweater; he her heart to her white Rally Club sweater with its aegis of a Lion's head. The audience seemed less interested in whether his hand would slip or not. After the Prince and Princess for Neatness, Sportsmanship, School Spirit, Friendliness, Loyalty, Dependability, Cheerfulness, and All-Round Athletic Ability had been crowned, Mr. Troutman gave the orchestra a signal. The drums rolled. The spotlights on the constructed heart blinked on and off. "Boys and girls" Mr. Troutman exulted, "the moment you've all been waiting for, your king and queen, Your Valentine Sweethearts, Vince Shelton and Olivia Kasper."

"Oh," gasped Darlene LeSueur, Princess Cheerfulness. "Vince is king and Olivia queen, and they're going steady, too." Olivia, legs rippling the yellow pleats of her Rally Club skirt, walked gracefully toward the heart. The football coach pushed Vince, his captain, in chino pants and letter sweater, onto the stage. "Don't forget to kiss her, dummy," he yelled.

In anguish of celebration, longing for both marches and waltzes, the orchestra marshaled its energies for a climactic "Let Me Call You Sweetheart." In great arcs Mr. Troutman's right arm led the school in song. Unless he was naked or in uniform, crew-cut Vince was bashful. Ordinary clothes meant ordinary transactions with the world, in which neither sex nor strength might prevail. Stiffly, swiftly, he kissed Olivia's cheek, the beautiful girl with whom he necked every Friday and Saturday night and Sunday afternoon after she came home from Mass. He kissed her again and touched the silver chain on which she wore his miniature football, basketball, baseball, and winged track shoe. "Attaboy," shouted the coach. "I'm in love with you," roared the school.

During lunch hour Harriet phoned her mother. "I was voted Princess Intelligence again," she said. "Olivia was Queen Sweetheart and Vince was king. People liked it, because they're going steady."

"I'm so glad you called," her mother said. "I got a phone call from Mrs. Jasper Rivers today. She's the local DAR president."

"What did she want?"

"Darling, you're the state DAR Good Citizen. Isn't that wonderful? Mrs. Rivers knows a member of the state judges' committee, and she called to tell me before the news was made public, because she knew I'd want to know. You had the only perfect test in the state. They were just thrilled with your answers."

"Even the part about the U.N.?" Harriet's body was like a metal casing for a vacuum.

"They thought your answer about the U.N. was liberal, but probably patriotic, and very well written."

"Oh," said Harriet. She stood in the scarred phone booth, the Lion's head and mane of the emblem of her Rally Club costume dropping over her breasts, the red paper heart crumbling on her left shoulder.

"We'll have your favorite dinner tonight," her mother exulted. "Roast beef and lemon cake pudding."

A month later Harriet and Mrs. Jasper Rivers, the rich widow of the founder of Rivers Lumber, were traversing the Cascade Mountains in the club car of the east-bound train. They were going to the Washington State Convention of the Daughters of the American Revolution. The cracked gray rock face of a mountain, a body's length away from one side of the tracks, transmogrified train windows into a mirror. Harriet saw the daughter of Mr. and Mrs. George Baxter Springer, 828 Apple Street, Northville, in her new tweed suit; small, gold-plated globes on ear lobes; matching choker around her neck. On the other side of the tracks was a one thousand-foot drop.

"I can't go, it's not right," Harriet had cried out to her mother the night before.

"I know how you feel, darling." Her mother had been pasting clippings about Harriet's victory from the *Northville News* into the family scrapbook. "I don't like their principles either. But you can't let people down at this stage and not go. It means too much to the school."

Harriet had felt an iron rod in her mother's hand, no less inflexible for being invisible. Nevertheless, her protest kept on. "But it's not right. It's a fraud. How can I be the State Good Citizen and be a fraud?"

"You may not believe in the DAR, but you do believe in good citizenship."

"Mommy, you don't understand. It's a fraud. That's all I can say. It's a fraud."

"But Harriet, it's not a fraud to represent people who believe in you. The school believes in you."

"You don't understand."

"All right," her mother had said decisively. "If it means so much to you you can cancel out of the ceremony. Phone Mrs. Rivers and tell her that you're not going to Wenatchee with her tomorrow to the state convention, and then go tell the people at school."

"I hate you," Harriet had screamed as the rod broke through to her flesh. She had run from the room.

"She's so temperamental these days," Harriet had heard her mother say to her father later when they were in bed and she on her way to the bathroom. "It's so hard being a parent. You want to do the right thing, and you never know if you are or not." Her father's voice was mumbling, soothing, as if he were passing papers for a renewed loan over his desk to a frenzied customer.

Harriet and Mrs. Rivers got off the train in the late afternoon. Towns in Central Washington must submit to heat and dust in summer, aching snow in winter. The six-story, yellow stucco hotel seemed tired; the room they were to share even smaller than Harriet had feared. It was stuffed with twin beds with bright blue chenille spreads; a dark, varnished bureau; a bedside table on which a Gideon Bible was opened to Isaiah. "I'm going to rest," Mrs. Rivers said. "I'm getting to be an old lady. Why don't you go out and have a stroll? Come back in half an hour, and we'll have dinner before the opening fun and games."

"Fine and dandy," said Harriet, ashamed of the clichés her nerves spewed forth.

Outside, Harriet sat in the town square on a slatted, wooden bench next to a trash barrel, beneath a pale-green and yellow willow tree, the hotel to the north. A vertical neon sign, spelling out "The Biltmore," had been turned on. It rose from the roof like an emaciated flamingo. To the east was a department store, to the west a movie theater and coffee shop, to the south a hardware store and Chevrolet agency. Weary, bitter grass, as tough and burnt as the pioneer women who had ridden across a continent to settle here, grew at her feet. She took, from her new purse, the index cards on which she had written the notes for her acceptance speech. "Why am I grateful to be the State Good Citizen for the Daughters of the American Revolution?" she whispered. I'm not grateful, I'm a fraud, she thought. On the bench across from her was a young man, built like David Patterson. His hands were hanging between his knees as if they had fallen from despairing prayer. He was wearing good clothes, flannel slacks, an overcoat, a tie. They glanced at each other, then at their feet.

Then she returned to the hotel room. Mrs. Rivers was lying

44

on the bed next to the window, in a flowered silk kimono and fluffy mules, smoking. Her suitcase was open on the stand. Before she could avert her eyes, Harriet saw a corset's impacted weave. "Hello, dear," Mrs. Rivers said. "You'd better get dressed. I suppose that the room service here couldn't rustle up a decent Martini even if it was a wet town."

In the bathroom Harriet put on a clean white bra and panties; her garter belt and stockings; her new gray dress; polished shoes. "You look as pretty as a picture," Mrs. Rivers said when she emerged, though Harriet knew, with mournful resignation, that if anything, she was handsome. In the dining room she ordered the medium-priced Cattleman's Cut. The waitress, in a black uniform and white shoes, poured Mrs. Rivers coffee.

"Western meals," she sighed. "First you get coffee, then salad, then the main course. There's never any point asking for a wine list. They think it's a new kind of seed catalog." Mrs. Rivers looked around the room. "I don't know many of the girls here. I usually don't come to these conventions, but I wanted to bring you. You do know that yours was the only perfect test in the state, don't you?"

"Mommy told me." Harriet's hands, trying to make her knife and fork cut her wedge of iceberg lettuce, turned cold.

"What will you do next year?" Mrs. Rivers asked. "You're an intelligent, well-mannered girl. Will you go to the university?"

"I've applied to Radcliffe and Wellesley and Harwyn," she dragooned herself into speech. "I'm waiting to hear from them. I want to go east to a women's college, especially to Harwyn."

"Do you? They're all good schools, but of the girls I knew when I was growing up in Boston, of those who were allowed to go to college, there was always something fine about the ones who went to Harwyn."

Mrs. Jasper Rivers confused Harriet. How could such a woman, who grew up in Boston, have permitted her son Eddie to sleep with the maids when he had been a boy? "When you get to Harwyn, you must go to the Biltmore Hotel there. The real Biltmore. There is a lovely court, where you can sit at a table and have cocktails and listen to a string orchestra and talk about the play that you have just seen. I stayed at this Biltmore once before, with my husband, while he was alive. He was looking at some timber property north of here. I asked the owner of this Biltmore if he had named the hotel after the one in New York. 'No,' he said, 'I called it the Biltmore because when it was built, it cost more than I thought it would.' Oh, Lord, here comes Mildred, the state president. She's a true believer in the DAR."

Pinned to the left breast of the gray silk dress of the gaunt woman now touching Mrs. Rivers' shoulder was an orchid corsage. Two medals flanked its mottled, off-white petals. On her right breast was a red, white, and blue rosette, "President" stamped in gold in the middle. "Helen," her voice throttled back its own imperatives, "I assume this young woman is our State Good Citizen."

Harriet stood up. "I shouldn't tell you," the president said, "because it's supposed to be a secret, but we were just as pleased as pleased can be with your citizenship test. My, we thought to ourselves, my, but that young woman has a command of American history and of the English language."

"Her family is one of the best in Northville," Mrs. Rivers interjected.

"I should think so, the way she wrote about her country. Is your mother a Daughter?" she asked Harriet.

"Most of my famliy came over after the Civil War," Harriet said. "There was one branch that was here in 1776, but they went to Canada." The president's face collapsed, as if it were a sea animal and Harriet's information a rancid plankton. "But," Harriet added hastily "that's only family legend."

"I see," the president said. "Helen, why don't you get our Good Citizen seated in the Wenatchee Room. We're about to begin. The girls can't wait for the opening ceremonies."

In the ballroom, red, white, and blue streamers were woven through the dangling prisms of the chandelier. A red, white, and blue cloth draped a front table. To the left was a piano. On the wall behind a felt banner proclaimed:

ANNUAL CONVENTION

DAR

WASHINGTON STATE

Harriet inspected her program. The State Good Citizen was the tenth event. The eleventh was the Beacon Prize for the best essay written about a Founding Father in a freshman composition class, to Greg T. Hanson of Cle Elum College. Looking around, being as dignified as possible, Harriet saw the boy she had seen in the town square that afternoon. Wearing the same jacket and slacks, in the same slump of despond: Greg T. Hanson. Suddenly Harriet feared that she was being obvious, noticing him more than he her. Both *Seventeen* and *Mademoiselle* had insisted that a girl must coax a boy out of his shyness after he has approached her. Only men throw forward passes, the *Northville News* advised. Women decide if they're going to catch the ball or drop it.

The rustle and murmurs of the sixty women seated behind Harriet abruptly hushed. A small woman—a grimmer Miss Hughes—had materialized at the piano. She lifted her hands and then flung them down into the opening chords of a brute Sousa march. In the back the doors opened. A procession, the president in charge, stormed into the room. Its stalwart members were wearing red, white, and blue sashes, two inches of gore and color across their breasts. The flags they were carrying slashed the air. At the top of the aisle the column divided, to unite again in back of the table. The members lowered the tips of their flags three times, then stood, panting but erect. "Ladies," the president ordered, "our National Anthem." "Oh, say can you see," sang the representatives of the Washington State DAR. A rhetorical question. Had they not inherited the vision, as well as the blood, of their ancestors? They prolonged the last, "Home of the brave," as if they might soar into ecstasy on the long *A* of the land they had wrought from heathens and the wilderness. Harriet looked at Greg T. Hanson. He was staring at the floor. "Amen," the president said. "Be seated."

As the report before the presentation of the Good Citizen Award began, Harriet felt her dominating, performing self begin to approach. "We have been vigilant," the blue-haired chairman of the Education Committee declared, stiff and forceful as a musket. "Believe me, ladies, your Education Committee has been vigilant, as alert as our ancestors who stood guard duty in Valley Forge. We have watched for the influence of atheistic communism in every school, in every book, in the state."

Even Mrs. Rivers nodded in agreement.

"This year we have trained our sights on one source of enemy propaganda. Across the Columbia River, in Oregon, there is a college. Its faculty is nothing more than an outpost of the Kremlin. They are helping Russia in its struggle to subvert our beloved

47

Constitution. They favor labor unions. They support free love. Why, some of them have signed petitions in favor of the Red Negro, Paul Robeson."

Her audience gasped. "However," their Education Chairman assured them, "we have our eyes on them. We're watching Robeson-loving, Red Reed College, and when it's time, we'll move."

Both of Harriet's hands clenched her speech index cards. Paul Robeson's deep voice on the record of *Ballad for Americans* had reached down to her to say that all people, no matter what their creed and color, were equal. Because of American democracy, redcaps and bankers marched together under the wind-swept flags of justice. Paul Robeson, a Negro, had led her to the top of a mountain. There they had saluted the earth, air, and sky of this, their common country. Rebellion flushed away Harriet's guilt about her cheating, her false perfection. She was going to refuse the award. She was going to rise up and ask how she could be a grateful DAR Good Citizen when the DAR was nothing but a bunch of narrow-minded bigots. If they still wanted to give her her $50 United States Government savings bond award, she was going to take it and start a Paul Robeson and Marian Anderson Fan Club.

Then Mrs. Rivers was whispering to her, "Good luck, dear. You deserve your moment in the sun." The president was introducing her. "Each year one of our special treats is to discover and to reward a young person of exemplary citizenship. This year our State Good Citizen is an outstanding girl. Her accomplishments in high school fill page after page. Her citizenship test was one of the best the School Citizenship Program committee has ever read. Would she come forward? Harriet Elizabeth Springer, of Northville."

Moral energy vaulted Harriet to the front. She regarded the rows of women in lace and satin; Greg T. Hanson; the photographers. Applause and flashbulbs popped. The president held Harriet's hand aloft. "Don't worry about the photographers," she whispered greedily. "We send pictures to every paper in the state. It's so inspirational." Then Harriet saw a three-column cut in *The Northville News*. A headline: SPRINGER GIRL INSULTS DAR TURNS DOWN AWARD. SCHOOL SHOCKED. She saw the Harwyn Admissions Committee. Groomed, omnipotent hands irrevocably folding up her application. She had been bad, disobedient, ungrateful,

rude. For a moment, fear silenced her. Then, a primitive auto-
pilot, the performing self, began to steer. "Daughters of the Revolution," she said, "I am grateful to be here, to inherit the dream
your ancestors baptized in the blood of 1776. I am grateful to be
your Good Citizen."

Safely home in Northville, guilt whistled at the State Good Citizen. She remembered another Harwyn: immaculate, moral. She
remembered the man who had told her about Harwyn, the only
real notable she had ever met. He had miraculously appeared in
the Springer house in 1948 to create grassroots support for the
United Nations. Eleanor Springer believed in the U.N. Big
George did not. He set aside ideology to sustain marriage.
    "You've got quite a spread for tonight, Mommy," he had told
her. The family was eating dinner in the kitchen before the meeting at which the famous man was to speak.
    "What if nobody comes?" Eleanor worried. She had food for
forty.
    "Don't you worry, Mommy. Everything you do turns out to
be a dilly." Big George was not a fan of personal catastrophe.
    "Why don't you believe in the U.N., Daddy?" Harriet had
asked belligerently.
    "I don't trust the Russians."
    "You believe everything you read in that stupid *American
Legion Monthly*."
    "That's not the only thing I read." Big George was peaceable.
"But I know enough about communism to know I don't want it
here. You wouldn't want it either if you had to live under it.
The Communists wouldn't put up with your sass for a minute.
Now do your old dad a favor and pass the catsup."
    The famous man had arrived. Martin Porter: a name on books
her mother kept in the living room; a name on the masthead of
a magazine her mother read. He had spoken to Harriet as he
had unsnapped his rubber boots. He had a daughter, back in
Connecticut, about her age. He wanted her to go to the best college possible for women—Harwyn, in New York State. "I want to
go there, too," Harriet had said instantly. Before Big George
could stride up and ask Porter if he wanted a bit to eat, Harriet
had asked, "What do you think of communism?" And he had said
fervently, "If we are to have a strong U.N., if we are to have

a safe, moral world, America and Russia must work together." That night Harriet had dreamt that she and Martin Porter's daughter were friends at Harwyn; he had visited them both. Martin Porter would not have submitted to the Washington State Chapter of the Daughters of the American Revolution.

Harriet longed to consummate an act of expiation. She read *Native Son*. She and her mother talked about how terrible it was that Bigger Thomas and his family had to live in one room in Chicago with rats. However, there were no Negroes in Northville whom she could succor. She followed the routine of her days miserably. Then, in late March, in gym class, the head of Girls Physical Education abruptly lined the girls up and demanded order.

"What's wrong with Old MacDonald now?" Darlene LeSueur whispered to Harriet. She fondled the silver miniature football that hung from a silver chain between her thrusting breasts. Darlene and Harry Joe Galter were going steady.

"Who knows?" Harriet shrugged. They surveyed the stocky teacher as if she were a mined potato field.

"Girls, I have a serious matter to bring to your attention."

"I wish I had said I had cramps," Darlene muttered.

"Someone in this class has done something serious. June Krajack has just told me that her wallet has been stolen."

Everyone stared at June Krajack, a subwheel, standing at attention at the end of the first row, pale and strained.

"I trusted you girls," Miss McDonald said. "And someone, in this room, has betrayed that trust."

"Yeh yeh yeh yeh yeh yeh yeh," Darlene mouthed.

"However, I've decided to give one of you a second chance. I'm going to blow my whistle. Then I am going to count to thirty. While I count, I want the thief to walk up to me and give me June's wallet. Is that clear?"

The whistle reigned over Harriet's eardrums; reverberated from the varnished floor, walls, fenced-over windows, the tarpaulin dividing the girls' class from the boys. "One, two three," Miss McDonald dragged out each syllable savagely.

"I bet I know who the thief is," Darlene said.

"Who?"

"The new girl, the one in the back row, with the funny hair."

"Did you see her do it?" asked literal-minded Harriet.

"I didn't have to. I can spot a thief, just like that. My father taught me how to do it in the store."

"Thirty," Miss McDonald proclaimed. "I'm sorry, girls, I'm afraid that I must take the next step."

Harriet intuited a prick of duty nearing her flesh.

"I am going to have to have the class searched. I am sorry that we have to spend time doing this, but we owe it to June. Sit down, all of you. Miss Jaronski is going to send you to my office, one by one. After we search you, you will show Miss Gunshaw your locker."

"I don't have June Krajack's old wallet," Darlene complained. "I don't see why they're picking on me."

"Harriet Springer, Olivia Kasper, I want you to help me with the search." To watch the class take off their clothes? Impossible. "Harriet, Olivia, come with me." Miss McDonald walked toward the door. Harriet straggled out of line after her.

"Teacher's pet," Darlene called after her. "I bet it's the new girl," Harriet heard her say. "My father told me how to spot thieves. Look how scared she looks." Then Darlene's voice was lost in the babble of the class, happy to give up an indoors softball drill for the chance to apprehend a thief.

Olivia was left in an anteroom to watch the girls strip to their underwear and to send them in to an inner office, where Harriet was to help inspect the clothes. Taped to the office walls were posture charts and nutrition guides. "Take your station," Miss McDonald said. The first girls entered.

Harriet tried to concentrate on the bundles she was handed. She pretended she was wearing gloves. When she saw a body, pubic hair often public through cheap rayon or thin cotton, she averted her gaze. Then the new girl came in. "Betty," Miss McDonald said, "give Harriet your clothes." The new girl did nothing. Harriet looked at her. "You might as well," she said, to comfort her. The new girl stood still, upper teeth grasping at her lower lip. Her body was a series of slumps and outcroppings. Eyes, ears, nose, mouth, hands, elbows, knees, and feet seemed twisted off other bodies and slapped on her passive frame. Her hair, the color of dirty broomstraws, stuck out stiffly. Even her thighs were freckled.

51

"You're new here, Betty," Miss McDonald said. "There's no point in getting off on the wrong foot in a new school now, is there?"

"It'll be all right," Harriet murmured.

"Get undressed," Miss McDonald said, a grim buttressed voice. "If you didn't steal June's wallet, you'll get dressed and go back to the class. If you did, you're going to get caught sooner or later."

Abrupt as a blow, clothes were thrown at Harriet. They smelled. The gym shorts were too dark a blue; zipper on the front, not the side. The sneakers were ankle-high black canvas, not low white Keds. The socks and shirt were gray. Harriet shook out each item and gave it back to Betty as quickly as she could. Then she shut her eyes and shoved her hand into the sneakers. The rubber insteps were rough and cold. To her dismay, she felt, in the toe of the second shoe, a wad of paper smooth enough to be cash. She opened her eyes, to confront Betty's yellow-brown fear, Miss McDonald's brute impatience. She thrust the wad even more deeply into the shoe. "Nothing here," she said.

"I don't know why you had to make such a fuss, Betty," Miss McDonald said. "Hurry up and get dressed. We haven't got all day."

Nancy Moberg was next in line. "Harriet," she said plaintively, "I forgot and went and left my Kleenex and my bobby pins in my shirt pocket. You won't throw them away now, will you?"

That afternoon, in the spring rain, in new raincoat and hat, body bent over her leather notebook, Harriet was waiting for her bus. "Hey, Harriet," the voice behind her was harsh. Betty Dowsey, the girl from gym class.

Her old tweed overcoat hung to midcalf. Her hair stuck out beyond the edges of a damp cotton scarf. She wore the same black tennis shoes and grayish socks she had for P.E. The edges of her oilcloth-covered cardboard notebook were fraying.

"Hi," said Harriet.

"I'm on my way home to get dinner for my folks."

"Is your mother sick?"

"No, she works. Besides, she's not my real mother. I'm a foster child." She spoke as if she had much to tell Harriet in a hurry.

"Is that so?" Harriet was unsure if she should express approval or sympathy.

Betty leaned closer. "Listen. Why don't you come visit me tomorrow night at my house?"

Harriet stalled. "I don't know if I can."

"Come meet my folks. I'd like you to meet my folks. I don't know anybody else that I can take to meet my folks."

"I have a lot of work to do this week."

"I guess you think I stole that wallet, don't you?"

"Of course I don't."

"Then why don't you come meet my folks. I live on Bush Street, Number 711, Bush Street."

"I'll ask my mother," Harriet said.

"I'll expect you," Betty answered. "Seven o'clock."

"What should I do?" Harriet beseeched her mother later. "I don't want to go there, but she doesn't have any friends."

Her mother was slicing apples. "Well, dear, it can't hurt you," she said reasonably. "You should be nice to people who need you, and she probably doesn't have any other way to thank you for being so understanding of her this morning."

At dinner that night, spooning applesauce over his roast pork, her father said the Dowsey name was familiar. "Frank Dowsey," he mused, "opened up a new account last month. Not much in it, though."

Eleanor Springer loaned Harriet her car to go to the Dowseys. She felt as she had at the end of World War II when her class had packed weekly parcels for Europeans for the Child-to-Child Rescue Program. She had conscientiously brought new clothes, unbitten pencils, and working toys. The single-story Dowsey house was on a corner lot. A battered pickup truck was parked on the broken concrete driveway. Betty answered the bell before the chimes ended their tinny run.

"Hi," she said eagerly. She had dressed up. But her clean white dickey was askew around her neck, and the yarn of her pink sweater was so thin that her bra showed. Harriet walked into a narrow hall. No carpet. To the left was a kitchen, to the right a living room. A hooked rug lay between the upholstered sofa and a table which a white, plastic radio dominated. A burly man lay on the sofa. He wore work boots, khaki pants, a plaid wool shirt. Big George kept his tie on until he went to bed.

"Hey, Dad," Betty said, "this is Harriet, my school friend."

53

"How do you do?" Harriet said.

"Can't complain." He went back to his paper.

"Come meet my mom." Betty led her across the hall. A muscular woman, in a chenille robe and mules, was heating water on the stove. "So you're Betty's friend," she observed. "I'm glad she has one. Moving around like we do, it's hard to make them. Betty, tell her to sit down."

Harriet took one of the wooden chairs. On a white doily, in the middle of the kitchen table, a porcelain shepherdess in frilly poke bonnet held a crook to admonish a bluish sheep.

"Want a Coke?" Betty stood in front of her.

"No, but thanks very much anyway," Harriet said. Her mother refused to let her children have gum or soft drinks, because they ruined teeth.

Mrs. Dowsey, with a cup of tea, sat down across from Harriet. "Get the cake you bought," she said.

"Where did you live before you came to Northville?" Harriet politely asked.

"All over," Mrs. Dowsey said. "California, Nevada, you name it. I met my husband in California. It was during the war. He was in the Army, and I was working in a shipbuilding plant. Look, over there on the wall, there's a picture of us on our wedding day."

The tinted photo in the gold frame showed a couple standing before light blue drapes. The woman, in a white suit, was carrying a bouquet of roses and baby's breath. The man, in a corporal's uniform, overseas cap pointed like a widow's peak, was holding her waist. "It's very nice," Harriet said.

"We got married before a Justice of the Peace." Mrs. Dowsey recollected. "The war was on, so we didn't have time for a big wedding, but we had all the fun that we could."

Betty put glass plates on the bare table. "I was in the orphanage then," she said.

"Probably making trouble, just like you do now, when your dad has to take the strap to you," Mrs. Dowsey said.

Harriet shuddered.

"Get the nice knife out," Mrs. Dowsey urged, "the good one, the one I got for a wedding present."

Betty gave them a colored paper napkin, a knife, and a fork. She put the chocolate cake, in a box, on the table. Then, from a cabinet, she brought down a bone-handled knife wrapped in tissue.

"Make an extra plate for your dad, Betty. I'll eat with him so you can talk to your friend."

As Mrs. Dowsey left, Harriet stood up. "It was nice to meet you," she said.

"The same, I'm sure."

"Don't pay too much attention to my dad," Betty said, eating rapidly. "He doesn't say much, but he's a good worker. We're trying to buy this house. It's only the second time we've tried to buy a house."

"Where's your room?" She disliked chocolate, but she wanted to keep Betty from noticing how hard it was for her to swallow the cake.

"Oh, I sleep in the living room."

"But where do you do your homework?"

"Right here, on the kitchen table."

Harriet meditated upon Betty. She might have stolen June Krajack's wallet. She was a poor foster child, but she had enough money to buy Harriet the cake. But, she slept on a sofa. She studied at a kitchen table. She had no friends. She was scrawny, ugly, flimsily dressed. Helping her would bring neither worldly credit nor glory to Harriet. Helping her was the right thing to do.

"Tomorrow night is a Y-Teen meeting," she told Betty. "I'm going to sponsor you for membership."

"Those girls will never let me in," Betty said, alert with want, wary with knowledge.

"I'll make it happen," Harriet promised.

The next evening she proposed Betty's name. "Ugh," Darlene LeSueur said. "She's a thief, a nasty thief."

"That's not fair," Harriet said. She was aroused. "That's not right. This is supposed to be a Christian organization. Besides, in this country you're innocent until you're proven guilty. You don't know that she stole that wallet."

"I don't like her."

"But she's new in town, and she needs our help."

The Y-Teen adviser supported Harriet. Betty was admitted. Every other Thursday, Harriet picked Betty up and sat by her in meetings as the club planned parties and paper drives. Betty was quiet until Harriet took her home, when she thanked her. "Gee," she said once, "I never thought I'd get into the club." Sponsoring Betty failed to wipe out Harriet's guilt about the DAR, but at least twice a month she enjoyed the quiet, steady walk of the virtuous.

"You're going to college, aren't you, Harriet?" asked Darlene LeSueur. Some of the girl wheels were eating lunch in their section of the clattering cafeteria.

"I'm going to a place called Harwyn." She opened her paper sack, trying not to revel in her pleasure at being accepted as a member of what she knew to be a legion of austere, intellectual, hushed women with high foreheads, eyes statue-blank under the pressure of wisdom, poetry, and ideals.

"Is that a Bible school? It sounds like a Bible school." Darlene knew Harriet was an atheist, but her question was genuine.

"No," said Harriet. "It's an eastern, women's liberal arts college, in New York, about sixty miles from New York City."

"Gee," said Darlene, "that's a long way away."

"Are you really going to Stanford?" Harriet asked Betsy.

"I can't wait." She was as sure of Stanford's Spanish arcades as Harriet was of Harwyn's Neo-Gothic arches.

"Aren't you scared to go so far away?" Olivia asked. She had chosen the University of Washington. Already sororities were discreetly wondering if she might pledge.

"I can't wait," Betsy repeated.

"Gee," Darlene said. She looked at Betsy and Harriet, but not Olivia, who was staying within the boundaries of the state. "You guys will go away and you'll never come back and speak to us hicks again. You'll get stuck-up.

"Well, I don't care. Harry Joe and I are going to have our house, and we're going to get a new car, and someday he'll get his gun collection. He's got a good job now with a beer distributor, driving the truck. Northville is the best town in the world to live in."

Harriet finished her sandwich, celery stick, brownie, milk. Outside, beyond the wall, car engines from driver education class started, missed, stalled, started again. She felt abused. She was not a snob because she had been admitted to one of the best women's colleges in the country. She had not betrayed Darlene. On the contrary. She had gone to four bridal showers for her, sitting gamely while Darlene and her sisters counted the number of different-colored ribbons that had come on the shower presents. The number of colors symbolized the number of times Harry Joe would do something to Darlene on their wedding night. Everyone ignored the fact that Darlene was already pregnant.

The girls began to list couples going to the senior prom. Harry Joe and Darlene; Vince and Olivia; Dirk Dennison and Betsy. But no one mentioned Harriet and no one. The girls would not talk about that in front of her. The code forbade such public humiliation. The class valedictorian, editor of the newspaper, three times Princess Sweetheart for Intelligence, vice president of the Rally Club, president of the Activities Merit Club, and State DAR Good Citizen got up, threw her garbage in a trash barrel, and started for her locker to get her Senior Civics book. Clive McGee was waiting for her outside the cafeteria.

"Hi, Harriet," he said. "Got any plans for the prom?"

Was he tormenting her? She had never discovered the truth about his Queen Sweetheart news.

"Don't you want to talk to me?" he asked.

"I've got to get to civics,"

"In that case I guess you don't want to hear the news I've got for you about the prom."

"What news?" Tension forcing her voice up a pitch.

"I'm going to ask Sherry Lynn Hill." She's only a sophomore, Harriet thought. "David may ask you," Clive went on, as bland as a clean bandage. "If he does, we'll double-date."

"Fine by me." Then she wondered if she should sound more hard to get.

"I've got to run," she said.

That night, during dinner, the phone rang. Harriet, staring down at her cream-and-brown bread pudding, told herself it would be for her mother or for Anne, who was getting up to answer it.

"It's for you, Hairy," Anne called from the kitchen.

Her father spooned himself more dessert. Her mother pretended to pluck a raisin from hers. Harriet walked carefully to the phone. "Hello," she said, controlling her voice.

"Hi, there." It was David Patterson. "You may have heard that there is going to be a senior prom at good old Northville High."

"So I've heard."

"I wondered if you would like to go with me."

There, at last, the words were there. "Yes, I guess I would. Thanks for asking me."

"That's okay. Well, I guess I'll see you in chem tomorrow."

"I'll be there."

"Okay. I guess we might as well sign off now."

"Thanks again."

"It's nothing."

She hung up, strolled back into the dining room, sat down. Behind her, beyond the picture window, was the bay, the mills, and piers; the clouds through which the sun was passing on its way to the icy ridges of Korea, the hordes of China, the brutalities of Russian communism.

"David Patterson wants me to go to the senior prom," she said. "I guess I'll have to buy a formal now." Her spoon slipped gracefully into the rich heap of her bread pudding.

"Oh, Harriet," her mother said, "we'll go to Seattle to get one."

She continued to eat quietly, but she wanted to shout. She would leave Northville proudly, not in disgrace; she would go to Harwyn, having touched every base. Head high, but still humble, she could manage through the festivities of graduation and June weddings.

The night of the dance, David Patterson stood resplendent to bow as he gave her a wrist corsage of red roses and ribbons. She inserted a white carnation in his lapel. They were the faculty choice to lead the prom parade around the gym. She in a white, strapless gown; he in a dark suit and new tie. Like royalty they marched beneath the crepe-paper-draped baskets into which he, as a substitute on the varsity basketball team, had flung shot after shot. They danced, closer and closer, until the bell of her skirt crumpled against the clapper of her legs. They went to a party with the wheels. The boys drank Olympia beer and let the girls sip from their bottles.

"Here, you want some? If you're good, I'll let you have some."

"Gee, I don't know if I should. I mean, after all, it's alcohol."

"Aw, come on, it's only a beer. Just this once, I'll let you have some."

"You really think I should?"

"Sure you should. I'll let you have some."

"Well, maybe this once. I mean, how many times in my life will I have my senior prom."

Then David drove her home. His hands beat a tattoo on the steering wheel of his father's car. For a moment they stood in the side entry of her house next to the high, gray Amana home freezer. She hoped he would do what desire and tradition suggested he might do—kiss her. He put his arms around her; hers collapsed around him. But she was unable to kiss him. An unwanted thread had suddenly, surprisingly, stitched her mouth shut. She feared betraying her parents upstairs, particularly her mother. She feared that David might stop when he found out how inexperienced and awkward she was. Her ardor was struggling against the restraint, trying to scissor it away, when he stopped. "Don't," she begged. She clutched at him, sweetheart roses melting on her waist. "Dammit," he choked out and left. "Don't go, I'll be good," she wanted to shout after him, even to run after him. But the same cablelike thread immobilized her. She heard his car motor. When he was no longer there to call back, she could move. She picked up her white skirt. She went upstairs. She heard her mother invite her into her bedroom to talk, but she pretended she had not. She could neither tell the truth nor disguise it.

She and David were next to each other on the stage at graduation. He ignored her. Luckily he was not invited to Darlene LeSueur's wedding. Harriet huddled correctly next to Betsy Metcalfe in a hot Methodist church with plain glass windows. She had had to dress up: girdle, of course; white spike heels; pink linen dress with precautionary shields pinned into it; gloves, pillbox hat. She wondered how pregnant Darlene was. Though she generally knew when someone was in trouble, she was ignorant of the details of other girls' adventures. When they had first French-kissed, petted, heavy-petted, or gone all the way.

At three o'clock, the organ music intensified. Ushers were bringing the parents of the bride and groom up the aisle. Mrs. LeSueur's lime-green brocade suit and Mrs. Galter's bright blue brocade suit were cut from the same pattern. As they were seated, a door behind the organist opened. The Blissful Aires, a quartet that performed at ceremonies and parties, emerged, to arrange themselves in a half circle between the organ and the front pews. Bending toward each other, they began to sing. Harriet pretended to listen to "I Love You Truly" and "The Lord's Prayer," but, without moving her lips, she tried to count the number of hairs in one square inch of the cropped head of the man in front of her.

Then the Blissful Aires began to sway from side to side, arms linked. They were crooning a medley of love songs from Broadway hit musicals. Harriet was astounded. She had heard "I Love You Truly" and "The Lord's Prayer" at four or five weddings she had gone to that year. At the fifth, where the oldest daughter of the Springers' family doctor had married a man from Seattle in the Presbyterian Church both families attended, the organist had played tasteful selections from the composer Johann Sebastian Bach.

As the Blissful Aires eased into "Some Enchanted Evening," Harry Joe Galter and his brother, Ted, emerged from the left side of the church. White evening jackets hung from their shoulders. Harry was rubbing his palms against his hips, as if he were still the center of the Northville football team, wiping the mud from his hands before bending to snap the ball back to Vince Shelton, his quarterback. The minister, in a plain black robe, at the top of the center aisle, stared, reproachful. Harry stiffened his arms, fingers pointed toward the floor.

The organist, with sweep and surety, struck at the Mendelssohn wedding march. Two little girls, in yellow taffeta dresses, white socks, and new shoes, stumbled up the red carpet of the center aisle. A woman, in loud anguish, called after them from the vestibule, "Throw the flowers, girls. Throw the flowers." The children reached into the yellow wicker baskets they were carrying to pull out paper roses to scatter through the pews.

Four bridesmaids and a matron of honor, Darlene's married sister, followed. The toes of their yellow satin spike shoes kicked at the flowers on the floor. Their gold brocade sheath dresses were wrapped around them as tightly as green waxed paper around the stems of bouquets. They held bunches of white chrysanthemum poms, as stiffly as if they were silver crosses before the werewolf. At the top of the aisle they formed an arc, facing Harry Joe and Ted. The boys' stare tangled in the lacquered heaps of their bouffant hair. "Oh," murmured a woman behind Harriet, "aren't they nice." "I'm getting out of this, I'm going to Harwyn," Harriet reminded herself.

A proud organ fortissimo triumphantly warned the audience to stand. Darlene, on her father's arm, marched between the rows of family, guests, and friends toward Harry Joe and the minister. She was wearing a gown, of Chantilly lace and peau de soie, that she and her mother had bought in Northville's best store. Simulated miniature pearls and sequins bordered the scalloped front neckline. A crown of pearls and crystal beads held her veil. She clasped a cluster of white orchids and yellow roses before her belly. In a miraculous dispensation she was again immaculate, innocent of the thrusts and pulls of sex, free from the tiny fingernails of the fetus that was scratching at the lining of her womb. "What a waste of money," Betsy whispered.

In the church basement the Blissful Aires were now sharing a pint of Canadian Whiskey with an accordion player hired to provide dance music during the reception. Together they were to perform "Ain't She Sweet" while Darlene and Harry Joe cut the three-tiered wedding cake. In the kitchen two of Darlene's aunts were making coffee in fifty-cup percolators and stacking wrapped squares of iced fruitcake in a large, yellow wicker basket for guests to take home and put under their pillows.

Drifting down from the ceremony came the opening chords of "Whither thou goest." To their surprise, though they had watched the rehearsal, they heard Darlene's solo soprano.

"Isn't it enough to promise to love, honor, and obey?" asked the younger woman. "Does she have to stand there in church and sing to him, too?"

"I think it's nice. Her father spent a fortune on her voice lessons. He should have something to show for it."

"But it's peculiar, to sing to your own husband at your wedding."

"It's nice. You never did have much of a sense of romance. We've got enough egg salad here to feed an army, don't we?"

Darlene's fragile voice trembled down; to touch the cake, sandwiches, mints, and nuts; the Blissful Aires, accordion player, and photographer, who did weddings to add to the salary he earned as a clerk in Ray's Foto Shop; the two aunts, in good clothes and aprons.

Upstairs, in her pew, Harriet felt her sweat overwhelm the underarm shields and ooze into the pink linen of her dress. "I'm going to Harwyn," she repeated to herself. "Things will be different there."

PART 2

Obviously this report is obeying the old-fashioned demands of chronological order. That means that I have come to Harwyn, to the part about us, that Susan Crawford Neall and Serena Bell and I will each remember, in our own ways. I am afraid that I might belittle Harwyn, but I might also be too kind. My account might yoke the faults of timidity and impertinence. If I am ambivalent now, it might be because I was ambivalent then. I was an outsider. I sought the status Harwyn might confer, but feared and resented the process. So, I think, did a Jewish postman's daughter from the Bronx; a black professor's daughter from Chicago; a doctor's daughter from Hawaii who wanted the territory to become a state. We did not recognize each other. Alienation was not a principle on which the ambitious organized a club. Making too much of certain differences was not a fashion of the time.

Harriet was enthroned in a carved wooden chair in a dining room with fifteen-foot-high mullioned windows and vaulted ceilings. Negro women were serving food in china plates and then clearing them away. Outside were six hundred landscaped acres; Neo-Gothic structures; tennis courts; a hockey field; a library with a collection of papyri scraps. Her brother had escorted her during the three-day train trip across America, over land and water increasingly susceptible to human organization. She had read F. Scott Fitzgerald. He had been bored. When he had gone away to Yale, he had worn a loud plaid suit; white shirt; a tie on which a palm tree was painted. Now he was in tweed jackets; chino pants; button-down-collar shirts; narrow ties. He had not approved of Harwyn. Wellesley and Smith girls were good-looking, those at Harwyn dogs. Harriet had not cared what he thought. Yale had failed to develop finer feelings in Georgie.

Of the people at her table, few were as beautiful as Olivia Kasper. These girls emanated other forms of aesthetic excellence. To her left was a thickset girl, with shoulder-length, straw-colored hair and bangs. Esther Reich, from Amarillo, Texas. She wanted to be called Amarillo. To Harriet's right was an exotic creature, fingernails painted the glittering scarlet of deadly nightshade berries. Naomi Weissburg, from Uruguay. Naomi wondered what a Texas was. American geography was so confusing. Across the table, hands in lap between courses, was a lanky, reserved girl. Her appearance was as alien to Harriet as Naomi Weissburg's. She wore no makeup, not even lipstick. Her brown hair was cut in a simple curve. She had a high forehead, large dark eyes. Her name was Louisa Lacey.

After dinner a Negro maid served the girls demitasse coffee. Louisa asked Harriet to come to her room to listen to music. Though Louisa's tone was casual, Harriet felt special, singled out. They walked beneath the covered arch that separated the dining and living rooms of Gould Hall from the bedrooms. Louisa had a first-floor suite. Its furnishings were in place. She even had two chairs.

"Didn't you find the conversation at dinner a disappointment?" she asked Harriet abruptly. "I don't want to sound like a horrible snob, but I had expected something more intellectual."

"I've never met anyone from Texas or Uruguay, though," Harriet confessed.

"Really? Where do you come from?" Louisa sounded genuinely interested.

"A little town you've never heard of, called Northville, in Northwest Washington."

"Oh, what a long way. You must be lonely."

"I'll be all right," Harriet lied. Louisa's concern was threatening to uncover a magnet of homesickness that would pull at her iron eyelids and release the cowardly tears.

"Well, my dear," Louisa said decisively, "we'll just have to take care of you. Now, what about some Mozart? Do you like the Mass in C Minor?"

In spite of her music lessons, Harriet could barely tell the Mass in C Minor from the Crab Nebula. "That would be fine," she said, as if she could. She was beginning to feel less weepy. Unexpectedly, she seemed to have a protector, a guardian whose questions symbolized the difference between Harwyn and Northville, between classical purities and Irving Berlin pumped out on an accordion. She was leaning back in her chair when a stranger knocked and entered. Her short, thick tawny hair was in two pigtails tied with colored yarn.

"Jane, my dear," Louisa said happily. She calls everyone "My dear," Harriet thought jealously. "I want you to meet someone in Gould Hall who seems tolerable. Harriet Springer, this is Jane Vanderbilt."

Harriet gaped. The Vanderbilt was less richly dressed than a Northville wheel. No cashmere sweater, but lamb's wool. No pleated skirt, but a khaki wraparound. No polished saddle shoes, but scuffed brown loafers. No socks to match her sweater; no socks at all. The Vanderbilt barely nodded at Harriet. Then, far more cheerfully, she arranged to play quartets with Louisa the next day and left.

On Louisa's desk was a colored photo of a middle-aged couple. He was wearing baggy, seersucker pants; she a cotton dress. "Are those your parents?" Harriet asked.

"Yes, they're sweet, aren't they?" Louisa answered with real affection.

"What does your father do?" Harriet asked carefully. She wanted to know, but she wondered if the question was indiscreet.

"He's a banker," Louisa said, as if it were irrelevant. "You'll meet both of them someday."

Afraid to wear out such a friendly welcome, Harriet left when the music ended. She immediately called home. She told her mother about Tally Merker, her sophomore adviser; about her need to buy Bermuda shorts; about the college president, who had called Harriet into her office to say how important it was for Harwyn to have a varied student body, including western girls. "Has Daddy ever heard of a banker from Boston named Lacey?" she asked casually.

"Daddy," her mother called out at home, "it's Harriet. She wants to know if you know a Boston banker named Lacey."

"Ferdinand Lacey?" Her father's voice was remote. "He could buy and sell me in a minute. He could buy and sell the whole town of Northville."

"I met a Vanderbilt in her suite," Harriet told her mother modestly.

"Oh, darling." Her mother was openly exultant. "I knew if I could get you out of Northville, you'd make contacts like that."

Returning to her room, Harriet felt better balanced. She listed things to buy. She put on her new, quilted bathrobe with the black corduroy collar. Carrying soap and towel, she walked down the hall to bathe. She was glad that Gould Hall had only one toilet and tub in the bathrooms and basins in each bedroom. She could be private. The stocky porcelain tub, set on four clawed feet, was like that of Grandmother Yates, except the hot and cold tap labels in Gould Hall were pressed from ivory. Back in her room, she sat on the single bed with the new cotton Bates spread. She had no sitting room. Through her three windows she could see the tangled branches of a spruce tree; the gray, mica-flecked stone walls and turrets of the library. This is my new life, Harriet thought. I'm lucky to be here.

That weekend, though, was the Freshman Orientation Mixer. The idea of such an event in the Harwyn gym had seemed blasphemous to Harriet, as if Darlene LeSueur Galter, in her Simplicity Pattern maternity dress, had asked Louisa Lacey if she thought Elizabeth Taylor should have married Michael Wilding. Louisa had refused to go. However, Harriet remembered her mother's prophecy that away from Northville she would discover men who would appreciate her. Perhaps, at the mixer, a boy would introduce himself at the beginning of the very first dance. On the floor, he would say, "Do you like John Donne?" She would answer, "My favorite line is the one Hemingway chose as the title for *For Whom the Bell Tolls*." When the dancing stopped, their hands would still clasp. Body and mind would have met body and mind: two shining beams, the searchlights of intelligence probing toward the sky of truth.

On the afternoon of the mixer, Amarillo and Harriet sat in the butterfly chairs in Naomi's sitting room. In the bedroom, breaking rules, Naomi had a hot plate. On it she was melting a square of yellow wax in a saucepan. A smell of candles and rotting eggs drifted out.

"My accent is perfectly good," she was insisting. "I went to the best English school in Uruguay."

"If your family had left Germany when mine did, and if you had come to America, your accent would be better," Amarillo asserted.

"When did you leave Germany?" Harriet asked, awed that people she knew could be victims of history.

"Nineteen thirty-six."

"We did not leave until 1939," Naomi said, "on a second-class cattle boat."

Through the doorway Harriet could see Naomi apply two strips of wax to her upper lip. It resembled the edges of a peaked roof.

"Why don't you use NAIR?" Amarillo challenged lazily.

"Because NAIR is for babies." Naomi's voice was strangled. "Wax is European. Now be quiet. I have to do a thigh."

Harriet fingered the remnants of her moustache. Compared to the rivulets of hair that ran down the inside of her thighs, it was but a drop.

After dinner, she dressed beneath the seventy-five-watt ceiling bulb—with its new shade—in her room. She missed her mother to help decide what to wear. She put on a purple wool dress with long sleeves and round neckline, designed for social events that were neither formal nor sporty. She brushed her short, springy hair. She applied a thin layer of Elizabeth Arden powder to her nose, bright-red Elizabeth Arden lipstick to her mouth. She pinned a name tag to her dress.

Naomi and Amarillo were waiting in the Gould lobby. The three of them, Harriet by far the tallest, stood in front of the shoulder-high, empty fireplace. Denver, the Negro woman who supervised the switchboard, inspected them. "My, my," she said, "you all look as glamorous as movie stars."

"What is a mixer anyway?" Naomi asked. "What am I supposed to do?"

"You just stand there, Miss Naomi," Denver said, "and look pretty, and a gentleman will ask you to dance."

Harriet worried that Amarillo's dress, black velvet with white linen collar and bib, might be more elegant than her own. They both seemed plain next to Naomi. Her dark blond hair was combed back from her forehead, to swirl around her ears and return to her cheeks. Nail polish matched her lipstick. Her pumps were covered in the same silk fabric as her dress—gorgeous red and purple prints of peonies. Gold bracelets shimmered on her wrists. Thick pancake makeup both concealed and rebuked her skin problems.

When they reached the gym, buses were braking in the parking lot behind it. "Hurry up," urged Claire Hazlitt, the chairman of the Orientation Committee,"we've got to get you gals in before we let the boys out." The gym lights had been dimmed, so that the running track fifteen feet above them jutted out from the walls like the visor of a dark helmet. At one end a small dance orchestra was tuning up. Student government officers and orientation advisers were organizing girls against two walls. Harriet, separated from Amarillo and Naomi, was put between strangers, unable to read their name tags. To stop her hands from scraping against her skirt, she grasped her garter straps.

Claire Hazlitt whispered to the orchestra leader. To a medley from *Call Me Madam*, boys entered through the gym doors. They looked more comfortable in jackets and ties than Northville boys. Harriet saw more glasses, fewer crewcuts, less robust bodies. A handsome, mature-looking boy, in dark slacks and tweed jacket, approached Naomi. She looked at Amarillo, who pushed her toward him. Hand on Naomi's back, he took her toward the center of the floor. As boys appeared, the orientation officers pointed at girls without partners. Amarillo was led off. The gym walls on either side of Harriet were stripped down to bare wood and brick. Harriet felt like an accident victim, who, recovering from a broken bone, must watch helplessly as a hammer swings down on the convalescing limb.

Then Harriet saw Claire Hazlitt grasp the elbow of a tall, blond, gangling boy and walk him toward her.

"Harriet Springer?" Claire asked brightly. "You're from way out west in Washington State, aren't you? This is Henry." She smiled at them, as if they were two matches she would enflame through the catching fire of her energy.

"Do you want to dance?" asked Henry. "I'm not very good."

"Neither am I," said Harriet, obeying *Seventeen*'s command to reassure the insecure.

Henry's right hand splayed against her spine. His left hand took hers. Harriet looked up at him, "Do you like John Donne?" she asked.

"Who?"

"John Donne."

"Sometimes."

"What are your favorite lines?"

"Now and then. He's a poet, isn't he?"

Perhaps, Harriet thought, it's going to work. "Yes, he is," she answered, trying to let him avoid bumping into other couples. "My favorite lines are in the sermon Hemingway used when he found the title for his novel *For Whom the Bell Tolls.*"

"Oh."

She shut up. *Seventeen* had told her not to push, not to frighten the shy. If she kept quiet, he would appreciate her sensitivity. Yet, as "Tea for Two" poured over them, and he silently stared over her head, panic beat at her ribs. "What do you plan to study?" she floundered.

"I don't know," he said. The music stopped. He took her back to her wall. He did not stay. Fearful that Claire Hazlitt might notice her again, Harriet pulled herself along the walls, to the door. She walked back to Gould Hall, feet hitting at leaves, and signed herself in. She did not want to be seen or to see herself. She was not going to be popular. Not being popular was like a third leg, dragging behind her like a tail. She had been foolish to dream that it might have deliriously atrophied at the mixer.

However, she was not home in Northville. Here Louisa Lacey alluded to Mozart; there Darlene LeSueur rhapsodized about Johnny Mathis. She would study hard and try to achieve success, on whatever terms she could. That night she dreamt she was in Northville. She walked, with her tennis racket, beneath the shadow of an evergreen-clotted hill. On her right was the house in which a mean lady lived. She had called a girl in Anne's class a dirty Jew and thrown potatoes at her. A plump man, in a flowered sports shirt, stroking the smooth top of his bald head, watched her as the muscles of her stomach and her legs loosened and fell apart.

In Northville her brain had worked with the self-effacing efficiency of the spleen. At Harwyn it faltered, grappled, stumbled. In English she perched stiffly, in a corner of a second-story classroom, next to an old fireplace. A small plaster cast of Athena on the

71

mantle. Engravings of Italian antiquities on yellowed, plaster walls.

"What image pattern does Hawthorne establish in the first paragraph of 'Young Goodman Brown'?" the shy instructor beseeched her shiny, sloppy, knitting students, yarn burgeoning from their fingers.

Silence.

"Do you think Hawthorne establishes an image pattern in the first paragraph of 'Young Goodman Brown'?"

"The man's last name is Brown. The story begins at sunset. It establishes a sense of darkness," Libby Molineux answered casually, contemptuously. She had gone to Foxcroft.

"Thank you, Miss Molineux. Why then is his first name Goodman and his wife's first name Faith?"

"Because Hawthorne is examining religious faith," Cornelia Lambert said. She had gone to Farmington.

"Thank you, Miss Lambert. Does young Goodman Brown pass the test?"

"Is the concept of irony useful here?" Molly Sonnenstein asked. She had gone to Midwood High in Brooklyn. Harriet wrote "irony" in her list of words to investigate. "I'm going to the library," she had written to her mother, "and read biographies of every author that we study. That way I may catch up."

Harriet hoped, too, that her first philosophy paper might redeem her. She nurtured it as she sat at a wooden carrel in the library, forty feet below brass-studded beams. High on slate walls, between leaded windows, were the large oil portraits of past Harwyn presidents. "The Pre-Socratics and the World" hypothesized that those Ur-thinkers of Western culture had three concerns: whether the world was unified or a series of unrelated fragments; whether the world was spirit or matter; whether the world was stable or in flux. She had listed the six possibilities in a left-hand column on a sheet of graph paper. Checking to make sure that her spelling was correct, she had printed the names of the Pre-Socratics from left to right along the top: Thales, Anaximander, Anaximenes, Pythagoras, Heraclitus, Xenophanes, Parmenides, Zeno, Empedocles, Anaxagoras, Democritus. She had drawn three lines from left to right: red for unity/disunity; green for material/immaterial; blue for stability/flux. If a Pre-Socratic had been on one side of the thinking about that concept, the line rose under his name; if on the other, the line dipped. She had a cartography of the history of early Greek thought.

When she had a typed draft, she wanted an upperclassman to confirm her diligence. She entered the Smoker, a wedge-shaped room over the Gould Hall arch, in which she liked to study. Its furniture was as worn as a stubbed cigarette; its walls the color of ash. Nevertheless, she would listen raptly to the tough, urbane talk that went on there, even on Saturday nights when girls who did not have dates gathered there and did not seem to care.

Her adviser, Tally Merker, was leading a conversation on a favorite topic: Harwyn and the Jews. "Of course Gould is a Jewish dorm. Look at the freshmen they put here. Amarillo *Reich*, Naomi *Weissburg*."

"Merker's not a Jewish name. How did they know about you when they put you here last year?" Rachel Diamond asked.

"They know." Cynical Tally. "They always know. This year they made a mistake, though. They gave us Louisa Lacey, who belongs over in Stuart Hall with the rest of the debutantes."

"I'm not Jewish," Harriet said, holding her paper, defending Louisa.

"But you're from the West," Tally said. "In their minds it works out to the same thing, unless you're a debutante from San Francisco or Los Angeles."

Bravely Harriet interrupted Rachel, a philosophy major, as she began to tell Tally about a sex dream she had had about a political science professor the night before. "Would you do me a favor?" she asked.

"Sure," Rachel answered, as if she had opulent leisure. She was wearing her lounge clothes: a dirty man's shirt, jeans, bedroom slippers.

"I'm taking Philosophy 1."

"That's good for a freshman. Who's your professor?"

"McMaster." A Scotch theologian who released his lectures as if they were sour grapes accidentally in his mouth.

"I'm writing a term paper on the Pre-Socratics, and I was trying to show how they all fitted together, so I experimented with a graph. I wondered if you'd look at it, to see if it was okay or not."

Rachel, in the afternoon light from the grimy, curtainless windows, regarded the paper impassively. "There's a lot of work here," she said finally.

73

"Thank you."

"Yeah, you've really got something here." Rachel scratched her rough yellow hair.

"I'm glad you think so."

"Any time." Rachel picked her Modern Library edition of Plato from the floor. Harriet left the Smoker for her room. For the first time that week homesickness did not adhere to her lungs like a slice of cold metal. She copied her chart, using a ruler to achieve the most pristine of angles and lines. She clipped it, as Appendix I, into a blue binder, behind the paper, an analysis of Thales' concept of water, and her bibliography. The next morning, in class, Professor McMaster received it as if it were hard bread.

Before philosophy, for the next two weeks, Harriet's heart pounded. One Wednesday, at the end of class, as the dead leaves of autumn were smashing against the ground floor windows, Professor McMaster handed the papers back and departed. His brogues pounded and smoothed the splintery wooden floors. She forced herself to wait until she was outside to open the binder. On the title page was an imperfect circle, a C minus. She closed the binder. This was how Darlene LeSueur must have felt when she had missed her period. Amarillo emerged behind her. "What a lousy class," she grumped. "How does that woman expect me to be interested in Babylonia? What's the slop for lunch today?"

"Grilled cheese sandwiches," Harriet forced an ordinary tone.

"Let's go get ptomaine then," said Amarillo.

After lunch Harriet waited until she saw Rachel alone, reading in a corner of a window seat in the hall living room.

"Rachel." She handed her the philosophy paper.

"I don't understand," Rachel said brusquely as she saw the mark. "Why don't you go talk to him?"

"Talk to a professor?"

"Sure, that's what they're there for."

The next afternoon she knocked at McMaster's oak office door in the library. He was sitting behind a wooden desk that stretched from wall to wall. Books, journals, file boxes, and papers jammed ceiling-high bookshelves, as guilt might an old church confessional. His figure blocked out most of the mullioned windows and the branches of dogwood and willows outside.

"Yes?" he said, not removing his pipe.

"My name is Harriet Springer. I came to see you about the grade on my philosophy paper."

"Oh, yes?" A grimace of recognition twitched at his ruddy cheeks. "It was a generous grade."

"A generous grade?" She checked a wail.

"Your paper is simply not philosophy."

"But, but it's about philosophers. Look," she opened the paper, as she stood before him. "I graphed all the Pre-Socratics. Look, here they are. I read about them all and organized them all, in one graph."

"Miss Springer, can you give me any logical reason why that should be considered philosophy?"

"Isn't philosophy about ideas? Isn't philosophy about the life of the mind? This shows the way in which the Pre-Socratics lived the life of the mind."

"The life of the mind cannot be graphed. It cannot be quantified as you have so deplorably tried to do."

"Deplorably? I really understood philosophy when I worked on this paper."

"I'm afraid not."

"But I don't understand what I did wrong."

"Someday I hope you will."

"Professor McMaster," she blurted, "I don't think the grade is fair."

"It's more than fair. It's just." He jabbed a little knife into the bowl of his pipe.

Her social sense told her to get out. "Thank you, Professor McMaster," she said. As she went, her loafers clamored against the library's slate floor. She had adventurously wandered into heterodox territory; except for geography, charts and graphs did not seem to be the thing to do. Very well, she would learn what it meant to be orthodox. However, for a week or two, she thought of the paper with bleak nostalgia. She could not tell her mother about the wretched grade. Indeed, she could not write her mother. Then Louisa Lacey invited her to Boston for Thanksgiving. Louisa was apologetic. She had to make her debut Wednesday night. She could not take Harriet to it, of course, but would Harriet mind terribly staying alone, because her parents would be away, in the house, until Louisa returned from her debut, which she did not want to make anyway. Of course not. Harriet instantly wrote her mother about a success.

Covered with a tan-and-gray laprobe, Harriet was plunging into a brown scene. Outside the car, square and black and called a Checker, to her left, was the Charles River; to her right, the brick, trim, and steeples of Harvard University. Inside, she was between Louisa Lacey and a woman Louisa called Aunt Gertrude even though they were not related. She had met them in the foggy cavern of South Station. Northville would have thought her sturdy shoes and stockings, her mottled tweed coat, her hair bun funny. She looked as if she were poor, but she did not talk as if she were.

"Louisa, dear, would you and your friend like to use my season ticket to the symphony?"

"Oh, I don't think so, though it's awfully nice of you to ask. I think Harriet ought to see Lexington and Concord and all that. It's her first trip to Boston."

"Perhaps you're right, but Kous is in fine form these days. We saw him at dinner the other night."

"Did you? That ought to have been fun."

"You're having Thanksgiving with your granny?"

"Yes, it should be very quiet."

"It's just as well. You'll need a quiet day after your debut."

"I wish I could stay home. Making a debut is ridiculous in this day and age."

"It will give your friends a great deal of pleasure to see you there."

Aunt Gertrude parked before a three-story wooden house in a crowded block. Harriet had seen such architecture once before: when she had gone to visit Mrs. Jasper Rivers to receive a going-away-to-college present. Behind two white columns was a front door with fanlight and brass knocker. Inside, on the right, was a parlor, to its rear a separate living room. On the left a dining room, to its rear a pantry and a kitchen. Hand-painted pictures of birds hung on the walls of the entrance hall. Louisa led her up a broad wooden staircase to a second-floor guest room.

"Get what you want from the kitchen," she said. "Make yourself at home. No, you don't have to put your suitcase on the floor.

You can use that rack over there. I'll come tell you good-bye when I've got my costume on."

Harriet hung up her coat, opened the suitcase, shook out her purple wool dress. She sat edgily in a rocking chair. She was confused. The Lacey family was powerful, affluent, famous. The furnishings radiated authenticity. The hurricane lamp on the tall bureau had lit a wooden house as real storms had besieged it. Louisa's ancestors had trimmed its wick as winds had howled off the Atlantic, over the marshes, testing the hemp tying the ships to the rocks that were generating the hardy Lacey fortune. In Northville, hurricane lamps were novelty items on sale in Bushwick Lighting Fixtures. Yet the Lacey home—if polished and pure—was not sumptuous. Where was the huge backyard, the long sofa, the wall-to-wall carpeting, the fat ceramic lamps, the three-car garage and carport that some of the rich in Northville had? Even Mrs. Jasper Rivers had plush pillows in her living room.

"Hello," Louisa said at the door. "Do I look like a deb?" She was wearing a long, white dress, simpler than the one Harriet had worn to the senior prom. "Look," she touched a necklace of dark-red stones, "Mother left this for me to wear. Wasn't that sweet? She and Daddy also left me the nicest note, saying they were so sorry that Daddy's business kept them from being here. Well, I'm off in a cloud of dust. Aunt Gertrude must be waiting to take me to the club."

"You look fine," Harriet said. "Have a good time."

"Are you sure you'll be all right?" Patrician and cajoling, Louisa hesitated in the white doorframe.

"I'm very glad to be here."

Harriet, bathed, huddled in her four-poster bed. Her conscience, vigilant and petty, interrogated her. Had she been grateful enough, polite enough, to Louisa? She was here, not in the Harwyn dorm left open for the holidays, eating with a Japanese girl who spoke with an accent; an Iranian girl who wanted to be a doctor; a West African who neglected deodorant; and Nadia, a plump, rich, homely Egyptian who was in her hockey class. All of them watching vacation loom before them as empty as the space between a butchered turkey's body and its head. She wrote Louisa a note, signing it, "Harriet the Handsome." She and her friends liked to give themselves aristocratic-sounding titles.

77

The next morning, at a long wooden table in the kitchen, Louisa said the debut had been grotesque. "We walked up and down the ballroom in this ancient club, on the arm of these wheezing old geezers. It's the only time they allow women to come into the place. Can you imagine it? At least it isn't New York where people go to dinner parties for weeks before the big event. Nelly Lambert says she can hardly stand it. Marmalade or honey on your English muffin?"

After breakfast Louisa took Harriet into the parlor to see a portrait of her mother's mother. Her face was shadowed, except for shrewd, enormous eyes. "She was a suffragette," Louisa said. "She marched through Boston when she was pregnant, though my grandfather told her not to do it."

Heroism suffused the chilly room. Harriet knew about the valor of the suffragettes. Her Grandmother Yates had given her a book once for Christmas, *Twelve Famous Women: Biographies for Girls*. She had discovered Empress Theodora, Elizabeth of England, Saint Theresa, George Eliot, and Susan B. Anthony, who had risked contempt and ridicule for women's rights, who had treated arrest as if it were déclassé. That afternoon she was excited as they drove through the countryside. Gold and scarlet leaves, as vivid as tropical fish, failed to hide its rocky angularities. Mrs. Alexander lived in a shingled, modern house. "She says she might as well enjoy conveniences while she can," Louisa said ruefully. Inside, at the end of the entry corridor, was a frail woman, leaning on a black cane.

"Hello, darling." She embraced Louisa. "Did you go through that dreadful debut without a hitch?" Her voice was tired, as if she had to carry her words over a long plain of silence.

"It wasn't so bad. You would have danced up a storm if you'd been there." Harriet marveled at Louisa's impudence with older people. "Come, Harriet," Louisa said, "meet my granny."

Harriet gently, respectfully shook Mrs. Alexander's hand. Its texture was as rough and fragile as a fallen leaf.

They sat in square-cut chairs. Beyond the window a grassy field ran down to a stone wall. An old woman in a uniform, whom Mrs. Alexander and Louisa called Margaret, served them sherry in glasses the shape of gladiola before they bloom. Mrs. Alexander and Louisa talked about the dance. They mentioned names that Harriet had read about in high school social science classes. She looked around the room. She hoped to find signs of the suffragette struggle: flags, buttons, sashes.

Holding her glass tightly so that it would not drop and break, leaving her reputation scattered among crystal shards, she finally spoke. "Wasn't it wonderful to be able to work for women's rights?"

The old woman gazed at her, huge eyelids unmoving. Harriet wondered if she had erred. "It was great fun," she said, quietly. "Great fun."

"But didn't Granddaddy hate it?" Louisa was helping Harriet out.

"Oh, yes, but he came around. It was dreadful, you know, not to have the vote, when every drunken man could stagger to the polling place. We were so sure that we were right."

"It must have been awful," Harriet said hotly. "You were right."

"Ah," said Mrs. Alexander, "here's Margaret. Our dinner must be ready."

At Thanksgiving the Springer family designed costumes for plays and pageants. They romped through hymns of praise, bellows of communal joy. Big George, as he carved the turkey, chanted to the table, "Who wants some juicy, tender meat? This is a good bird, a wonderful bird." Harriet suppressed the thought that this Thanksgiving feast was stingy, the turkey carved in the kitchen, the dish of cranberry no bigger than a scoop of ice cream. She was also glad that her mother had taught her how to unfold heavy napkins, to handle a broad-bladed butter knife. Mrs. Alexander and Louisa talked about the family. Louisa's father wanted to go to Africa.

"What," Harriet did not want to fall behind in the conversation, "do you think will happen in Africa when Albert Schweitzer dies?"

"I fear great turmoil," said Mrs. Alexander. "Shall we have our pie? It's one of Margaret's special recipes."

Single portion finished, they returned to the living room. Twilight was changing the field outside to the color of the stone gravemarkers of the founders of America.

"Did you ever belong to the DAR?" she asked Mrs. Alexander.

"I did, once, but, of course, I had to resign, over their treatment of poor Marian Anderson."

Her body, like that in the portrait, was in shade, except for the eyes and upper part of her face. Harriet's muted criticism of the meal buried away. Before her was a suffragette, a rebel. If she was old, fatigued, she was still awesomely there. "I was the DAR Good Citizen for the State of Washington last year," she blurted out, "but I cheated on the exam that won the prize."

Shame suffused her. She wanted to crawl, to erode the flush that was recording her pain, to rub herself into the Oriental rugs and wooden floors. Instead, she sat, holding her demitasse, an empty token in a suppliant's hand.

"Did you? Did you really?" Mrs. Alexander brooded over her. "I don't know. I never thought an exam could measure patriotism and citizenship. What a silly thing to have a child do." Then, as if moving from a last duty to a final pleasure, she smiled at her granddaughter. "Louisa, love, play the piano. I would so like to hear some of your music." The strong, melancholy invitation of a Thanksgiving hymn entered the room. Harriet wanted to sing, to shout out, "Come ye thankful people, come, raise the song of harvest home." She had been a pilgrim, too, and she had been rewarded in a suffragette's forgiveness.

Harriet had refused to believe that Harwyn would have Hell Days, even though her *Freshman Guide* described it as an annual March event. Freshmen might be hazed at the University of Washington or Washington State College. Even Olivia Kasper had been blindfolded during her sorority initiation and forced to put her hand into a toilet to feel a soft, squishy cylinder that turned out to be a peeled banana. Surely Harwyn would despise such cruelty.

Yet, one Monday, the hall president rose at the head table after lunch. A weak spring light glinted off the condiment pots. "Freshmen," she announced, "Hell Days have begun."

"Freshmen," the other seniors shouted, "stand up. Stand up and sing."

"What is a Hell Days?" Naomi asked. "I am confused. I haven't done anything bad."

"Freshmen," the seniors repeated, "sing 'Mary Had a Little Lamb.' Three times."

"It's childish," Louisa said. "I'm not going to obey."

"Neither am I," said Harriet.

"Nobody's going to force this Texan to sing," growled Amarillo. Only Harriet had linked Amarillo and Naomi and Louisa.

Amarillo and Naomi thought Louisa stuck-up; she thought them common. Now they were together.

"But I'm scared," whispered Naomi.

"Act like an American," Amarillo said.

They stared at the other four freshmen at the table. Cecily Dain, in love with a West Point cadet, at Harwyn to be near him. Fifi Trevisi, engaged to a dentist doing his military service in Korea. She wore the first tooth he had ever pulled, bronzed, around her neck. Joan Golden and Margy Epstein, industrious premeds. "Freshmen, obey," the seniors commanded. Cecily, Fifi, Joan, and Margy stood up. "Mary had a little lamb, little lamb, little lamb," their voices lurched and called.

The Negro maids had disappeared behind the heavy swinging doors between dining room and kitchen. As the song ended, they returned carrying trays of fruit cup. Cecily, Fifi, Joan, and Margy sat down.

"Swine," Amarillo said.

"I don't see why you're calling us swine," Joan said defensively. "All we did was sing."

Hands in the pockets of her class blazer, the hall president approached their table. "Hello, rebels," she said. An orange slice caught in Harriet's throat. "I'm going to ask your advisers to talk to you," she went on. "I'm not sure you really understand Harwyn traditions."

"Fine," said Amarillo.

"I know that you wouldn't want to do anything you might regret later," the hall president said before leaving for her bridge game.

"How ridiculous," Louisa stood up, "how simply ridiculous."

Harriet wanted to ask if they were going to get in trouble, but her contempt for Cecily, Fifi, Joan, and Margy was too great to permit them to hear her doubts. "I'm going to geology lab," she said defiantly.

"Ugh, geology," Naomi shuddered. "I am going to break my fingernails on those rocks. I am going to flunk out and be sent back home. My daddy will be furious."

"Anyone can do geology," Margy said. "It's not half so hard as bio."

Harriet spent the afternoon in the science building. She lacked a geologist's eye. Unless instructed, she could not tell if a mass of rock was talus or moraine. At five, worried that she was not doing well, she stored away her samples; put on her boots; and crunched across the shadowed ice to Gould Hall. Tally was waiting for her in her room. "I know why you're here," Harriet said, hanging up her loden coat. "But I'm not going to be hazed."

"You're taking this too seriously," Tally told her, pushing her glasses back on her hair. "Nobody's going to hurt you. It's only a tradition."

"But Tally," Harriet was choking back tears of frustration, "if I had wanted this sort of thing I would have gone to the University of Washington. I wouldn't have come all the way east to Harwyn, where I thought people were going to be the kind of people who hated Hell Days."

"Look, I'm your adviser. I'm on your side. I'll get people to leave you alone if you just stand up and sing at meals. Will you do that much?"

Cross-legged on her bed, Harriet wrapped herself in honor. "I won't," she said.

"Singing at meals isn't going to hurt you," Tally bargained. "And, when it's all over, you'll see the point of it all."

"Like what? Like being tarred-and-feathered in front of the statue of Athena in the library?"

"Oh, for God's sake," said Tally. "If you're going to be so stubborn, I'll tell people to lay off, but I think you're going to be sorry."

As soon as she left, Harriet went upstairs to Naomi's suite. Amarillo was there.

"Did your adviser tell you that all you had to do was sing?" she asked.

"I said I wouldn't," Harriet told them. Modestly. Proudly.

"I think I will," Amarillo said. Carelessly. "It doesn't seem like much, and I'm going to absolutely refuse to do the rest of their stupid stuff."

"I am going to sing, too," Naomi giggled. "And sound so dreadful that they will be tortured themselves."

"If you're going to do it, I guess you're going to do it," Harriet said. "I've got to get my skirt for dinner now."

"I've got mine right here," Amarillo said, too aggressively. Though Harriet's feet struck resolutely on the corridor floors, a heavy resignation clung to her. She could not go back on her principles, but she had been deserted by her friends.

She looked for Louisa, but Louisa was out. Between the meat and pudding at dinner, the seniors shouted, "Freshmen, sing. Freshmen, sing 'Mary had a Little Lamb.' " Amarillo and Naomi rose. "Mary had a little lamb, little lamb," they bawled. "I hate this place," Amarillo burst out when she sat down. "The food is lousy. I wouldn't give it to a dog."

On Thursday night Harriet stood alone in front of the brass urn in the living room as Denver poured her demitasse of coffee. Fifi Trevisi, on the hall president's command, was crawling back and forth in front of the fireplace. The bronzed tooth was dangling on a plumb line from neck to floor. Roots seeking the rug as if it were a gum.

"Harriet," Tally was speaking to her for the first time since she had refused to go along with Hell Days, "come to my room for a while, would you? Rachel and I have to talk to you."

They walked through the arch, down the hall. Naked bulbs flickered in the lamps where gas jets once had burned. Tally's room was done in plaids. Over her desk was a Harvard banner. On the desk a framed picture of her Harvard boy friend. Harriet took a straight chair. She would not pretend this was a friendly visit and sit on the floor and read Tally's *Time* magazines. Tally and Rachel were on the window seat.

"Harriet," Tally came to the point, "I've got to make sure that you don't leave your room tonight."

Harriet was astonished.

"It's in your best interest," Rachel said quickly.

"What's going to happen to me?" Harriet asked. "Do I get bread and water for breakfast?"

"Harriet, shut up and listen," Tally said. "I've done what I said. I got everyone to leave you alone, didn't I?"

"Yes," Harriet said. Grudging but fair.

"I won't actually lock you in your room if you promise me not to go out after the ten o'clock milk break unless one of us blindfolds you and goes with you."

"But why?"

"You'll see," Rachel said, as if Harriet's questions were logging off her patience. "You've got to take our word that it's in your best interest."

"Come on, Harriet," Tally cajoled. "I went out on a limb for you. Now why don't you do something for me?"

The hint of Rachel's anger, Tally's distress, sawed at her. "You promise you won't lock the door?" Wary Harriet.

"Honest. You'll be glad tomorrow."

Back in her room Harriet tried to read William Faulkner. The narrative was upsetting. She couldn't tell who was talking to whom. She went to bed. During the night, noises fluttered in the hall. She wanted to go to the bathroom, but she would have preferred to have her bladder excavated without anesthesia than to call Tally to blindfold her and take her to the john.

Then, at six, the odd, muffling noises of the night cohered into music. Up and down the hall girls were singing an old melody. "Good morning, good morning, come and see the sun," they were calling cheerfully. Harriet wondered what new torment this lyricism previewed. "Open up, Harriet." Tally was shouting out and knocking on her door. "Open up. We've got a surprise for you."

In the corridor a score of upperclassmen were standing in a semicircle. They were smiling, proudly, beseechingly. At their feet, on the floor, was a thick, mysterious pile.

"What's this?" Harriet asked. Tally had betrayed her. "Why have you left your garbage here? Do you expect me to pick it up? Screw you and your Hell Days."

"Garbage?" The sophomore song leader puckered into hurt. "Garbage? Oh, Harriet, look at them. They're for you. We want to show you how glad we are to have you here."

"Look at them, Harriet," Tally ordered.

She bent down. The loafers, sneakers, and bedroom slippers of Harwyn were guarding a mass of fresh flowers. Pinned to the daffodils, rose buds, and gladiola were handwritten notes. On a card taped to a pussy willow, Tally had scrawled, "See, kid, I told you it would be all right."

"This isn't so bad now, is it?" said the hall president.

Harriet picked up the flowers, the petals and stems wetting her pajamas. The group gazed at her, as if they would will her appreciation of their sentiments. She stared back. She could not forgive them. A Mrs. Alexander would not consort with people who ran Hell Days and who then tried to win them back with dainty bribes. "Thanks," she said tightly and relentlessly. She shut the door and threw the flowers in the trash.

Later that morning she passed the Smoker. Tally was there. "Harriet," she said, "come on in. Have a cigarette on me." Harriet still distrusted her, but Tally was her sophomore adviser and her friend. "Relax, Harriet," Tally said. "We'll all put Hell Days away someplace. Forget it. Have a cigarette. You're all right." Harriet accepted the Pall Mall. She had stood upright for principle and not lost the Smoker Crew. She did not think she might inflate the lesson into a moral law, but it pleased her nonetheless.

Summer in Northville between Harriet's first and second Harwyn years was like a visit to a decaying town. It was being abandoned, but people and officials still lived there to exact annoying tribute. The buildings, her home, her room seemed diminished. The new world into which she had entered trivialized them. She got off the train in a beige suit she had bought for ninety fear-wracked dollars at DePinna, a New York department store. She and Nadia, from Egypt, had been spending spring vacation in the city. They had shared a small room in the Biltmore and walked as quickly as possible through the lobby so they would not hear the music from the lounge.

"You're grown-up," her mother said. Before her embrace muffled speech. "You've done so well." Despite the lack of dates, she had. Her average had gone up from C plus to B. She had wept as she had read about Lear, a mad old king who, sanity restored, if kingdom lost, asked his good daughter to come away to prison so they could sing like birds in a cage. After several losses, she had become second sophomore representative to the Student Governing Council. Louisa had nominated her, a last act of friendship before moving from Gould to Stuart Hall.

At their first dinner together, her family irritated her. "Why does everyone have to rush so with their food? Why can't we eat in a leisurely way and have good conversation?" she complained.

"I'll bet my bottom dollar you didn't eat like this at Harwyn." Her father cut his rolled flank steak.

"We didn't have to. We had better things to do."

"Well, next week," he pointed his knife at her like a sword, "you're going down to the bank and fill in for the girls who are on vacation."

"I did that last summer."

"You're going to do it again. My kids are going to learn where they get the wherewithall to go off to college so that they can come back and try to chickpeck their old pa."

85

"But I want to spend the summer studying." She had her list: Dante, Schopenhauer, Nietzsche, Homer, and haiku.

"You can study at college."

She appealed to her mother, in vain. She spent the summer at the bank hand-cranking an adding machine. Once she overheard a conversation between a teller and the credit manager's secretary. Her Uncle Charles was trying to push through a funny loan. He was under some pressure to meet interest payments on his land. Her father had stopped it. Blood might run thicker than water, but her father was an honest man. Harriet listened and paid little attention. She wanted to escape once more from Northville and return to Harwyn.

There again, she felt at home. Her rituals of work and friendship enveloped her. A few days after classes began, she and Amarillo were sprawled after lunch on the window seat of the Gould Hall living room. Naomi was standing in front of them. Her clothes had gotten more and more disheveled. Now she was wearing Italian loafers, a French shirt, a Harwyn gym tunic. "I don't understand," she was wailing. "Why do I have a letter from the medical office? I spend every summer in Switzerland. I have massages. I eat yogurt. I am very healthy."

She gave the letter to Harriet, who conscientiously read it to Amarillo:

Dear Naomi:

We are always, at Harwyn, particularly concerned about the health of foreign students, especially those who have spent their summers away from America and American medical facilities. We are, of course, interested, not just in the health of our foreign students but in the remote but dreadful possibility that they might bring, without knowing it, something back with them that might harm the entire Harwyn community. Therefore we are asking you, at your earliest convenience, to come to the medical office for a Wassermann test.

Sincerely,
Georgia L. Peabody, M.D.
College Physician

"A Wassermann? What is a Wassermann?" Naomi moaned.

"I don't know exactly." Amarillo sounded sober. "But I think you'd better get to the medical office right now."

86

"I'll go, I'll go." Naomi took the letter back. "I don't want to get into any trouble. I could lose my visa. My daddy would be furious." Holding the paper between two long, scarlet fingernails, she ran out of the dormitory.

"She fell for it," Amarillo exulted. "She really fell for it."

Harriet grinned conspiratorially. However, she glanced up and down the window seat to see if anyone had overheard Amarillo. She did not want it known that she had stolen the stationery from the dean's office when she was turning in an attendance monitoring report, her job that paid thirty-five cents an hour; that she and Amarillo had written the letter to plague Naomi. She and Amarillo had been proud of their practical joke, but Harriet was also guilty. Her mother would have said the joke was cheap.

The only person who might have heard was the girl sitting in a wingback chair next to the piano—Sloan Trouver. Harriet had already noticed her. She was in a science class Harriet monitored. She had been elected freshman hall president. Slender, six feet tall, she limped slightly as she walked, swinging her right leg impatiently. Her long, fine dark brown hair was usually drawn back in a loose mound at the nape of her neck. Though her face was round, high strong cheekbones hardened its planes. She appeared to be engrossed in *Harwyn Happenings*, the campus paper.

Harriet ought to have been glad to have been ignored, but she sensed a quick, sharp ache of disappointment. It was as if a nerve had both been touched and lost its ordinary relay system. She was equally excited and disturbed. Forcing herself to look away, she recognized the sensation. Only a few women provoked it. Olivia Kasper had. So had Vivian Clare, when she had walked with her Uncle Charles into the Springer kitchen on that sunny morning during the war. They made Harriet feel in the presence of an aloof but powerful force, more beautiful than she. She longed for them to notice her. If they did, she might be judged and dismissed, but they also inspired her to act distinctively, attractively, at her best. To seem more relaxed than she was, Harriet leaned back against the wood paneling. She looked down at her Bermuda shorts, her knees, her loafers. She was remembering the curious stability of her response to these special women. Once there, no matter how surprisingly, it held, as if her nerves had quickly found a new, compelling pathway.

"Let's have a game of gin," Amarillo said lazily. Harriet shuffled the cards. She was relieved to do something, but she was aware of how much she wanted Sloan to see how expertly she could handle the deck.

She was studying her hand when Naomi scurried back. "I am going crazy," she cried. "I am going really mad. Do you know what a Wassermann is? It is a test for a horrible disease, for syphilis."

"Naomi," Amarillo stared at her. "How could you get syphilis in Zurich when your daddy was there?"

"Of course I did not get syphilis. I am a virgin. My daddy would kill me if I was not a virgin. I went to the medical office, and they said they never sent this letter. They said it was a cruel joke, or a mistake. I tell you, I am going crazy." She slumped next to the card table, gnawing at the end of her shirt collar.

"What's wrong with a good dose of the clap?" Sloan Trouver asked unexpectedly from her chair.

They all looked at her. "What is the clap?" Naomi asked despairingly. "I tell you, I am a simple Latin American. I have language difficulties."

"Naomi, clap is just another word for syphilis," Harriet said quickly. She wanted to keep Sloan in on the joke. "Some of the best people have had it and survived."

"But I don't have it," Naomi protested wildly.

Suddenly Sloan was standing over them. "Don't worry, Naomi," she said. "It's probably just a mistake. Bureaucracies make them all the time. It doesn't matter if you're a foreigner or not. Bureaucracies screw up."

Harriet looked up at her. "Do you want to sit down?" she asked as casually as she could. "We could do with a fourth for partner hearts."

"No, thanks," Sloan said. "I've got to get ready for a class." Then she looked at Harriet. "You know that class. You check the attendance. I see you keeping track of us."

"I'll see you later then," Harriet said. She felt as if she had been given a small but vital signal. When she did her job that afternoon, she wondered if Sloan would notice her. Her heart was beating rapidly when Sloan waved surreptitiously at her. Over the next weeks she began to put the science building at the end of her rounds. She sat, clipboard on lap, smoking, waiting for Sloan. She read Gerard Manley Hopkins. He pulled the breath out of her body toward a dazzling, luminescent, dancing world. "Glory be to God for dappled things," she whispered to herself. She hoped Sloan, inside near a window, would see her: serious, mystical, poetic. Sloan's own speech was often that way. "Look at the dogwood trees," she said once. "In the spring they'll flower. Did you know that the dogwood was the flower of Christ?"

Harriet had not. She hoped Sloan would not think her crass.

"In the spring we can see marks on the petals. They'll be brown, like scars, like stigmata. That's why they're called the flower of Christ."

"That's interesting," Harriet said, though she considered it macabre.

"I wonder if my stigmata will ever show," Sloan asked, softly, impersonally. Harriet experienced a gash of Sloan's pain, as startling as a slash of red on the gray walk. This strong girl needs protection, she thought.

In November they met a slender, blond girl, hair twisted in a severe French knot. Face a long, austere oval; the line of brow, nose, and mouth sculptured straight. Even in a London Fog raincoat and light blue-and-white Yale scarf, she reminded Harriet of portraits in the campus museum of Renaissance princesses known for learning, piety, and money.

"Hello, Sloan."

"Hello." Sloan sounded as if she had stepped behind a shield.

"How do you like it here? Is it as we imagined it would be?"

"No."

"Why don't you come over to Stuart and have dinner with me tonight?"

"I have to work."

The blond stranger flicked the end of her scarf over her shoulder. "Okay," she said. "I'll ask again. Bye for now." Her smile puzzled Harriet. It seemed designed to force Sloan to remember something.

"Who's that?"

"Someone I knew at Prideworth. Her name's Sophia. I don't like her. She's a troublemaker. I was on scholarship at Prideworth. It trained me for this place, how to be poor in a rich girl's school."

They neared the stone arch of Gould Hall. Ten more steps— they would have to mingle with the others. To slow them down, Harriet gave Sloan a present: the news that she had discovered a private place to study, where they could smoke without the noisy crowd of the Smoker, a seminar room in the library. Legally, it was reserved for majors and professors in the anthropology department, but it was rarely used. Red and beige Northwest Indian masks hung on the walls, their pursed lips preparing for whistles and kisses that never would be given. Sloan promised to meet Harriet there after her lab.

By five she still had not come. The pages of *The Making of the Modern World* were blurring for Harriet when the door opened, "Sorry," said Sloan. "I had a hard time dissecting my dogfish. Hey, this place isn't bad." She sat, the sleeves of her black turtleneck shoved up. "She's beautiful," Harriet thought. "She looks like a French intellectual." Surreptitiously she scrawled a joke/poem and shoved it into the pool of light from Sloan's green glass-shaded reading lamp:

> Fish died.
> Why?
> Formaldehyde.
> Shall we cry?
> Weep, weep said the bird.
> Harwyn cannot bear very much reality.

Sloan smiled. "Call it 'Requiem for a Nun's Dogfish,' " she said. "I like this place." Harriet was rapt.

Because Sloan had dreaded going home for her Christmas vacation, Harriet worried about her while she was in Northville for hers. It took nearly twenty-four impatient hours to fly back from Seattle to Idlewild. Because of storms, the plane made unscheduled stops in icy airports in Montana and North Dakota, so barren that even the tin postcard racks were empty. She waited in her room until Sloan appeared, minutes before the end-of-vacation curfew was to go into effect, gaunt, haggard, the sleeves of her old winter coat too short for her arms. She pitched herself on Harriet's bed, long fingers spanning and cradling her head; bone thin, wounded legs stretched out before her.

"I can't stand them," she said. "They were drunk the entire time. My father, the Army officer. My mother, the last of the bankrupt Virginia Sloans. Drunk, cruel, horrible. You can't know what they're like, mothers so drunk that they can't get their kids to the hospital when they have polio."

"But look at all you do. You can dance. You play basketball. You ride horses."

"You're so goddamn naive."

"I'm not naive." Harriet was too hurt to be angry. "Here, I brought you a present. I thought that maybe, in beauty, you might find a momentary peace." She had rehearsed the speech in the crowded plane. She handed Sloan a white gull's feather, as shapely as a newly forged knife, the tip as soft as water from a fern.

Sloan ignored it. "I'm so unhappy I could die. Do you know what it's like to want to die?"

"When I was fifteen, I found a gun in the basement. I wanted to commit suicide."

Volatile Sloan laughed. "You wouldn't know a gun barrel from your elbow," she said. "Where's that present you brought me. I don't know why, but I tell you things I've never told anyone else." That was Sloan's gift to her. It was more than enough.

Harriet had learned basketball in the valleys of Northville. She had once beaten her brother George in several games of Four Horses. Angry and impotent, he had paid two other boys to beat her up. She had been shoved against a fence. Gary Podges held her arms. Terry McBridge hit her in the stomach. She had screamed, "Scared of me, aren't you? Scared of me, aren't you?" at her brother until sobs of pain had thwarted her.

Now she and Sloan discovered they both played. They decided to go out for the varsity team together. The rules were confining: forwards on one side of the court, guards on another, no player permitted to dribble more than twice. However, Harriet loved practicing with Sloan. Her body had a reason to move, to jump, to reach out. She and Sloan were no longer isolated beings but part of an organism, responding to the field of force in which they were immersed. When they were chosen for the varsity as guards and given their tunics of official Harwyn green, Harriet bought Sloan a forbidden beer.

Before the first game of the season, they sat, side by side, contemplating the competition: the girls from the Academy of Our Mother of the Sacred Crucifix. Across the lacquered gym floor, they were praying in a circle around a nun. "My heavens," Susan Crawford, a forward, said. "They're all wearing little crosses."

Miss Pritchey, the Harwyn coach, clapped her hands. "Okay,

team," she called out tensely, "on the floor. Guards, go to it. Forwards, shoot when ready, but when you're ready, shoot."

In the center circle Susan Crawford adjusted her red headband; heard the whistle; and leaped. The extended fingers of her right hand reached the elbow of Our Mother's center. The ball was rammed to Harriet's forward. Hands shaking frantically, Harriet flung herself after the girl. "Argh, argh, argh," she growled.

"Snobby bitch," the forward hissed. She feinted to the right, slipped to the left, and passed laterally to a forward who scored on a jump shot.

"What happened?" Harriet whispered to Sloan as they regrouped.

"They've been trained," Sloan said. "They're all P.E. majors."

In center court Susan passed off the referee's toss. The second forward dribbled and handed the ball back to Peggy. Her shot landed five feet short of the basket, into the net of the arms of an Our Mother guard. A series of cross-court passes flashed through Amy, Sloan, and Harriet as if they were dust. A lay-up. Our Mother 4, Harwyn 0.

At halftime the score was Our Mother 27, Harwyn 6. As they left the court, Harriet's forward muttered, "Harwyn girls. Think you're so smart."

"You've got us all wrong," Harriet protested.

"They really hate us," she exclaimed to Sloan as they sat on their bench and sucked orange sections.

Sloan leaned against the wall, rubbing a towel around her neck. She's so brave, Harriet thought. Stricken with polio when she was a child; adulterous father away at war; drunken mother too irresponsible to take her to the hospital on time; paralyzed legs yielding to her will, so that now she could float over the world as if she were Diana.

"Are you all right?" she asked.

"I'd be better if our forwards would get some baskets."

"We're trying," protested Susan Crawford.

At the beginning of the third quarter, Susan outjumped the rival forward. A Harwyn substitute took a pass and stood in the right corner. "Shoot, you fool, shoot," Sloan shrieked. The girl, squinching her eyes shut, let the ball go. Landing on the far rim of the hoop, it vibrated then dropped for two points. The Harwyn team, surprised by joy, leaped up and down. To punish them for premature glee, Our Mother scored three quick, vicious baskets.

Exhausted, too far into defeat to feel responsible, sure of Sloan's nearness, Harriet looked at the score, on a blackboard. She wanted to laugh. Chasing a ball down the sideline, she slipped and fell. As she lay on the floor, the laughter threatened to break loose.

"Springer," Miss Pritchey knelt beside her. "Springer, are you hurt?"

"I'm ready to go," warrior Harriet began stoically, but delirious Harriet triumphed.

"Springer, I'm going to bench you for a while," Miss Pritchey said sternly. Sobered, Harriet slunk off. As a spectator, she saw burlesque again. When Sloan was given a rest break, they sat together, legs and sweaty shoulders touching. As Our Mother scored its sixtieth point, they buried their faces in Sloan's towel so that Pritchey could not see them laugh, the mocking music of their own disaster.

For the last minute, Pritchey put the first team in again. Scrambling, Harriet slapped the ball away from her forward toward Sloan. She grabbed it, whirled, and threw. The ball arched down court, hit the back board, and plunged in. The referee's whistle ricocheted against the harsh tweeds of Miss Pritchey, burrowed into the black habit of Our Mother's coach. "No basket," she shouted. "Snobby cheats," Harriet's forward whispered. "Sore winners," Harriet whispered back. Thirty seconds later the game was over. The Harwyn girls, forty points behind, chanted:

> Sport, sport,
> Yea, yea,
> Thanks for coming
> Here to play.

"Let's go," Sloan urged Harriet. "We don't want to stay here for any more of this gracious crap." Still in uniform, they escaped outside. The wind, carrying scythes of snow, cut against their legs. "Come on," Sloan said. "Let's run."

She seized Harriet's hand. They raced over the quarter of a mile of the campus to Gould Hall beneath the stringent moon. At first Harriet ran to show Sloan that she could transcend the rule that said she should not hold a woman's hand, but then it became as easy a thing to do as to run alone. When they reached the slate floor underneath the arch that connected the two halves of Gould Hall, it seemed dank, claustrophic. Reluctant, sad, Harriet let Sloan's hand go.

"Come on," Sloan said, "the roof." She led them to the second floor where a small door gave way to a flight of stairs to the roof over the arch itself. Rubbing and blowing on her hands, Sloan rested on the stone wall between two turrets. To light their cigarettes out of the wind, Harriet squatted in front of her. When she stood up, she was cold. Her loden coat came only to the middle of her thighs. She was still in her short tunic. She willed herself not to let something as mundane as being cold quench the fire in her nerves.

She handed Sloan a cigarette. She wondered why Sloan was staring at her so openly, but she held out the cigarette slowly so that Sloan would not stop.

"Harriet?" Sloan's voice flowed toward her, around her. "How are you?"

"I'm fine," Harriet said. "What about you?"

Then Sloan's right sneaker was stubbing out the cigarette. Her hands were following her voice. She was pulling Harriet toward her and roughly wrapping them both within her coat. Harriet stood rigidly, her head like a stiff bush against Sloan's neck. Then slowly, fearfully, because she could not bear the distance if she did not, she put her arms around Sloan. "Harriet?" Sloan's voice was distant but still entwining. "Can I trust you?" "Of course," Harriet's voice cracked with promise. "I'm a spy," Sloan said. "What?" Harriet leaned back in dumb wonder.

"I said, I'm a spy. My father works in Intelligence for the Pentagon. He makes me work for him. That's one of the reasons why I hate to go home. I never know what I will be asked to do."

Harriet was stunned beyond acceptance or skepticism. "I never guessed," she said.

"That's good." Sloan's hack of a laugh was dull, mirthless. "It shows I've kept my cover."

"But why are you telling me?"

"I've told you. I can talk to you. I need someone who will never ask me any questions but who will understand, if I'm secretive, or if I have to go away. You've got to promise that you will never ask me any questions but that you will understand."

94

"You can trust me." Better to die than to fail that trust.

"Now, you mustn't be surprised." Slowly, Sloan kissed Harriet, her forehead, her mouth, as if she were bearing a sacred brand.

"Are you surprised?"

"No." False.

"Are you happy?"

"Yes." True.

As Sloan brought her closer, Harriet sensed her own body releasing itself, muscle by muscle, then, abruptly, Sloan became tense. "What the fuck? Naomi, what the fuck are you doing here?"

Naomi was shivering, in jeans and bedroom slippers and cotton shirt, in the doorway. "I just wondered where you were," she said miserably. "I just wondered why you didn't come into the Smoker to say hello to me."

"Go away," Harriet glowered.

"Go on, Naomi," Sloan was more gentle. "We'll be down in a minute."

"That goddamn interfering bitch," Harriet raged.

"She's harmless."

"I don't give a damn. I don't want her around."

"I like her," Sloan said. Harriet lapsed back. "Listen." Sloan held her as if an embrace would breed obedience. "Do you promise to keep my secret? I could die if you told anyone. I mean that literally. I could die."

"You can trust me, darling." The word came out as if her mouth had broken open to reveal a sealed treasure.

"Then let's go down." On the stairs, Harriet again rejected the impression that she had been cold. She and Sloan had consecrated themselves to each other on the roof. How could she have been uncomfortable?

For the rest of the semester, until she had to go home to Northville for vacation again, she was happy. Her world was complete. One night she was in Sloan's small room, the size reserved for scholarship students. Sloan on the bed, Harriet leaning against it, Sloan's hand on her hair. Rachel Diamond, knocking only once, came in, to see Sloan's hand in flight from Harriet's skin. "I'm so sorry," sarcastic Rachel. "I really didn't mean to separate the Bobbsey Twins."

"That's okay, Rachel." Emergencies calmed Sloan. "What can I do for you?"

95

"I wanted to borrow the copy of Sartre that you have from the library."

"Sure, take it, it's on the desk."

Rachel picked up *Existentialism and Humanism* and left. "Goddamn it," Sloan said. "The bitch. I wish I could lock the doors around here."

Harriet waited for the hand to touch her neck again. "Don't worry about Rachel," she said.

"I won't, but I hate this place. Sometimes I think I should leave. I could work for my father full time."

"Don't leave," Harriet said. She felt ravaged.

Sloan, hands behind her head, said nothing.

The next day Tally stopped as she was about to walk into the library. "Let's just sit here on the steps," she said. "It's a nice day to be outside." Honeysuckle was beginning to show white among the dark green of the ivy on the walls. Azalea, wisteria, and the dogwood were close to bloom.

Tally hunched over, arms folded around her knees, staring at her scuffed loafers and sockless legs. "Look, Harriet," she said. "You can't live your life with a woman; you've got to live your life with a man. That's the way life is."

"Of course, Tally," Harriet said. "I know that." She was surprised that Tally would sit so awkwardly to cite the obvious.

"Just because men don't respond to some people as often as they respond to other people doesn't mean that some men won't respond to them at some time."

"Sure, Tally. I know."

"Someday you will meet a guy who really likes you. I know you haven't had a lot of dates here, but that doesn't mean much. You'll meet the right man soon enough, and then everything will be all right."

"I'm glad you're my adviser, Tally," Harriet said. Though Tally was confusing her, she wanted to be appreciative.

"I'm not very good," Tally said. "If I were, I wouldn't have to be talking to you like this." She stopped, uncertain. Then, grasping her knees even more firmly, went on. "You know those girls who are over in Pinkham Hall, the ones who work on the stage crew?"

"One of them is in one of my classes."

"Well, look, I don't want you to be like them. I don't think you ought to dress like them, or behave like them, or look like them, or be seen with other women like them. You may not know this, and it's hard to talk about, but April Phelps and Jennifer Cochran were seen kissing each other in the library stack, just last week. You're too good to do that sort of thing."

"But Tally, I'm not one of the Pinkham girls."

She wasn't. April was fat, Jennifer thin, and both wore filthy jeans and T-shirts and hammered on flats for the Stage Crew.

"All right," sturdy Tally stood up. "But just remember, you've got to live with men in this world."

After she left, Harriet sat alone, still confused. The mystical loveliness of her union with Sloan had as little to do with the raw, grubby world of the Pinkham girls as kingfishers with mud turtles. She didn't even like April and Jennifer. Neither did Sloan.

Harriet, when not substituting in the bank, spent the next summer in her bedroom. She typed letters to Sloan, pretending they were notes about English literature, and sneaking them off to the post office. In August, a fellow from Georgie's Yale college visited, a Frenchman, even though Georgie had a job on the Olympic Peninsula in the woods. Eleanor and Big George had met him when they had gone to Georgie's graduation. Harriet hated the frantic preparations for the event. Her mother might talk about opportunities for women, but when the beds had to be made, the clothes washed, the dining room table polished—she and her daughters did the sweating.

Jean Maurin was shorter, darker, older, flabbier than she had expected. His pants had a funny waistband. His black shoes were pointed. His teeth were ragged, stained from the Gauloises he smoked, their pungent smell spewing through the Springer house. He sat at the dining room table, judiciously tasting fresh salmon and homemade meringues. When he praised the food, Eleanor Springer relaxed.

After dinner Jean asked to play Ping-Pong at the table in the basement. He had discovered it in New Haven—an amusing game. "I'll take you on first," Big George stretched, got up. "The girls have to do the dishes, but then they can come down and try to replace the old man."

97

Exhaling smoke from mouth and nose, Maurin smiled at Harriet. The gesture was old, not the split-level innocence of northwestern men.

In the kitchen Anne loaded the dishwasher. Harriet scrubbed the pots and pans. "Do you like him?" Anne asked.

"I think he's creepy."

"I've never met a Frenchman before."

"I have, at Harwyn. I don't care if he is on the Yale faculty and a fellow of Georgie's college, I still think he's a freeloader."

Anne had a date. He wanted to go steady with her, but Eleanor Springer thought it would be unfair for Anne to accept his miniature silver basketball. The next year she would go to college; he, a poor boy, not athletic enough to get a scholarship, would enlist in the Marines. So Harriet, in blue denim pedal pushers and checked Peck & Peck shirt, descended alone to the basement. Her father, though over fifty, beat Maurin easily. "I guess your old dad still has some zip left," he said, handing Harriet the paddle.

Harriet, too, defeated Maurin. He seemed indifferent to both the chance of victory and threat of loss. He laughed at his mistakes, as remote from the competitive storms of Springer sports as silky Alexandrine from a private curse. Yet, as she put the equipment away, she was nervous, a gauge trembling under visible pressure. As he followed her up the wooden stairs, his hand almost touched hers on the bannister; his belly threatened to swell toward the small of her back; the Gaulois smoke played around her neck and thick, untamable curls. She left him with her father, to write her letter to Sloan. She usually revised them, worried that her prose might be insufficient oxygen for the high places of Sloan's soul.

A Frenchman who is a fellow at my brother's Yale college is visiting. He seems to find Northville *trés amusant,* and his Gallic suavity flatters my mother, who usually has to be content with being called Sweetie Pie as a compliment. Tonight we played Ping-Pong, and tomorrow I am to take him for a sight-seeing trip. He had to have his bed made for him. *Quel dommage* that you are not here.

I was thinking about you. You are not the mirror image of my soul, nor I of yours. Yet we are both serious people who take the risk of willing ourselves to laugh at ourselves, though in laughing we may score our own dignity. If we perceive something beautiful vanishing before us, we would resent its lacks. We both run through forests, strong in the joy of seeing the sunlight break through the green prisms of the trees. Yet I miss you as the earth would miss the rain, the rain the earth; the sun the moon, the moon the sun. Loneliness is the cessation of immediate understanding. I am lonely. Good night.

The next afternoon her father released her from the bank to give Maurin his tour. He wore foreign sunglasses. "I am so sorry," he murmured, "that I must go to Canada tomorrow. Northville is very beautiful, and your family is very charming."

Harriet planned to show him both scenery and local curiosities. On the way to the Nookagillish Indian reservation, she turned beneath a high, iron arch. Screwed to it were the metal letters *Northville Cemetary*. Six-foot-high clusters of green and yellow Scotch broom lined the asphalt road. To the east were the white humps of mountains a hundred miles away. They passed the small, detached, fenced-off plot where Jews were buried. Near the center of the cemetery was a grassy plot. Embedded there, in concrete, were two antiaircraft guns, pointing toward the sky, mountings and barrels painted silver-gray. Surrounding them was a triple circle of helmets.

"The American Legion and the Veterans of Foreign Wars paid to get the guns here," Harriet said, stopping the car. "Isn't it idiotic? Every guy in the two posts brought a helmet here. Now they come out and have picnics with their kids."

Enigmatically, Jean got out of the car and opened her door for her. They stood together near the circle of helmets. I must do something, I must say something, Harriet thought. She kicked out at one of the helmets. It clattered against its neighbor.

"Don't," Jean said mildly. "Leave the dead alone." He took her right arm, fingers against the ribs beside her breast. She stood, unsure of what to do, until his hand lapsed away. "You funny American girls," he said, his voice casual, amused again. "You funny American girls. Show me the rest of your tour." Next, the graves of her mother's parents. Their markers were upright granite rectangles; the only inscriptions names and dates. Harriet changed the water in the tin funnels in which her mother kept fresh flowers. Jean leaned against her Grandfather Yates' tombstone. He undid the top buttons of his shirt. Curls of black hair bordered the tank top of his ribbed cotton undershirt. All the other men Harriet knew wore white T-shirts. "How did your grandmother die?" Jean asked.

"Old age and cancer." Her voice, as he watched, seemed to struggle like water in a clogged pipe.

"And your grandfather?"

"I really don't know. It was during the Depression."

She jumped over the privet hedge separating the Yates plot from its neighbor to brush bits of leaves and grass from the stone there. As a preschooler, she had played there while her mother had tended her Grandfather Yates' grave. Before, the letters of the alphabet had been abstract, confusing, but suddenly, as she had studied the stone, the letters had straightened into sense. She could read:

Interred here
in one coffin
MARY AUGUSTA
WIFE OF
Lewis S. Roberts, M.D.
& daughter of James W.R.
Phebe R. Harley
& her infant son James Lewis
she died
Feb. 6, 1919
aged 18 years
her son
the following date
aged 11 days

Jean wandered around the edge of the hedge, humming tunelessly and sunnily. He squatted down beside her: "Would you like to make love with me?"

"I beg your pardon?"

"Never mind." He took her hand, fondled it, released it. "Tell me," he said, "why have you all gone to such good colleges. Surely it is very odd to go from here to Yale, or from here to Harwyn. And your pretty sister, Anne, she wants to go to the university, I believe."

100

"Mom believes in education. She thinks that if she and Daddy give us the best education they can, it's better than leaving us money. She thinks education really helps in getting through life." I'm babbling, she thought self-consciously.

"Americans are so optimistic about education." He opened her car door.

"You don't believe in it?"

"It can be useful, but a nice Yale degree, or a nice Harwyn degree, can never keep you from real harm."

Heretical.

"I've shocked you." He shrugged, then tucked her skirt inside the car before shutting the door. She could not tell if his touch was an impersonal courtesy or a pass. He settled himself on the other side. "Finish the tour," he suggested. "I did not really want to see the town but to be with you, but you should probably show me the rest of the town."

The next evening, after he had gone, Harriet and her mother were doing dishes.

"Do you like Jean Maurin?" Harriet asked, a preliminary skirmish.

"He's a fellow of Georgie's college."

"He made a pass at me."

Her mother's face blanked out, as if it were a mask over fright. "Did he?" she asked numbly.

"Yes, I was showing him Grammy's grave."

"I didn't know that."

"Now you do."

"It's hard to believe that one of your brother's teachers would do a thing like that."

"Well, he did. But don't worry, I didn't do anything back."

"That's good." At last her mother seemed certain of herself again. "Why were you showing him Grammy's grave?"

"There's not that much else to do in Northville." Harriet paused, scrubbed at the sink. Then, deliberately, she asked, "How did your father die anyway? Jean asked, and I didn't know what to say."

Her mother shoved a frying pan into a drawer as if she were upset. "He was hurt in an accident. I've told you that. I wish you'd stop dawdling so we could get out of the kitchen."

101

"Okay, okay," Harriet said, angry to be under attack when she had been trying to talk. "I was just asking." She went upstairs to write to Sloan and to refer vaguely to continental manners.

A few days later she received a handwritten letter on Harwyn stationery from the president of the Student Governing Council:

Dear Harriet,

Bad news. Muffy Gallagher, who was supposed to be our delegate to the national meeting of the Student Government Association of America, can't go. She has a bad case of mono. Could you go as her replacement? We thought you might be able to, since the meeting is going to be in St. Paul, Minnesota, at the University of Minnesota, and you live out west. You would have to go to the meetings and then report back to us. I *really* hope you will be able to.

Harriet was delighted. The honor was reported on the society page of the *Northville News*. Her father released her from the adding machine and ledgers of the bank.

The night before she was to catch the train to St. Paul, Olivia Kasper and Betsy Metcalfe dropped by. Olivia in white sandals, a white pleated skirt, and pink shirt. She was pinned, to an athlete, a university hero. Betsy was dressed like Harriet—pedal pushers; old Keds; no socks; a white sweatshirt with the sleeves cut short. She had a day off from her summer job at a resort. She was seeing the golf pro there. "Her parents are wild," Mrs. Springer had told Harriet. "They're scared to death she'll have to get married and drop out of school. He's divorced and eight years older than she is."

The three of them sat, in canvas lawn chairs, drinking iced tea, in the elongated shadows of the grape arbor.

"I like it that Stock is older," Betsy said toughly. "It's great. He knows exactly what he's doing. No fumbling around. I know I won't get pregnant or anything."

"I saw Darlene Galter," Olivia said. "She looks terrible. She has two kids now. She was driving them around in a pickup truck."

"My mother says," Harriet added, "that Harry Joe gets drunk and beats her up."

"Do you like it back east, Harriet?" Olivia asked. "Do you get to go to New York a lot? That should really be fun."

"I don't go in as much as I should, but I think I'll get a job there when I graduate."

"Not me." Betsy pushed at the ice in her glass with her finger. "Not me. Not for a million dollars. I'm staying in California. I love it. I just don't understand, Harriet, how you can go back there where it's dirty, and you don't know anyone, and everybody's so snobby."

"I feel like I belong," Harriet said. "And a Frenchman I know is interested in me."

"A Frenchman?" Olivia was respectful. "I guess that's what happens when you go east. Betsy and I just see Americans."

"Stock's traveled around the world," Betsy said. "Just because you're an American, it doesn't mean you're a hick."

"No," Olivia said, softly, "but I wish I could travel. Bill wants to stay in the west, too."

"He's right," Betsy declared. "You'd never get me east. Never."

When Olivia and Betsy left, her mother called Harriet into the living room. "Why can't you dress like Olivia?" she asked. "You have good clothes. You could be so handsome."

"I'm wearing what Betsy was wearing."

"But you could be ever so much more handsome."

"The hell I could."

"There's to be no swearing in my house," her father said, putting down the latest *Time*.

"Don't swear. Look pretty. What a set of directions," she said bitterly.

Because her train was in the afternoon, she could check the mail for something from Sloan before she left. Sloan rarely wrote, but when she did, Harriet preferred not to let her mother see the envelope and ask who Sloan Trouver was. Sloan had written. As soon as the train left Northville and was bumping over the roadbed next to the bay, Harriet tore the letter open. It was short:

Harriet,

My mother has found your letters. She made me burn them all in the backyard. Please don't write anymore this summer.

Sloan

Harriet's body turned icy, shriven without penance. Her letters, her poetry, was in ashes. Sloan, her poetry, was imprisoned with

103

her ghastly, drunken parents. In a panic she wondered if she should get off the train and phone Sloan. But if she did, Mrs. Trouver might answer. She thought she might write, but Sloan had explicitly ordered her not to. Overnight, in her berth, anxiety and doubt bullied her. She dreamt that she and Sloan were sitting on a floor, but it opened up so that they fell toward the stony bottom of a canyon. She woke up choking, thinking she had bits of rock in her throat. Finally, at a stop in Cut Fish, Montana, she wired Sloan:

BE STRONG. RED, BLACK, AND SILVER WILL TRIUMPH OVER JEALOUSY AND FEAR.

Because she had acted, she felt better. She was sure Sloan would be consoled. Still, for the rest of the trip, as she sat in her compartment, the panic would rush at her. To calm herself, she repeated the telegram over and over. At the University of Minnesota she was assigned a room in a women's dorm. She attached her name tag to her blue cotton dress and went outside to study her program. Sweat gathered around the tops of her nylons and oozed between her legs and the slats of the wooden bench on which she sat. She selected an afternoon workshop about the relationship of student government to college presidents. While she was there she listened dutifully, but she made notes in her steno pad for Sloan that she would give her when they were safely together at Harwyn. When it was done, she stood in line for macaroni and meatloaf in a huge cafeteria. Over the steam tables hung a banner: WELCOME GUYS AND GALS OF THE S.G.A.A. Old phrases from advice columns urged her to forget herself; to break the ice; to remember that everyone was shy; to smile so that the world would smile with her. She took her tray to a table at which a girl with an efficient-looking haircut was sitting.

"Hi," she said firmly, brightly, "I'm Harriet Springer from Harwyn."

The other was Stella McComber from Idaho State. Harriet unrolled tinware from a paper napkin. "Did you come by train?" she asked.

"Oh, no, that's too much money. We came by bus."

"Are you going to hear the keynote after dinner?"

"Of course. I think anyone who's in Congress really has to have something on the ball, don't you?"

"Shall we walk over together?" Harriet smiled over her forkful of yellowish pasta.

"You go ahead. I've got to go up to my room. I'll look for you in the auditorium."

Am I a loser, a dog, Harriet wondered, as she walked beneath shade trees to the evening session. There on the auditorium's limestone steps, cigarette dangling from lower lip, briefcase in hand, coat loose, was Jean Maurin.

"Harriet, Harriet," the fervor of his reproach was welcome. "You did not tell me you would be here. I could have driven you here. I have a car now."

"I didn't know you would be here."

"You don't want to hear this guy talk. It will be hot. It will be boring. Come for a drive. It's very pretty here. A big river, and bluffs, and many trees."

She hesitated. If Harwyn had sent her to the S.G.A.A. convention, she was obliged to attend. "You won't miss anything," Jean said. "I have met this congressman. He always says the same thing. It will be a much bigger honor for you to be with me. I am an international adviser."

I can, Harriet thought, include a section on S.G.A.A. foreign activities in my report. She went with Jean. They drove away from the Mississippi River toward open farm country. Clumps of trees and silos rose from the fields. Jean was humming as he had in the Northville cemetery. Harriet felt increasingly out of control, and in his. She almost never touched Sloan unless Sloan touched her first. That gave Sloan power over her, but Harriet also believed that she and Sloan had become equals, equivalences, self to other self. When Sloan did touch her, her excitement was refined to a pitch almost too high for the body to hear. She would not touch Jean until Jean touched her. That, too, gave him power over her, but she could not imagine that they would ever be alike. And if he were to want her, her body threatened to unravel, to succumb to a warm passivity. She thought of Sloan's painful letter, in her purse at her feet, but Jean's casual, immediate, physical authority could wash even over it.

"Do you think foreign students have a hard time in America?" she asked. She wanted to reassert some will.

105

"I'm off duty now," he answered.

He stopped on a patch of dirt between road and ditch. He turned her body to him. His tongue entered her mouth, hoed her teeth, raked the inside of her lips. His hand stroked the top of her stocking, pulled at the elastic straps of her garter belt. "Jean," she said. "I'm a virgin." Confession, plea for mercy, cry for help.

He pressed the inside of her thigh. "Then we will stop for now. This is no place for a nice girl to lose her virginity." She was relieved, but his words emptied her. She rubbed his waist. The flesh gave beneath her hand.

"You like me to kiss you, don't you?" he said.

"I don't think you should," she said conscientiously.

"Come to my room day after tomorrow for lunch. You'll like it. I'll feed you lunch."

"But what if there's a session I should be at?"

"By then you will know more about student government than any girl as nice as you should know. I'll feed you a nice lunch and tell you things you can tell your Harwyn friends."

She agreed. The next day she went to more workshops and then, in the evening, to a business meeting. Stella McComber saw her in front of the auditorium. "Hi, there," she said. "We just never caught up with each other last night, did we? Wasn't the congressman wonderful? He's got a great career ahead of him."

"What's tonight going to be like?" Harriet asked, to divert more questions about the night before.

"Lots of important resolutions."

Inside, three thousand delegates were finding seats. They were at once orderly and exuberant, like disciplined sports fans. At eight a tall boy, in a suit and tie, took the podium on the stage. Several men and a woman with a steno pad occupied a table behind him. As the tall boy welcomed the delegates in an earnest baritone, Harriet was convinced that he had won his regional speaking contests. The first agenda item was the Resolutions Committee report. Its recommendations were so dull that Harriet subversively asked Stella why the delegates were bothering to vote on them.

"Because this is a democratic organization," a surprised Stella reminded her. Harriet tried to suppress her restlessness. She

106

wished Sloan were there, but from time to time the memory of Jean, an older European trying to seduce her, if in the front seat of a car on an American back road, overwhelmed her. Then she noticed that the people on the stage were cupping their hands over their eyes and glaring into the auditorium. Two students were walking purposively down the side aisles toward the floor mikes. To Harriet's left was an angular boy, red hair rising from his head like rocket exhaust. To her right was a husky girl, her brown hair falling in long braids. She was dressed like avant-garde Harwyn girls in the spring: white peasant blouse, ballerina skirt, sandals. "Mr. Chairman," she announced firmly, "we wish to present a resolution from the floor. Be it resolved that the Student Government Association of America support and work actively for racial justice and Negro equality on all its campuses."

"So move," the boy shouted. "Second," someone behind Harriet called out. Around them delegates whistled and yelped in disbelief. "What in heaven's name are they talking about?" Stella asked. "We don't have any Negroes in Idaho."

"Order," the chairman shouted. "We have a motion on the floor." The liturgical phrase calmed the unruly house. "Debate is now in order." His voice was straining to be judicious.

As delegates lined up in the aisles, Harriet looked for Negroes. She saw none. The first speaker, a blond boy, held the floor mike with tender rectitude. He favored the resolution. "As students and officers of student government," he concluded, "we have a special commitment to racial equality. We cannot permit ourselves to perpetuate the selfish injustices of the past." Harriet applauded. Stella shook her head disapprovingly.

The next speaker began neutrally. "I am as committed as my colleague to equality. However, I am also committed to individuality and liberty. We cannot dictate to, impose upon, the many excellent institutions we represent." As he talked, his voice became more impassioned. Stella leaned toward Harriet. "He's got the right idea," she said.

"Have you ever read *Native Son?*" Harriet asked her. Stella looked confused.

Now a short girl, in a striped dress and white heels, was speaking tersely, as if human silliness were worth but brevity. "We have justice in America," she said. "There's no reason to

107

support this resolution. We might as well go on record to support turning the Mississippi River into water."

Harriet wanted to get up and speak, but a young man was offering a brisk amendment: to delete the word "racial" and substitute for the word "Negroes" the word "American." Harriet no longer understood the debate. Crouched and intense, supporters of the resolution were going up and down the aisles. "Vote *against* the amendment," they were whispering. But Harriet reasoned, if she voted for equality for all Americans, that would certainly include Negroes.

"Oh, for Pete's sake," Stella said. "I wish we'd get this over with."

"Question," the crowd shouted.

Hesitantly, Harriet voted for the amended resolution. She was part of a great majority. Then the radical girl, her voice low and hard and angry, claimed a mike. "You hypocrites," she began, "taking refuge behind meaningless words . . ." Her sentence ended as her mike went dead. "The next item of business is the expansion of the office of international activities," the chair declared.

"What was that all about?" Harriet asked Stella. "I hope I did the right thing."

"I don't know, I'm sure," Stella said. "But some people sure know how to waste other people's time."

Harriet gazed around the auditorium again. She thought Jean would be there, but she could not see him. Dutifully she settled back to take notes about the rest of the plenary session. The next morning she dressed carefully: a white blouse, an artificial red carnation on its mandarin collar; a green bolero skirt, famous paintings reproduced on the cotton fabric. She reminded herself that she was only going to have lunch with Jean. She attended a workshop on health services. Then, at twelve, she walked down a slope to the faculty club where he was staying. Her heels plunged into the earth.

Jean had a corner suite. Light from two walls of window commingled on the varnished floorboards of the living room. On a desk were sandwiches, some olives in a paper cup, a bottle of wine. "Sit down," he said agreeably. "Do you like my room?"

"It has a nice view," she said, though she saw only buildings, trees, a road.

"Tell me about your workshops. Have you been good? Have you been industrious?" Sitting on the arm of her chair, he gently tugged at the curls at the back of her neck.

"Every place seems bigger than Harwyn," she said. Because tranquillity was abandoning her, she went toward the food.

"Do you mind ham-and-cheese?" Jean said. He stayed on the chair arm, smiling, humming.

"No, it's fine, thank you." However, she could not remain standing, eating ham-and-cheese as if she were at an outdoor picnic. She had to return to the chair, in the center of the room. The sun was flowing toward it, stippling Jean's trousers, lap, hands. She wondered why her nerves were making such a fuss. When she sat down, he stroked the back of her neck, beneath the curls. "You are very sweet," he said. "You mustn't be frightened."

"Why should I be frightened?"

"No reason. You are a sweet girl, and you should enjoy your afternoon."

Then he got up and went through a door behind them. The creaking floorboards told her that he had returned. He bent over the back of the chair to caress her arms and hands. His own arms were covered in white terry cloth. Coming around the chair, he pulled her up. He half carried, half led her into a small bedroom, onto a twin bed. She lay there, as he slowly undressed her, touching the skin as he revealed it. The blouse and skirt and her underwear were hung over an open bureau drawer. "Lie still," he said quietly, as he put a pillow under her hips and opened her legs. He had stopped humming. His face, moving close to her, was intense and abstracted, as if he were casting runes. His eyebrows were dark and heavy. She touched the wing of his nose, the pocked and stubbly cheeks. When he opened his mouth, she saw gold and dark-edged silver in his teeth.

Then he lowered his body over hers, his robe falling on either side of her, as if it were a curtain. His right hand guided something into her. He had not permitted her to see his body, wanting her to attend to his hands, her sensations. She was aware of a force inside her, but as he gathered his energy, her excitement seemed to flee from her into him. His eyes were shut. He was gasping and sighing and moving, as her body became stiffer, flatter, dumber. She felt sun on her feet, his sweat on her stomach.

"You're going to be safe," a new calculating voice said. "You're due for the curse in a couple of days." Suddenly he withdrew. Kneeling on the bed over her, he pulled at his penis, left hand holding the robe to keep her from seeing it. "Ah," he sighed and sat back on her thighs. The wine bottle was next to the bed. Swallowing some, he bent to kiss her and release it into her mouth. She gagged in surprise before it went down. He drank some more, touching her breasts.

"They're too small," she said.

"Oh, no." He was comforting. "More would be vulgar." Then, still on her thighs, he pressed his hand down on her stomach. "Now," he said, "I will let you go back to your workshops so that you may carry out your duties. I would tell you to come sleep with me tonight, but I must start the drive back to New Haven. So, you see, if you had not come to me this afternoon, I would not have been able to please you at all. This fall, perhaps I will come to Harwyn and rescue you from all those girls."

"It's a pretty campus." She was gathering her clothes, surprised at how matter of fact it all was. She tried to see Jean in the Smoker. Improbable. He kissed her before she walked down the four flights of stairs and over the grass to her dormitory. "Please, dear God," she prayed, as if she were a baptized Christian child again, "let the shower room be empty." She had to be alone with her new body. Undressing, she noticed blood on her nylon briefs. "Don't worry, it's only natural," she reassured herself. She was thinking of the sex book that had passed around the Gould Smoker. She placed the square mirror from the dresser on the desk. She looked at the image of her stomach, thighs, thin line of hair running from navel to her shaggy pubic curls. "I'm not a virgin anymore," she said. "I'm not a virgin anymore." But no matter how gravely she uttered the words, her body looked the same. Even the blood on her pants could have been the beginning of the curse.

The bathroom was empty. She stood beneath the shower. She washed herself with the Ivory soap she carried in her traveling case. "I'm not a virgin anymore," she repeated. "I'm not a virgin anymore." When she got out, she wiped and dried her genitals over and over again, until the towel hurt. Despite that, her body did not feel radically changed either. She was no longer a virgin,

110

but after the romantic tales, the hints, the jokes, her mother's warning, it came to this. Big deal.

In theory, Harriet disapproved of deceit. Practically, she enjoyed secretly storing the story of the loss of her virginity away. She thought she might be punished if the world, or Harwyn, or her family knew how easily Jean Maurin had taken her to bed. With a stealth she would have disclaimed if she had recognized it, she also knew the event could be a weapon in a battle beyond prediction. More immediately present in her consciousness, if never spoken about, was Sloan's cold warriorship. The anguish it caused Sloan sharply spurred Harriet's chivalry.

Sloan had craved to be elected sophomore representative to the Judicial Honor Board. She was. Yet she was languishing at Harwyn. She would lie on her bed, feet dangling over the edge, arm crossed over her eyes, wishing she was dead.

Before the novel class they took together, on a wet day, when the buildings smelled of damp wool, Harriet saw Sloan talking to Sophia Herrick. Sophia appeared controlled but worried; Sloan admonitory but amused. As Harriet approached, Sophia glided away. "You'll never guess," Sloan was actually laughing, "you'll never guess what she wanted to know. She was asking how far the little sperm could swim. She spent a weekend at Yale, and now she's worried about the little sperm."

Harriet smiled politely. She preferred the Sloan who talked about Gerard Manley Hopkins to the Sloan who used barracks talk learned on the Army bases on which she had grown up. Still, she was pleased to see Sloan cheerful.

"I told her not to worry, considering the time of month she said it was. I'm always having to pass out medical advice to people from my old school. I'll never forget the time when a girl put a Tampax up, and forgot that it was there, so when she put another one up, she couldn't get anything out. She had to go to the infirmary, and because I was the school president I had to stand up in front of the whole school and tell them how to use a Tampax. It was gross."

Sloan grew more depressed as Thanksgiving approached. Harriet, impetuously, supportively, invited herself home with Sloan for the vacation. "You won't have to be alone with your family," she argued. "Will they have to know that I was the person who wrote you those letters?"

"How couldn't they? Those letters were a real mess."

"I don't know, but I'm sure it could be arranged. Maybe they could know, and it would be all right. They could see that I'm not such a monster."

"Don't be an ass." Their worst insult. "Let's go to the Smoker. I want to see Naomi. She's the only amusing thing around this place."

But two weeks later Sloan, in the Smoker, abruptly wondered why both Harriet and Naomi could not come home with her for Thanksgiving.

"Naomi, too?"

"My dad will like her. He'll think she's sexy."

"Is there room for us both?"

"My little brother will be away. It'll be more fun if Naomi comes along. She'll distract my parents."

"What about my letters?"

"I've decided that I can't worry about them anymore."

Each weekday night at ten was a study break. The Negro maids put out bottles of milk to pep the students up. While Sloan searched for Naomi, Harriet went to her room with Ensor, *England to 1914*. She preferred to read alone than to hear Sloan ask Naomi to come where Harriet could neither welcome nor veto her. Fifteen minutes later Naomi appeared in her room in baggy jeans, French silk shirt, Italian belt, and mock-leopard bedroom slippers from the town of Harwyn. "Did Sloan ask you for Thanksgiving?" she asked.

"Yes."

"Do you want to go?"

"Do you?"

"I would like to see her house, but her parents scare me."

"Well, make up your mind." Relentless Harriet.

"Oh, I can't. My Daddy is coming to New York. I have to stay with him at the St. Moritz."

Harriet enjoyed her silly, refugee, Latin-American friend again. "Let's go to the Smoker," she said. "Ensor is putting me to sleep."

Sloan and Amarillo were in the Smoker. "Reading Ensor?" Amarillo asked. "Thrilling, isn't it. Doesn't anyone want to go to the movies tomorrow night in town? *Giant* is playing. I want to see Rock Hudson and Elizabeth Taylor and James Dean in the drama of my state."

"I've got a midterm," Sloan said.

"Elizabeth Taylor for one night won't interfere with that," Amarillo told her.

Sloan slapped the pages of her book together, gathered up her Harwyn notebook and clipboard, and walked out. "Temper, temper," Amarillo mocked. "We've been naughty. We've upset Sloan."

"She's got a big test," Harriet was defensive.

"Don't we all," Amarillo said. "Could you care less about Irish Home Rule? Did you know that Alison Clark goes over to Professor LeClerc's house every Saturday night after she has signed out to go baby-sitting?"

"But he's so short, and she's so tall," Naomi was titillated. "I wonder how they manage."

"Anything can be managed," Harriet said.

When vacation began, Sloan, Harriet, and Naomi took the commuter train to New York together. Naomi's face heavily powdered to hide the red reminder of a too-aggressive wax job. Sloan and Harriet treated themselves to a taxi to Penn Station to catch the crowded Washington night train. Mottled, stained windows held back the dark outside; Sloan's body barred Harriet from other people. "Do you think your mother will like the present I got her?" Harriet asked. She had shopped for an hour before choosing a Spanish tile on which hot dishes could be set.

"Sure, it'll be fine. She'll be too drunk to notice."

"You really think now that they won't connect me with the letters?" Harriet's anxiety was flourishing now that her project was becoming real.

"I told you, I'm not worried any more. I threw away the envelopes. I'm not sure that my mother even read the name at the end of the letters.

In Washington another taxi to Chevy Chase. The dark city bewildered Harriet: the traffic circles; the grand, looming buildings that looked like stage sets; and then, in the suburbs, the brick houses too close together. Sloan's home was on a little slope, a front yard no more than thirty feet across. No porch light shone between its two white colonnades.

113

A straight flight of stairs led from the hall inside to the second floor. Going up, Harriet tried to keep her suitcase from banging against the bannisters. They turned left. Sloan's room was simple: White spreads on the twin beds matched white, dotted swiss curtains. The chest of drawers, dressing table, and desk looked as if they were bought, then painted. Sloan pointed to the striped rug, "My father brought that to me from Greece," she whispered, "He was on duty there once."

"It's pretty," Harriet said.

From down the hall came a tremendous snore. "I wonder if that's my father or my mother," Sloan said. "I'm going down to the kitchen to see if there's a message."

Quickly, before Sloan could return, Harriet undressed. She was sitting on the edge of a bed when Sloan came in with a piece of grocery sack. Written on it in blunt pencil, "Welcome home, darling. News about tomorrow. Dad and I have to go to the general's for dinner. You and your friend can go to the Army/Navy Club. I made arrangements. Your brother stayed at school. Sleep in if you want."

"Well," said Sloan dully, "she's more organized than usual."

Because it confused Harriet to watch Sloan undress, she looked at her bookshelves. Then Sloan was crouching beside her, hair loose, wearing a bathrobe that looked like a floor-length poncho. She put her arm around Harriet. "Come on," she said, "have a cigarette. Tell me how you like my wonderful, friendly family."

They sat on the floor together, the hard edges of the shelves cutting into Harriet's spine. Her left hand held her Lucky Strike, her right hand was free if Sloan wanted it.

"I hardly ever invite anybody home," Sloan said.

"I'm glad it's me," she said. She's moody again, she thought.

"Sophia Herrick was here once."

"But I thought you didn't like her," Harriet was surprised.

"I thought she was okay for a while," Sloan said cryptically.

"There, right over there," Sloan pointed to her desk, "that's where my mother found your letters."

"How did it happen?"

"She said she was looking for something."

"I want to kill her," Harriet said. "How could she do that to you?"

Without touching Harriet, Sloan stood up. "Let's go to bed," she said. "You get to meet them tomorrow. Oh, shit, we'll have to put clean sheets on."

During the night Harriet kept waking up, to wonder where she was, to remember when she saw Sloan, in the other bed. Early in the morning she fell fully asleep. At ten o'clock she was flustered to find herself still in bed but Sloan gone. If she had been in Northville, she would have been having Thanksgiving Day breakfast of waffles and sausage. But she was in Chevy Chase, uncertain of her welcome and her tasks. She put on skirt, shirt, knee socks, loafers. Carrying her hostess present, she descended. Sloan and her mother were in a dining room, to the left of the stairs, both in caftans.

"Hi," said Sloan, "meet my mother."

"How do you do?" Harriet advanced, extending the present. "I thought that perhaps you would like this."

"My God," Sloan's mother said, "it's so early in the morning for formalities."

Harriet stood, in the silence, until Sloan told her to sit down and have some coffee. "It's a beautiful pot," she commented politely.

"Some of my good things survived all our moves, even if I didn't," Mrs. Trouver said. Unwrapping the package. "Well, now," she examined the tile, "that's nice."

Her hair, except for the fact that it was graying, looked more like a student's than a mother's. Parted on the side, it fell to her shoulders. Her face and arms were tanned. Her features were more beautiful, more generous, than Sloan's, but dark circles under her eyes and a jagged-looking nose took their toll of her charm. "So you go to college with my baby?" Her husky voice reminded Harriet of that of an actress.

"We're in the same hall."

"She's something, isn't she? Three inches taller than I am, sober, brilliant as they come, and my baby."

"They think a lot of her at Harwyn."

"Everyone always thinks a lot of my baby." Mrs. Trouver blew her daughter a kiss. "Sloanie," she said, "can you get your raddled old mother the pitcher of tomato juice from the frig?"

"I'll get it," Harriet said, eager to be a good guest.

"What's her name?" Mrs. Trouver whispered as she went into the kitchen.

115

"Harriet," Sloan muttered. "Harriet. I've never mentioned her to you before."

"Here you are, ma'am," Harriet said with a flourish when she returned.

"Look, Sloan, no vodka." Mrs. Trouver held up the pitcher. "Not even on a holiday. Have some, Harriet, it'll do us all good."

"What time do you and Daddy have to be at the general's?" Sloan asked, as if she were organizing her mother.

"Around two. We'll have to get him up before one. He doesn't want to go to the general's at all, not at all. You all are going to be all right at the Army/Navy Club, aren't you? Sloan, honey, charge it to your granddaddy. Her granddaddy," she turned to Harriet, "her granddaddy is my daddy. He's a general. I've been in the Army all my life, first an Army brat, then an Army wife."

"It must be interesting."

"Interesting? Honey, you don't know the half of it. Harriet, that's a familiar name. Harriet, I once knew someone named Harriet. A woman who worked for us on a base in Texas, before you were born, Sloan. Harriet, if I were a good mother, I'd be cooking Thanksgiving dinner, but we've got to go asslick a general."

"I've never been to an Army/Navy club," Harriet said.

"You and my baby should have a good time," Mrs. Trouver said. She peered at the glass of tomato juice against the light from the window. "I'm going to get some ice," she told them, "What's tomato juice without ice."

"Let's go to the basement," Sloan said. "I want to see if she managed to get the piano tuned." As they left, she called to her mother, "Make sure it's only ice. You've got a long day ahead of you."

"Don't worry about me, baby."

Harriet and Sloan stayed in the basement, reading. Sloan wanted to let her mother wake her father up. "They'll probably have sex," she said. "It'll be good for them both."

"I like your mother," Harriet answered, embarrassed by Sloan's frankness.

"She's all right," Sloan said, with belligerent pride.

They left before Colonel Trouver was up. On the way to the club, Sloan showed Harriet Washington monuments, more familiar now in the light. She noted them dutifully, as if they were illustrations for a required course. The club was a comfortable hotel with Oriental waiters. Harriet watched Sloan, trusting in her skills, wary of her own, as Sloan ordered oysters, turkey, whiskey sours. "I thought more people would be wearing uniforms." she said.

"God, no, but you should see my father when he does. He's got medals all over his chest. He'll never make general, because he's too much of a renegade, but he's a real hero."

That evening they were slouching on the living room sofa when Colonel and Mrs. Trouver came home. He was in a gray civilian suit; a hard, muscular man, with short hair, an inch or two taller than his daughter. Horizontal line slashed into his face. "Hi, honey," he kissed Sloan. "Glad to see you again." He shook Harriet's hand. She was trying to stand, but the gesture pushed her back on the sofa. "Christ," he said to his wife, "get us all a drink. I can't stand that bore. What a way to spend a day, watching old movies of Army/Navy games."

He brought a chintz-covered wing chair closer to the sofa. "See that?" he asked Harriet, pointing to his tie clasp. "I had it made out of a bullet that went through my canteen once in the Yugoslav mountains. It bounced off a rock, went through my helmet, and came to rest, like a little dog, at my feet. I decided it should stay with me."

"You were lucky," Harriet tried to admire him.

"Sure I was lucky."

"Chow time," Mrs. Trouver announced sarcastically, swaying and pushing a cart with bottles, glasses, and an ice bucket. The colonel poured four Scotches. "Drink it neat," he gave Harriet one. "It's going to go into you whether you dilute it or not, so you might as well have it pure."

Harriet winced as she tasted it. "Still a virgin?" the colonel asked. He raised his eyebrow, just as Sloan did.

"Come on, Daddy," Sloan said. "Tell us more about the general."

"He is a fart," the colonel pronounced distinctly, "A first-class fart, without redeeming qualities. If he didn't have a say about my career, I would suggest that he be assigned to special latrine duty in Korea. But," he stared at Harriet as if she were an item on a souvenir stand, "I've got a real opportunity here to find out what college students are thinking about. Korea, that reminds me of international communism. What do college students think about international communism?"

"Well," she rummaged for composure, "I don't think they know about it, but I don't think they're as scared as somebody like the American Legion might be."

"The American Legion? Do you have anything against the American Legion?"

"You've never had much good to say for them," Mrs. Trouver reminded him. Harriet was grateful for her support, but she had, Harriet noticed with horror, a highball glass full of neat Scotch.

"I will remind you," the colonel said, still looking at Harriet, "that I am not concerned with my opinions now, but with this young student's. She is going to give me an idea of what her fellow students are thinking. What are they thinking? What are they thinking about international communism?"

"I can't speak for all of them," Harriet temporized.

"Then why did you think you could speak for the American Legion?"

"I read its magazine. My father is a member. I get some idea of what it thinks."

"Mama," the colonel said to his wife, "Mama, this young lady's father went to war. What do you think of that?"

"I hate war," Mrs. Trouver announced. "Robert, why don't you go down to the basement and get some wood and build a nice fire? It's Thanksgiving. We have our baby home. We should have a little celebration."

"We are having a little celebration," he told her. "We're having a little nightcap with our daughter and her friend. What did you say your name was, friend?"

"Harriet," her voice less steady than it should be. "Harriet Springer."

"Harriet," he said, "that's a familiar name."

"That's what I told her." Mrs. Trouver, though her glass was still half full, went to the cart to replenish. "Remember that Harriet who worked for us in Texas? Come on, Robert, build a fire."

"I can't interrupt this important conversation, Mama. If you're bored, go up to bed and wait for me."

"I'm not bored," Mrs. Trouver stood over him, "I just want more family celebration."

118

"Well, I want family conversation."

"Then," Mrs. Trouver steadied herself on his chair, "I'm going to bed. Sloan, baby, why don't you come with me and brush my hair, like you used to do?"

"Don't get too Black Irish, Daddy," Sloan said, standing up. She held out her hand to him. Taking it, he kissed the palm.

"Night, night, night, night you-all, you-all," Mrs. Trouver called as she and Sloan walked out.

"My wife gets very southern after a party," the colonel said to Harriet. "You stay here. You haven't instructed me in the virtues of communism yet. I'm an old officer, and they've got me sealed off in the Pentagon. I'm going to get another drink, and then you can teach me."

"I didn't say communism had virtues," Harriet swallowed. Being alone with the colonel scared her. "I only said that it might not be as frightening as people say."

"My, my, my, my, my," the colonel said to his glass. "Do you suppose that this battle-scarred old soldier, whose ears have been ruined by years of listening to exploding shells, is hearing right? Do you think that this young student could be saying that communism is not frightening?"

"The Russians have taught a lot of people to read," she said, "and the old czarist regime was very corrupt."

"And do you believe that there is no corruption in Russia now?"

"I don't know," she said. She had her opinions, but they seemed to shrivel before she could speak.

"Oh, Lord," he groaned. "To think that I'm saving the world for you. You've barely started your drink. Don't you appreciate your nightcap?"

"It's fine," she said, trying to filter the Scotch through her teeth, as if they might dilute the taste.

"How long have you known my only daughter?" the colonel asked, pulling the cart toward him.

"A year and a half. I was a sophomore when she came to Harwyn."

"Oh? So you're older than she is?" His voice was lower, less jeering than it had been.

"I guess so."

119

"You guess so? You should know about things like age. It's easier to know about age than communism."

"I'm a year older than she is. Almost exactly. Our birthdays are almost on the same day."

The colonel seemed to yawn. "I'll say good night now," Harriet said hastily.

"You haven't told me about communism yet," he said, "but I think I know enough already." When she got up he did, too, and took her elbow, as if he were going to escort her to the stairs. "So you're a year older," he said, and then, without warning, he shoved her against the wall. "Are you the dyke that wrote my daughter those letters? You are, aren't you?" he went on before she could deny his accusation. Then, pinning her shoulder, he began to kiss her. She felt as if a pile driver were attacking the rock of her mouth and body, but his voice was hideously guttural and cheerful. "You little lesbian, I'll straighten you out." Silently, she began to struggle, twisting against him. He relaxed his hold, but only to laugh, before he pressed himself against her again, his mouth forcing her head against the wall. Then, unexpectedly, he released her. He slapped her right flank. "Go on," he said, "I think my daughter and I can manage you."

Distraught, she ran up the stairs. Sloan was lying on her bed, wearing her caftan, holding a book. "I saw my father kissing you," she said neutrally.

"I didn't want him to," Harriet found breathing hard.

Sloan was silent. She might have been torn between loyalty to her guest and to her father. She might have been supporting her father, whose impulses were, at base, a sign of his incorrigible energy. "It's his house," she finally said. "I'm going to read some bio before I go to sleep. We've only got two days of vacation left."

Harriet still looked at her. She needed help. "He probably won't be around tomorrow," Sloan admitted. "He's got some special duty for the next few days."

"Where's your mother?"

"Passed out on the floor in their bedroom. Take a shower, would you, or go to bed and read. You're making it hard for me to study."

Harriet obeyed and went to bed. She did not know what else to do. That Sunday she was glad to be back in her safe Harwyn territory. Naomi came to her room. She had hand-dipped chocolates from New York. "What are Sloanie's parents like?" she asked eagerly.

"Her mother drinks, really drinks, but she's attractive."

"What about her father?"

"He's very hard-boiled," Harriet said. "He drinks, too." She told Naomi nothing more. The incident with Colonel Trouver was too humiliating to talk about. He had bullied her with his masculinity. He had assaulted and ridiculed her. Labeling her a Lesbian, he had reduced her immaterial passion for Sloan to something ugly, perverted, loathsome. Her parents, if they knew, might wonder about the intensity of her friendship with Sloan, but they would, at least, dislike Colonel Trouver, his brutality, his kiss at the bottom of a flight of stairs in a home that drunkards ruled. But Sloan had accepted everything her father had done to Harriet. She neither protested nor sympathized. Still, Harriet clung to their intimacy. She knew better now what Sloan endured. If Sloan faltered in their private world, Harriet would simply work harder to sustain it. If Sloan gave less, Harriet would give more, and the equilibrium of their emotional calculus would, she hoped, remain.

Despite Harriet's efforts, where once she and Sloan had had secrets they now began to have silences as well. About Colonel Trouver, about Compton Francis, a man Sloan had met at a Christmas party. Compton had been in the Army. He was now a graduate assistant in history at the University of North Carolina. Naomi kept Harriet informed about him. "He writes to her and tells her he is in love with her," Naomi said gleefully.

"Is she is love with him?" Harriet knew she should be happy. Comptons and Sloans were supposed to have romances.

"She says she isn't, but she likes his body."

"Are they sleeping together?"

"He won't sleep with her unless they get married."

"I don't believe it."

"That's what she says, but you know Sloanie. Sometimes she exaggerates."

Harriet worried, but she was distracted. Molly Sonnenstein asked her to audition for the Harwyn Junior Show. Ebullient, imperative, gregarious Molly Sonnenstein. As tall as Sloan; hair as dark and unruly as Harriet's; a great, theatrical, beaked nose;

in fur-collared tweed coat and fur-lined books. A grades in philosophy, physics, literature. Plans to be an opera singer. A prodigy. Director of the Harwyn Junior Show.

"But I can't sing," Harriet demurred.

"You've heard of *My Fair Lady*, haven't you? Well, we've written a show just like it. You don't have to sing. All you have to do is talk, like Rex Harrison."

"But it would be a waste of everyone's time."

"Come on, boobala, try out. We think you're going to be terrific."

She went to Woolbrith Auditorium, arched and buttressed like a Gothic cathedral, severe as a Romanesque chapel. She took her abridged edition of *Clarissa*, in case she had a moment to study. Molly—in tweed skirt, black tights, and her boots—was standing on the slate floor of the orchestra pit. "Okay," she announced to the girls sitting in the front rows, "we've got a plot that Shakespeare wouldn't have scorned, so you Harwyn snobs can accept it. We're also going to spoof academic life. There is this Prince Rhetorissimus. He wants to create an ideal princedom of the mind, a little Platonic realm. Across the meadow is a convent, and in the convent there is a beautiful princess. She's brilliant, too. She really likes the arts and sciences, but she doesn't like the prince, because he's a pompous ass.

"When the prince proposes to her, she turns him down. He is crushed. He had never thought that anyone could turn him down, and besides, the mother superior of the convent has been on his side, because she thought he would endow the convent if he married the princess. To get over the blow, he goes on a pilgrimage through the streets and taverns of his principality. He learns about life. Then he goes back to the convent and asks the princess to marry him again. She does, but only if he agrees to let her be his coequal in running the entire kingdom, including all the schools.

"So it's a happy story, but that's only the main plot. You've got enough to set the scene. Harriet Springer, you do Prince Rhetorissimus."

Harriet took a carbon copy of some lyrics. At an upright in the orchestra pit the pianist put out her cigarette in a half-full milk bottle. She and Molly had done the show's book, music, and lyrics. Harriet slouched up to the bare stage, stood before a gray backcloth, looked out at Molly and rows of empty orange plush seats. "Okay, Harriet, sing to the princess. You're trying to woo her, but your idea of wooing her is to tell her how great you are," Molly instructed.

The chords from the piano were heavy, somber. "Remember, Harriet, don't try to sing, just talk your way through," Molly shouted.

Feeling silly, Harriet began:

> Crown me, crown me, prince of words.
> Aristocrat of nouns and verbs.
> I rule the world of men and speech,
> Through language ethics I shall teach.

But, as she continued, she stood more confidently, the adrenaline of performance charging her. When she was done, she was aloof, haughty.

"Harriet," Molly approved loudly, "do it again. I knew I was on to something." "Crown me, crown me, prince of words," Harriet declaimed, with authority, with laudable condescension. She got the part.

She researched her performance. She observed the male professors at Harwyn. Adopting a walk from psychology, a voice break from history, a gesture from French, a pointed finger from physics. She usually stood in front of mirrors to reassure herself that her face was still a part of her, but now, she posed to check on Prince Rhetorissimus. She was growing fond of him: his quirks, his pride, his movements, his humiliation and eventual triumph. She was rehearsing her/his lines when Naomi and Amarillo appeared in her room.

Naomi sat in Harriet's armchair. Her mother had upholstered it in the same material as her curtains before shipping them to her. Amarillo took the bed.

"Harriet," Naomi said, as if she were stripping the pale pink polish from her nails, "have you thought whether or not you're going to the dance after the Junior Show?"

"Of course not. Who would I ask? My brother?"

"If you had someone you wanted to ask, would you go?" Naomi inquired delicately.

"Maybe, but then I'd have to worry about what to wear."

123

"That's no problem," Amarillo said. "I've talked to Tally, and she's got a dress you could borrow. One of the maids could fix it up for you."

"And we could go to the branch of Saks and buy shoes. I'll help." Naomi was enthusiastic. "And I'll fix your face for you. We'll wax the little hairs off and put on eye shadow and everything."

"I don't want all that junk," Harriet insisted. Back to her dresser, script in hand, she gazed at them irritably.

"You sound just like Sloanie in a bad mood," Naomi rebuked her.

"Look at the big picture, Harriet," Amarillo said. "You're one of the leads, if not the lead, in the Junior Show. You just can't, when it's over, take off your costume, come back to the hall, have a Lucky Strike and go to bed. You owe it to yourself to go to the dance afterward. I'm going with Eddie Jacobs from Columbia. I've asked him to find one of his friends for you. Tally says that if that doesn't work, she'll ask Hank to find somebody at Harvard."

"You've been talking this over behind my back, haven't you?" Harriet accused.

"Because it's important," Amarillo said. Her bedroom slippers are dirty, Harriet thought. I wish she weren't sitting on my bed.

"Are you going, Naomi?" Harriet asked.

"I'm going with a friend of Judi's boy friend." Judi was her adviser. "You know, don't you," her tone was delicate again, "that Sloanie plans to go with Compton. He's going to drive all the way from North Carolina to go with her."

"She didn't tell me that," Harriet said.

"Everybody's going," Amarillo asserted. "You'll be glad when you get there. Eddie will find you a really nice guy."

"If everybody's going," she said, bitter in submission, "I guess I'd better."

The Junior Show ran for two nights: On Friday the audience would be heterogenous, but on Saturday it would be mostly girls and dates going to the dance. The Thursday dress rehearsal had been difficult. The sweat-shirted Calibans of the stage crew were still working on the sets and lights. On Friday Harriet, whispering her lines to herself, walked to the Woolbrith dressing room. Naomi was with her. She did the cast's makeup.

The last items for her costume had arrived only that morning: black tights; a black, turtleneck shirt; a black velvet doublet with slashed sleeves; a long open bright-red sleeveless coat; heavy rings, a gilt chain, from which hung a gilt medallion three inches in diameter; and finally, black suede knee-length boots. When she stood, in front of the mirror, she saw Naomi, holding a stick of rouge and a powder puff, astonished, next to her. "Harriet," Naomi said, "you're a beautiful man." She looked at herself. Even in a mirror that naked bulbs framed she saw a person whose body and clothes flared into the world like a dark sun. Her hair was no longer frizzy, but curly. Her large nose and square jaw were no longer irregular, but strong. Her body was no longer too flat, but trim and fit. Her walk was no longer out of control, but energetic and bold. She was no longer a misfit, but a colossus. As she went up the concrete stairs to the wings, two at a time, she noticed girls staring at her, with surprise, with respect. She sat in the wood-and-leather chair near the light board. "Don't sprawl," her mother had always instructed her, but to sprawl in tights and boots was to stretch. Is this, she wondered, how Olivia Kasper had always felt: this balancing of brain, will, and body in peopled space?

Arranging themselves on the stage were ten Harwyn juniors: the male citizens of her kingdom, in little peaked caps, tunics, cloaks, and tights. They had the show's opening chorus. Across the stage, between pulleys, ropes, and cables, was the Princess Linguistica, in a white gown. Next to her, in black habit and wimple, was the Spanish major who had been cast as the mother superior. As the heavy, burnt-orange curtains slid open, Harriet's citizens began to extol her in four-part harmony. She stood up and strode; the spotlight that had been blinking during dress rehearsal now fully caught her face. She turned toward the audience, left arm uplifted. "Prince Rhetorissimus, the genius, c'est I," she proclaimed. The arm came down. "It's Professor Wortsley," a girl in the audience yelped. Then she knew she had them: beyond interruption, intervention, interference, and fear.

The next morning she slept late, Friday's shouts of bravo still lulling and exciting her. She got up to have the final fitting of her dress for the dance. She placed herself in panty girdle, stockings, three-hooked padded, strapless bra, and satin heels and went to Tally's room. Jennie, a middle-aged maid from another hall, was waiting there. As Tally watched, Harriet put the dress on so that Jennie could do the final pinning of the hem.

"Turn, please, Miss Springer," Jennie said, kneeling patiently on Tally's rug.

"You're going to be glad you're going," Tally said.

Still in her bathrobe, Harriet found Sloan in a tea pantry, ironing her formal, a green silky dress with spaghetti straps.

"I'm surprised this thing hasn't been torn apart," Sloan said. "I borrowed it from my mother."

"It's pretty."

"I never have enough clothes," Sloan said, rubbing the iron angrily against the cloth. "I can't even buy my own formal."

"When's Compton arriving?" The first time she had said his name to Sloan.

"Around six. We're having dinner at the Hunting Hart Inn. We may not come to the dance. Compton doesn't like to dance."

"That's okay."

"He'll probably ask me to marry him again."

"I didn't know," Harriet's voice had to struggle against the knife in her throat, "that he had ever asked you to marry him in the first place."

"Oh, sure, the first night we met at that party in Washington."

"But he's ten years older than you are."

"Only eight. But I'm not in love with him."

The knife withdrew, the broken edges of flesh cleaved again.

"Hurry up, will you?" Judi, Naomi's adviser, was in the door. A thin, precise girl, she wore makeup even on Saturday morning. She planned to work in fashion when she left Harwyn. After lunch, Harriet was too nervous to study. She and Amarillo and Naomi and Sloan played partner hearts. Then Harriet went to her room to whisper the prince's lines to herself once more. She was there when she heard the bellmaid. "Miss Springer, Miss Springer, gentleman in front for you." Walking to the tip of the stairs, she looked down to see Amarillo facing two boys. Though about the same height, they seemed to reverse each other. If the back of Eddie's blond hair was smooth, that of Harriet's blind date was dark and tufty. If Eddie was wearing a dark brown tweed jacket, dark brown pants, and calf-high snow boots with metal clips, the second boy had on a light brown tweed jacket, light brown pants, and black rubbers. Between the cuff of his pants

126

and the back of his rubbers was a line of light-blue and white checked socks.

Unskilled in not doing what she ought to do, Harriet descended. "Come meet the fellows," Amarillo shouted. Her date's hair cow-licked out over his forehead. He, too, wore glasses. His skin looked as if he had been nibbling on it.

"Harriet," Amarillo growled encouragingly, "this is Carl, Carl Jacobs. You should have a lot in common."

Harriet extended her hand. His was wet.

"Let's sit down," Amarillo said. Because men were allowed in the girls' private rooms only between 2 and 4 P.M. on Sundays, they went into the public living room. Carl and Harriet bumped into each other and separated swiftly, as if each were a live lobster and the other boiling water.

"The damn heater conked out on Highway 9," Eddie said. "We nearly froze our asses off."

"How terrible," Harriet said, voice false even to her. "How do you like Columbia?" she asked Carl.

He was wrenching at his left thumbnail. "It's a good school," he said, sticking the finger in the neck of his sweater. "It's as good as Princeton or Harvard or Yale. It's got some of the best departments in the world."

He was majoring, he said, in poli sci.

When Amarillo volunteered to take the boys to their hotel, Harriet said she would stay in the dorm to work on her lines.

Naomi was waiting for her in the Smoker. "I saw him," she said, as if she had spotted a grotesque crustacean through a glass-bottomed boat, "I was peeping over the stairs. Those awful little rubbers. But at least you don't have to watch the show with him. If my date is a weenie, I have to be with him all the time after I put on your makeup and you turn into a man."

That evening she stood again in the wings. Molly, like a cheerful eggbeater, was whisking about. Shards of voices and the detritus of laughter piled up in the auditorium, sounds that seemed to exist beyond her. If she had not felt boards beneath her boots, a medallion in her hand, breath passing over the soft flesh of the inside of her lips, she would have believed herself separated from her environment; inside a transparent, but inviolable, sphere. Then the curtain was drawn. As the chorus of her citizens commended her, she marched on majestically. "Prince Rhetorissimus, the genius, *c'est* I," she declaimed. In the middle of the center section of seats was Sloan, not withdrawn but alive, pounding the arm of her chair. Beside Sloan was a dark man with a heavy face, hair combed back. Other men were in tuxedoes, but Compton had on a tweed jacket. That's no competition, Harriet thought. "Prince Rhetorissimus, the genius, who found the square root of pi," she boasted, "*c'est* I." Like a black/silver/red rocket she slid cleanly through the atmosphere of her opening number, into the purity of performing space, circled, shot pyrotechnic colors into the dark of the void, and brought the house down.

When the show was over, after four curtain calls, she left the stage for the last time, flicking back the panels of her coat. She leaped toward a canvas and timber flat and touched the top. Girls surrounded her; Molly hugged her; a professor sought her out. "We're fighting," he said deferentially, "to see which of us you imitated the most."

"It wasn't any of you," she said. "It was all me."

In the dressing room she slipped the medallion off, but for a moment she let it fall back, before her next program called for her to rub cold cream on her face, strip off the costume, and abandon Woolbrith for the dance. Outside she jumped over unmelted swatches of snow. She wanted to swing from the bare limbs of the trees. The same blood was coursing through her veins and the stars. As she passed the gym, she heard the arpeggio of a piano. On the walks were couples, in coats, the long skirts of the girls flaring beneath furs and rich cloths. I'll be late, she thought. Her blood jet-pulsed more sluggishly.

After a bath, Harriet dressed as if she were assembling a layer cake. Body powder, deodorant, Tabu perfume, underwear, dress, dangling rhinestone earrings and necklace that Naomi had loaned her. Carl was to meet her in the gym. He was wearing a dark blue suit but the same light blue sweater. "Eddie and Amarillo are already dancing," he said. She waited for him to help her with her coat. When he did not, she hung it herself on the iron-pipe rack. As he led her in the first dance, his left thumb rested on the top of her zipper. "Dear God, let it stay there," Harriet hoped. She began to feel herself curl up, as if she were the lobster that had been immersed in the boiling water. Then Sloan, though with Compton, touched her back. "You were great," she said. "I'll see you back in the hall when we're through with this idiot

128

dance." The next day they planned to room together for Harriet's last year.

As if it were the ancestor of a graceful child, endurance was often necessary before Harriet could be victorious. With the two hundred members of her class, she sat in a Harwyn lecture room. Custom gave the juniors the duty to elect all-college officers. They had selected the presidents of the Student Governing Council and the Judicial Honor Board. They were casting paper ballots for the first vice presidents. As the votes were counted, the class practiced its group singing. "Down by the Sally Garden," the songmistress announced, unbuttoning her official blazer. "Who is this Sally Garden?" Naomi whispered indignantly. "Who are we singing about? This is ridiculous, this Harwyn democracy." After "Harwyn, Harwyn, Queen of Thought," Harriet learned that she had lost both first vice presidencies. Though her heart congested into a hailstone, she congratulated her triumphant rivals.

Then loyal Amarillo put up Harriet for the second vice presidency of the Student Governing Council. As she waited for more nominations, Harriet clutched her Kittredge edition of *The Complete Works of Shakespeare* and tried to survey the room maturely. There were no further names. Though by default, she was an officer. Dubious but thrilled, she tested her happiness. If there had been more candidates; if Louisa Lacey were not away, spending her junior year abroad in Spain; if Molly Sonnenstein had not refused to run for anything—she might not have made it. But still, she, Harriet, had endured. She was now entitled to carry the black, leather-bound notebook that outlined her duties. She was now to have her name engraved on a plaque in the Student Governing Council room. She went to telephone her mother the good news.

Later that afternoon she went into the Smoker. Her friends were there. Sloan stretching her legs across a chair, right knee smaller and knobbier than the left. "Look who's here," she said. "My next year's roomie, dragging her triumph behind her."

Harriet felt happiness backsliding. "I was only elected second vice president of S.G.A.," she said, as if self-defense were self-deprecation. "You're going to be elected to the Judicial Honor Board. You never lose an election."

"God, student government. You act as if it had something to do with the real world." Sloan limped out, sullen, gritty.

"What's wrong with her?" Harriet asked Naomi. She privately wondered if Sloan's father had pressed an unwanted assignment upon her.

"Nothing. She's just a moody pig sometimes. She's mad, too, because she saw a note on your door from that girl with the stupid blond French twist from Stuart Hall, the creepy girl Sloanie went to school with."

"I've got a note from her?"

"But don't ask me what it says. I don't read people's mail."

The sheet of parchment on her bedroom door surprised Harriet less than she let Naomi know. After the Junior Show, Sophia Herrick had begun to visit Harriet in the Anthropology Seminar Room. One day she had given her a copy of the campus literary magazine that had published one of her poems, "To Georgia O'Keeffe and the Desert."

Harriet had never heard of Georgia O'Keeffe. "You make me see the sand," she had said. Seeking safety in deserts, which she had at least visited.

"It took a great deal of work," Sophia had told her seriously. "I had to get the rhythm of the wind and not lapse into the confines of old meters."

"I can imagine," Harriet had answered respectfully.

"Do you want to be an actress?" Sophia had asked another time. "You took the campus by storm in the Junior Show."

"I didn't do anything much," Harriet had demurred.

"Everyone said you were wonderful."

"But I'm not a real actress, and besides, I couldn't make it a career. It's not what you should do with a Harwyn degree."

"You underestimate yourself," Sophia had said. "You're much too modest." Then she had rearranged her Yale scarf and left Harriet beneath the Indian masks. She confused Harriet. She sounded flattering and sincere, but her smile was odd and sly.

Sophia's note was an invitation to dinner at Stuart Hall. Harriet was curious. She had never eaten there, where Harwyn's richest, oldest, nicest money lived. Stroking a jade seal that she wore as a ring, Sophia welcomed her in Stuart's pillared lobby. "I wanted to celebrate your latest triumph," she said. Harriet thought she sounded nervous, but the perception was too alien to her sense of Sophia and of Stuart to be acceptable. The manners at the refectory table in the dining room where they sat were more elegant

130

than those in Gould Hall, but the casual lapses in them more extreme. Across from Harriet the daughter of a steel company president threw her bread at the daughter of an investment banker.

"Oooh, Bitsy, you'll be sorry," she was warned. With light, shivery laughter. Harriet watched as if she were benignly accustomed to it all.

After dessert and demitasse, before Harriet could do the right thing and go home to Gould to work, Sophia said that she and Harriet ought to go to the Edwin Muir reading.

"Is it here?" Harriet stalled. She was as unsure of Edwin Muir's identity as she had been of Georgia O'Keeffe's.

"It's in the Common Room," Sophia said. "We really should go. I like the way he's trying to keep English nature poetry alive."

"It's ambitious, all right," Harriet extemporized.

Outside the leaves of the tough-vined honeysuckle were greening. White-horned flowers would blossom soon. The petals of the dogwood, which time had scarred purple, were about to realize themselves as Sloan's lustrous stigmata. If Harwyn had transformed nature into such a garden, an alumna gift had changed the Common Room into an Oriental bazaar. Tapestries hung on the stone walls. Rug washed over the slate floors. Brown velvet chairs, their bronze arms shaped like lions, flanked a red velvet swing with a fringed canopy. Edwin Muir sat in a chair with gold-studded legs. Old, frail, the bristles of his moustache soft, he wore a three-piece suit and round-rimmed glasses. He regarded his audience with plaintive respect, as if, with luck, they might join him in making the most of a strange, exhausted world.

Sophia knelt against a brass urn in which a huge fern grew. Her long slender hands flat against her thighs. Her French twist carrying on the vertical, snake-thin line of her spine. Harriet sat against the wall. Fern fronds seeding her hair. The presence of a poet, even if she did not know his work, claiming her upright respect.

"Here penned within the human fold," he began. But then, as if his speech had been stolen by the same force that had drained the world, he sighed into inaudibility. Only an isolated word or two continued to boom out, as if a leftover air pocket in his lungs were propelling it. "Horse." . . . . "Love." . . . . "Children." . . . . "Road." . . . . "Alone." . . . . "Private"

"Mine are itching," Sophia muttered.

131

Harriet was shocked. To deny the spontaneous eruption of Northville prudery, she raised her eyebrows and depressed a corner of her mouth.

"Let's go," Sophia said. To prove further her sophistication, Harriet went with her. "Come back to my room," Sophia suggested. They were standing next to a Japanese cherry tree. "I have a new Telemann record I want you to hear. You don't have to go back to Gould to sign out, do you? It's still too early."

Pleased to be wanted, Harriet was brave. "If it gets late," she said, "I'll crawl into my room through a window."

Sophia had a whole suite. On the living room floor were shag rugs, cow hides, a leopard skin. On her window seat were silk, leather, and velvet pillows. On the mantel of the fireplace, in which fires were forbidden, were silver candlesticks. Sophia gestured Harriet to a high-backed, carved chair, put a record on her turntable, and then like a flower seeking its own vase, sat on the arm of Harriet's chair. Harriet shut her eyes. She had to close out the surprise of Sophia's body, smaller than Jean Maurin but less explicable. Then Sophia's hand was moving on her neck, as if tracing the notes of the mercurial flute cadenza. "Harriet," Sophia said, "are you and Sloan good friends?"

"She's my best friend here." Be calm, Harriet urged herself. Pretend you're talking about the structure of a John Donne poem.

"Is that so?" said Sophia. Her hands stopped moving but stayed on Harriet's uncertain flesh. "I know Sloan very well, you know."

Harriet opened her eyes as if this were an ordinary conversation. "She told me you've stayed at her house."

"Have you?"

"Last Thanksgiving."

"Then it's gone very far."

Harriet wondered what "it" could be. "Her parents make her suffer," she said bitterly.

"All parents make their children suffer," Sophia answered, to correct Harriet's sad superficiality. "Sloan and I were very good friends. She's popular and gets elected president of every school she goes to, but she doesn't let herself have many friends. People are attracted to her aloofness." She stroked Harriet's throat as if the gesture ornamented memory. "I once made her a little drawing. She was holding a gavel. She made me a little drawing, too,

132

but I wasn't a person. I was a leopard. Sloan liked my leopard skin. That was at Prideworth, where we were roommates."

"You were roommates?" Harriet felt a sharp gasp of betrayal. Sloan had never told her.

"For several years." Sophia's finger was now tracing with careful dispassion the grooves around Harriet's collarbone. "But you mustn't worry. That was a long time ago, in another country, and the wenches both are dead, or at least, very different."

"I really should go home and finish *Pericles*," Harriet said, grasping at the solid ground of a clean, familiar duty. "Loomis is giving us a quiz next week."

"Who wanteth food, and will not say he wants it? Or can conceal his hunger till he famish?" Sophia lifted her hands gently—so that Harriet could leave if she wished, if she were so foolish. But Harriet was only flustered by not knowing what those hands meant. "Thanks for dinner," she said. Standing clumsily. "I'm glad we went to Edwin Muir." Then, free of Sophia's touch, she wondered, insecure, excited, if Sophia were angry with her. "I really am glad," she added. Sophia, still sitting, answered, "Come back sometime if you want. We might have a great deal in common."

Confidence restored, Harriet went home.

In old turtleneck sweater and jeans, Sloan was waiting for her.

"You weren't at dinner," she said. Eyes as cold as hubcaps.

"I was at Stuart Hall. Sophia Herrick asked me to dinner. We went to the Edwin Muir reading and then we sat around in her room."

"What the hell did you do there?"

"Listened to music. Talked," Harriet said cautiously.

"But I've told you that Sophia Herrick is a menace. You don't have any idea what she's like."

"I guess not." Harriet sat down in her armchair. "I wasn't her roommate."

"Did she tell you that?"

"Yes. I don't know why you didn't."

"Did she make a pass at you?"

"A pass?" Harriet discerned a new Sloan, pacing up and down the room as if she might grind Sophia into the floor.

"A pass. Don't you know she's a Lesbian, despite all the talk about the little sperm. Those cute little Yale sperm. I guess you

133

wouldn't. You're so fucking dumb that you wouldn't know a Lesbian if she raped you."

"Oh, for God's sake." For the first time since she had begun to love and shelter Sloan, Harriet was mad at her. "I'm not a virgin."

For the first time Harriet seemed to have surprised Sloan. "You're not a virgin?"

"You're goddamn right I'm not. I've slept with a fellow at my brother's Yale college. A Frenchman. If you're ever going to lose your virginity, do it with a Frenchman. He was very good."

"Compton won't sleep with me unless I marry him. He respects me. Why didn't you tell me?"

"I didn't see why I should."

"You're not a virgin? Jesus Christ. You can't be trusted after all," Sloan said harshly and walked out. The slamming door sucked Harriet's moment of triumph dry. Arid with fear, she followed after Sloan. She stood outside her room. "Sloan, it's me."

"Go away."

"But it's Harriet, it's me."

"I don't care. Go away."

Harriet's hands began to prickle. "Sloan," she said quickly, before anyone could pass down the corridor and hear, "it didn't mean a damn thing. It really didn't. And if it matters so much to you, I won't see Sophia Herrick again. I won't go near her."

Sloan permitted her to come in.

Six weeks later Harriet was on a small plane, scuttling around a thundercloud. Next to her a crew-cut priest was fingering a cross. Below them, waiting, were the forests and lakes of Northern Michigan. There was no reason for her to be here, for her to have gotten off the New York–Northville train in Detroit, to be risking death to fly to a summer camp for underprivileged children. Except—she had stayed at Harwyn after exams were over to help plan the next freshman orientation week. Her responsibilities of power. Sloan wanted her to bring some things to the camp where she was a counselor. Sloan could not trust her mother to fill a shopping list and mail a package.

Harriet's mother had not wanted to trust her daughter with money for a wild-goose chase. "I don't understand," she had said. "Daddy needs you here in the bank. It's not fair for you to spend his hard-earned money to go off and visit a girl."

134

In a Gould Hall phone booth, Harriet's stomach closed over her guilt. "That's not what I'm doing," she protested. "I'm going to visit a camp for underprivileged kids. They come there from Chicago and Toronto and Detroit. I thought it was your big plan for raising children that they should have broadening experiences."

Eleanor had sent a check.

Harriet was saying multiplication tables, as she did on roller coasters, when the plane landed at a one-strip airport. A station wagon from Camp Community took her and another passenger to a log reception cabin. Gravel walks and geraniums surrounded it. There she waited for two hours for Sloan to return from a canoeing lesson she was giving on the lake on which the camp was sited. When Sloan appeared, she was wearing a uniform of knickers, middy blouse, knee socks, and sneakers.

"What are you grinning about?" Her first words.

"Your costume." Tactless Harriet.

"It's a good idea. It gives the kids a sense of tradition."

"Okay, I'm sorry. Here are your things."

Sloan took the package of books, paints, and a small portable radio. Hardly mollified. "I had a hard time getting you in here," she said. "They don't like many visitors. It upsets the kids. I managed to wangle you a place to sleep in my cabin."

Bunk beds lined the walls of the cabin. Standing in the interior gloom was a stocky woman, red hair shingle-cut. Sloan introduced her as Barbara Brentson, her cocounselor. "Hello, Barbara," Harriet said.

"Most people call me Birch," she answered. Then, tone less grumpy, she asked Sloan if she had gotten a report on one of the kids in their cabin from the infirmary.

"Her temperature is down. It's not as serious as we thought."

"Good, I'd hate to have her really sick after we'd gotten her in pretty good shape."

Their intimate, professional voices excluded Harriet. Calm down, Harriet told herself, and changed her clothes to help Birch and Sloan prepare a marshmallow roast. At eight thirty they were in their bunks: Harriet below Sloan, Birch across from them. Before they slept they sang, ending with a round about farms. Each little city girl was a different animal. "Your turn now, Lorraine,"

135

Sloan urged a tense, skinny child of eight. "You can be a cow. I know you can be a cow."

"Moo," the child bellowed in fear and defiance. "Moo."

"Lorraine is a good moo-moo," Birch praised her. "Lorraine is the best moo-moo in the cabin."

Harriet was uncomfortable, cold between the harsh sheets, her trench coat covering her. The grain of the plywood on which Sloan's mattress lay swirled over her. Outside the crickets cheeped corrosively. Inside a mosquito whined. She tried to control a growing delirium of impatience; to listen to the children falling asleep; to permit Birch to inspect her until Birch turned, huddled on her side, and apparently also slept.

Around ten o'clock Harriet thought it might be safe. She scratched the bottom of Sloan's bunk; the wood was splintery, as if a homesick camper had once clawed for help. No response. She stood. "Sloan," she whispered and touched her face. Sloan must have been awake, because she reached up, felt Harriet's hand, turned on her side to face her, and put Harriet's hand on the side of the bunk.

"Hello," she said, eyes large and wary.

"I've got to leave tomorrow. Can't we talk by ourselves? This is our last chance for three months."

"Sssh. You'll wake the kids."

"Sloan."

"Please stop making a fuss. You're here, aren't you?"

"Come outside, just for a minute, please."

"Go to sleep." Sloan was both imperative and on the fringe of panic. A child coughed. "Do you hear that? You're waking the kids."

"Sloan—" Lorraine was pulling at Harriet's legs. "I go shit-shit, I go shit-shit, I go shit-shit, what about you?" she was saying. Hoarsely, wildly. Then she raced out of the cabin. "Goddamn it," Sloan swore at Harriet. "See what you've done now." She followed the child, Birch following her. A minute later, one scream. Harriet cowered back in her bunk. Much later Sloan appeared. Carrying Lorraine tenderly, Birch's hand on her neck. "I went shit-shit," the child was crooning sleepily, "I went shit-shit, and I buried it myself." Harriet felt sick.

Seven days later, five days after being home, Harriet was in a private room in the Northville Hospital. Her body ached persistently, as if someone had wrapped bicycle chains around it and pulled. Hot packs shrouded her. "It may be a very mild case of encephalitis. It may not be," the doctor had told her parents. "But we shouldn't take any chances. We'll treat it as if it is." Reveries drifted in and out of Harriet's consciousness like thin vapor from a basin of dry ice. She wondered if Sloan would mourn if she died. If Sloan, walking along the Michigan lake, would smash her head against one of the pines growing in beach sand. Harriet hoped she would.

In the corridor was a heavy sound. Then her mother, fuming in tumult, ran into the room. "What have you been doing?" She was waving a piece of paper.

Harriet's head turned, as if it were one of the bandages being unraveled. Her mother must have gone mad. She and Anne, last Christmas, had asked each other if she were having her menopause, because she was so crabby, but this was new.

"What are you talking about?" she asked slowly.

"This, I found it when I was going through your purse, looking for your glasses."

A dumb IOU from a sophomore to whom Harriet had sold the curtains and pillows from her old room. She and Sloan were going to get different-sized ones for the suite—a living room and two little bedrooms—that they were to share next year. "What about it?" she asked.

"Those just weren't your things. They were mine, too. Daddy and I have put everything we have into seeing that you had the best things possible to take to Harwyn."

"I'm going to room with Sloan Trouver." Her vocal cords, like her limbs, seemed partially immobile. "I don't need those curtains anymore."

"You're giving up your independence?"

"Oh, for God's sake."

"Don't swear."

"For God's sake, I will swear. I'm twenty-one. What difference does it make if I live alone or with someone? I'm lying here like a dummy, and you pull this scene on me." No need to add that she was no longer a virgin either.

Her mother collapsed into a green leather visitor's chair. Speech

137

and sobs in conflict for the upper hand. "You're giving yourself up. You're giving up the start we gave you. I don't know what's happening to you kids. Georgie failed a course at business school. I don't know if he's going to stick it out or not. You're turning your back on what we gave you. Only Anne is managing to stay on the straight and narrow. You may think you expect your children to break your heart, but when it actually happens, it hurts."

"Tough luck." Harriet closed her eyes. She heard her mother leave.

That evening both parents visited. "I talked to Phil this afternoon," her father said. "He says the packs will probably come off tomorrow. We're out of the woods, and nothing bad has really happened."

"I still think," her mother said, "that you picked up whatever bug you got on that trip to Northern Michigan."

The next day, as the nurses stripped her of her wrapping, Harriet wondered why they were so cheerful; why she was to be glad that her limbs were hale and hearty. She went home, with her mother, two days later. Because she had been sick, she was excused from her bank job. The house was quiet. Georgie had a summer job again in the woods on the Olympic Peninsula. He was supposed to be thinking about his career. Anne spent the days packing salmon in the fish cannery. Harriet watched the mail. In early August, she received a letter from Sloan from Camp Community.

Dear Harriet,

I may not come back to Harwyn. Birch has gotten me catalogs for the University of Michigan. Compton has sent me catalogs from Chapel Hill. Both schools would be much cheaper than Harwyn, and both of them good premed programs. I haven't heard from the Harwyn Scholarship Committee yet, which will make a difference, I suppose.

I will miss this place when I leave. The children, my campers, have more reality and brains than anyone at Harwyn.

Sloan

"I'll write the Harwyn Scholarship Committee," Harriet thought. "I'll write on Student Governing Council stationery," but when she went upstairs to do it, she could not. Students did not write letters for other students at Harwyn. Instead, to Sloan:

Dear Other Self:

Please don't leave. If you need money, I have some in a savings account, and we can share the allowance my father sends me. Harwyn is the right place for you; it's a better school than the state universities. Don't worry. We'll work things out.

Harriet

Because her mother was at a club meeting, she could walk safely to the corner letter box without being noticed. During the next week she waited for a letter; one did not come. A dull, weighty sensation blocked out a nervous, buoyant sense of expectation. Both her father and mother had to wake her up to get her out of bed in the morning. She would sit, at her dressing table, looking into the mirror. The picture of Elizabeth Taylor, which she still kept there, smiled back, the sweet mouth in proportion with her curls and frilly peasant blouse.

A month before Harwyn was to begin, Harriet, her father, and her mother were at lunch. Her father was using a toothpick to get at a piece of cold lamb.

"I can't go back to Harwyn," she abruptly said.

"You've got to," her mother said.

"I can't."

Both parents gathered their attention.

"Got any particular reason?" her father asked, as if he were being calm with a mortgagee trying to circumvent a payment though he had money.

"I'm not happy there." She stared at her plate. "That's all I can say. I'm just not happy there."

"Is there any place you want to go?" Her father was still calm.

"Maybe a state university, to get a different kind of experience."

"Never." Her mother burst out.

"Why can't you go back to Harwyn? You're a student government officer. You've got good grades. You've made wonderful contacts, like Louisa Lacey. Why can't you go back?"

The three of them sat, in golden-oak and leather chairs, at the polished table. Northville Bay, through the window, was spacious, glittering, capaciously blue.

"You've got an investment in Harwyn," her father said. "You've got to have a pretty good reason to pull out. I haven't heard one so far."

139

Without planning, Harriet went for broke. "I'm afraid of homosexuality," she said. Her parents seemed not to recognize the word. "There's this girl named Sophia, who tries to make passes at me. I hate it. I want to get out."

Her father, rubbing his knees, stared at his hands. Her mother looked at her plate. They might have been at silent prayer. Finally her mother said, "You'll just have to stay away from this, this Sophia. She's not in Gould Hall, is she?"

"No, she looks for me in the library."

"Well, let's not talk about it anymore. We've all got too much at stake for you to pull out now."

"I know some homosexuals," her father said. "Just stay away from them. Some of them are harmless enough, though."

"Let's clear the table, Harriet," her mother suggested. "I need you to help me paint the lawn furniture this afternoon."

Performing domestic rituals during the next weeks, Harriet's sensation of carrying soft-edged bricks inside her stomach grew worse. Then, in late August, Naomi wrote to her from Switzerland:

> I suppose you know about the trauma with Sloanie and money and coming back to Harwyn. The Scholarship Committee gave her $1,000 more when she threatened not to return. She has so much nerve, your roomie.

"I guess I don't mind going back to Harwyn after all," she told her mother later that day.

"I'm surprised, dear," her mother said. "I thought we had settled that ages ago."

Harriet had dreamt that her last year in college would unite friendship, learning, and lyrically ordered exaltations. But whenever she entered the first-floor suite she shared with Sloan, she felt isolated among gnarled, dark-red vines. Sloan spent evenings at Branson, Harwyn's brother school. Its students signed honor pledges that they would not use their rooms for immoral, dishonorable, or sexual purposes. And girls would be out by midnight. Sloan would appear around twelve thirty and march without speaking into her separate cubicle of a bedroom. She was dating two Branson seniors. One was the only Negro student there.

Naomi told Harriet that Sloan said her parents would kill her if they knew. The second was an economics student who had a withered arm, a legacy from polio. Naomi referred to them as Othello and the Crip. Harriet told her she was prejudiced. A Harwyn freshman also had a crush on Sloan and gave her poetry books. Both Naomi and Harriet called her the Leech.

One afternoon, Naomi, streaked hair tousled, wandered into the suite. "Where's Sloanie?" she asked, too casually.

"At a lab."

"What are you doing?"

"Reading Shelley for my honors paper."

"Oh, how boring and poetic." Naomi sat, on the window seat, covered in nondescript cloth left over from a Trouver house on an Army base. She examined one sandaled foot. "You didn't have a very good time when you saw Sloanie at that camp, did you?" she asked.

It's her revenge for the night she was excluded from the tower, Harriet thought. "Not very," she said.

"Did you meet the girl called Barbara, who called herself Birch? Did you know that she and Sloanie had a big thing going?"

"Why should I care?" Harriet asked, bending her Parker pen as if it were a pencil.

"No reason. But now listen." Both eyes and mouth opened wide, "Here's the big news. Sloanie's not a virgin anymore."

"How do you know?" As soon as she spoke, Harriet shut her eyes, as if that might black from her mind the picture of a naked Sloan on the floor, among the trees, with another body.

"She told me after lunch today. She said it was Compton Francis. She said, and listen, Harriet, this is the real part, she said she made him do it, after she came back from that silly camp. She said that if he didn't sleep with her she'd find someone who would. She was tired of being a virgin and she wanted a man."

"My God," said Harriet.

"Why are you so shocked?"

"I'm not shocked."

"Yes, you are. After all, you're not a virgin, either."

"How do you know that?"

"Sloanie told me. I think she just wanted to keep up with you. She's very competitive, you know."

"Well, I got there first."

141

"Weren't you scared?"

"It was with a Frenchman. He was very good."

"I never thought it would be you to be the first to lose her virginity."

Harriet shrugged. When Naomi left, she ripped open an inhibiting veil of honor and went into Sloan's bedroom to see what she could find. She searched through books, bureau, clothes. In a box of writing paper she found a half-finished letter to Birch. "We were like two ships that passed in the night," she read. Then she huddled, a bun of misery, on Sloan's bed, hands clutching the red/white/green-striped Bates cotton bedspread.

Sloan spent the evening at Branson with the economics student, Edward DeVore. "You should have seen the shirt the Crip wore tonight," Naomi reported to the Smoker. "He came to pick Sloanie up in a wool shirt with big plaids on it, like people wear to go hunting."

At eleven forty-five, Harriet bathed and lay awake in bed. In the room's corner her marble basin, on its old-fashioned wooden legs, glimmered from a light on the sidewalk outside. She wished she was as stolid and cool. Early, at twelve three, Sloan went into her room. Harriet heard her closet door; the water in her basin; the metal sigh of her bed.

"Sloan?" she said. "Why, if we room together, aren't we happy?"

She repeated her question.

"Speak for yourself," Sloan said.

At least Harriet enjoyed the prestige of her student government duties.

Because of it, the Career Office asked her to come to a special meeting. The office was in two basement rooms in the main classroom building. Wooden bannisters on the stairs hung from plaster walls like blazer buttons coming loose. In the outer area, on chairs and on the floor, were the leaders of the Harwyn Class of '59. At two, a thin man appeared from the inner office. The Career Office director in escort. He was wearing a blue suit; a striped tie; a white button-down collar shirt. The girls inspected him cautiously, impassively, deferentially—as if he were a male professor.

"Good afternoon," he said, an olive-smooth voice. "My name is Shaw. I represent the Central Intelligence Agency."

The Central Intelligence Agency. Harriet was alert. This was something. However, Molly Sonnenstein was knitting with un-usual fervor. "The CIA?" she asked, without waiting to be recognized. "You mean you want us to spy?"

Harriet thought her rude. Mr. Shaw was unfazed. "Oh, no. Each year we recruit a highly selected group of the top graduates of America's finest schools. Because Harwyn graduates have an excellent record with the agency, we talk to a few rigorously chosen seniors each year, to see if one or two of them might be right for us.

"Not all our employees do field work. Indeed, only a specialized few do. The bulk of our most intelligent, educated, and valued employees work in our central office. They may be historians, linguists, political scientists, economists. Intelligence work, as the name implies, demands hardworking intellectuals. Most of it is very close to the scholarship that Harwyn girls do so well."

"I know three languages," said a bouncy girl from Stuart Hall, related to two United States senators. "Would that be acceptable?"

"It depends on the language. But you must remember that simply knowing something is not enough. We need people of character, stamina, devotion, discretion."

"What I don't understand about the CIA," Molly said, "is how much you expect people to give up their lives for you. If I came to work for you, for example, would I have to lie about what I do?"

"It would depend on your assignment." Over Mr. Shaw's shoulder was a window cut high into the wall. Through it Harriet could see the roots of an azalea, sheltered by a mound of snow as calm as Mr. Shaw. "But most of us think of ourselves as civil servants. We work for the United States Government. I should add, however, that we also think that the demands on agency members are more stringent than those on civil servants in something like the Department of Commerce."

Harriet shrank away from the meeting. She was an English major, with enough rudimentary French to pass her language requirement. Her love for Gerard Manley Hopkins was not enough to get her a job with the CIA. Nor was she as brave as Sloan, enmeshed in secret duty with her father.

The next week she had a personal interview with the Career Office director.

"You left the meeting with the Central Intelligence Agency recruiter early," Mrs. Bennett noted reprovingly. She wore expensive tweed suits and pastel blouses that buttoned to the neck. Her body was jogging to fat on the surface and around the edges.

"Yes," Harriet said guiltily, "but I didn't think there was any point in staying. I didn't seem qualified."

"The agency accepts only our best graduates," Mrs. Bennett said. Then she sighed. "Do you have other plans?"

"I want to do something worthwhile."

"What is your major?"

"English."

"Oh."

"I've always wanted to live in New York." To walk down Fifth Avenue, in a Peck & Peck suit and pigskin gloves, hair breezing behind her. To share the wind with writers, actors, the publishers of *Life* and *Time*, Tallulah Bankhead.

"English majors in New York might try editorial work. Do you know typing?"

"Yes," Harriet was glad she could offer some skills.

"Are you engaged?"

"No, I'm not."

"Most of our girls ultimately are, you know. A Harwyn education is a wonderful background for an enduring marriage."

"I can imagine that it would be."

"Here," Mrs. Bennett said, handing Harriet a card, "If you are interested in publishing, go to this office when you go to New York. It's an employment agency that pays particular attention to the graduates of women's colleges. Make sure that your recommendations are on file and that you have a resume. It is a pity about the Central Intelligence Agency, of course, but if you are not qualified, you simply are not qualified, are you?"

"That's how I felt." Truthful Harriet.

She now saw her future, as she had seen Harwyn when she was back in Northville. That purity of vision was strong enough to help squire her through the rest of her year, miserable in her suite, mildly prosperous outside of it.

But by February the winter was boring for her, for everyone. Walking into town—for a movie, a beer, a break—was too cold to be worth it. The snow was too old to be clean, too new to melt. In the Smoker even their own invective failed to amuse them.

144

"Don't bother to eat," Amarillo said wearily at Sunday dinner. "Today's train wreck has horse blood in it."

"The meat is all gray," Naomi added squeamishly. "Let's throw it at Miss Pratt." The elderly hall supervisor, Miss Pratt ate alone at a little table near them.

"Don't be mean, Naomi," Harriet admonished. She was wondering where Sloan might be. She had left their suite after breakfast dressed in her boots and gloves and winter coat. As the Negro maids were serving apple brown betty with whipped cream, Sloan walked in. She looked exalted, healthy. "Where's she been?" asked Naomi.

"How should I know?" Harriet answered tensely.

"Finish the sewer scrapings," Amarillo said. "I want to play partner hearts."

Amarillo and Naomi went into a living room to claim a card table. Harriet walked to the junior table where Sloan, against all rules, had cajoled a college-seal-stamped plate of food she had missed. "Want to play?"

"I'll be there," Sloan spoke, but did not look up.

A few minutes later she joined them. Hundreds of loafers, saddle shoes, sneakers, and leather pumps had kicked the wooden card table legs. Thousands of Lucky Strikes, Camels, Kools, and Parliaments had burned its leather top. The Leech, Sloan's freshman crush, sat on a stool next to them and looked morosely at Sloan.

"Hey, Naomi, we'll be partners," Sloan said.

"What's the matter? You sick of Harriet?" coarse Amarillo asked.

"I want to change," Sloan smiled. That's what books mean, Harriet realized, when they talked about wolfish grins. As if it were a hallucination, she saw a tantalizing world washed clean of tall, arrogant, tormented, vicious Sloans, with their ludicrous, leechy followers.

"Cut the cards," she said. Voice convoluted.

She was dealt the queen of spades. The principle upon which hearts is organized is simple: win big through collecting all the shit. The queen of hearts means thirteen penalty points; each individual heart card means one penalty point. However, if someone ends with both the queen and all the hearts, shoots the moon, that person earns twenty-six bonus points. Harriet passed

145

three cards to Naomi on her left, collected three from Sloan on her right. Not enough strength to shoot the moon. On the third round, she dumped the queen on Sloan. "A little present for you, roomie," she pointed out unpleasantly.

Two rounds on Sloan deliberately picked up a trick that had two hearts in it. She was going to try for the moon. "Don't worry," she assured Naomi cockily. "We'll be fine." Harriet studied her cards. If Amarillo, her partner, could play a club high enough to take a trick, Harriet, void in clubs, could throw a heart on it. She would guarantee them a penalty point but deny Sloan triumph. Finally, on the tenth round, Amarillo did so. Sloan's bullet to the moon fell back, trajectory severed. "Well, roomie," Harriet said, "didn't make it, did you?"

They finished the game silently. Harriet added up the score. "We smashed them this time, Amarillo," she said casually.

"My deal." Sloan said. Her eyes looked like her father's.

Each card came to Harriet as if it were a bit of shrapnel. She stacked them neatly with both hands, willing herself to wait to look until she had them all. When she did, she forced herself to remain calm. She had a perfect hand for shooting the moon. She played as if she were Elizabeth Taylor taking National Velvet over jumps in a sunlit glade. For the last rounds she had control, watching the others unable to break her power. Reining in the final trick, she bowed ironically to Sloan.

"Worm turning?" Sloan asked. Some storm was gathering, but jaunty in victory, Harriet ignored it. "I'm going to work on my honors paper," she said nonchalantly. "See you, Amarillo. So long, Naomi. Maybe we can play again some time, Sloanie."

She walked beneath the winter-blasted arch and down the corridor. She was standing in the middle of the suite when the door opened, and suddenly Sloan was hard on her back, shoving her toward the floor, left arm across her throat, collapsing her windpipe and neck bones. "You bitch," Sloan was cursing her, "I'll kill you for doing that to me."

Harriet did not resist, did not want to resist, the pressure of Sloan's body. Then she started to gag. Involuntarily she pulled at Sloan's arm, scratching, wrenching the flesh. She got to her knees, though her forehead still scraped the carpet. Sloan, repeating "I'll kill you," pushed her back again. Breath and breathing almost gone, Harriet rolled on her side and broke away. "You tried to kill me," she panted.

"Halfway through I decided you weren't worth it," Sloan said. "That's why I set you free."

"You used to say you loved me."

"I did? How queer." She left.

Harriet was still on the floor when she heard a knock on the door. "It's Sloan," she thought. "She's sorry. She's come back." The walls of the suite seemed to spring back into place. "The door's open," she called, roughly, eagerly. Standing there was Sloan's crush, Mary Matthews, the Leech.

"What the hell do you want?" Harriet choked out at her.

"I heard noises. I was worried."

"What the hell were you doing standing outside?" Harriet shifted herself up to the window seat.

"I wasn't standing outside. I just heard noises."

"It was nothing," Harriet said pulling at her clothes, "Go away, will you."

God, she's ugly, she thought. The Leech's light brown hair hung in hanks and bolts. Her mouth was loose, thick-lipped. Acne maggoted her skin. Her father was a famous professor; her mother had been crazy. When the Leech was little, she had discovered her mother's body, tongue out, neck askew inside a noose, dead in a closet. From time to time a light would glare from behind the Leech's glasses, and she would go up to the roof of the arch and throw things off.

"I was worried," the Leech said tautly. "I thought something was wrong."

Then she was scrambling on the floor near the window seat, head burrowing and nuzzling in Harriet's lap. "I'm worried," she was sobbing. "Tell me Sloan's not hurt."

Touch her, Harriet told herself, touch her, help her. But her hand recoiled from the hair, the face, the grimy clothes. "Go away," she tried not to scream, "everything's all right." She stood up, but as Mary slipped down, she clung to her legs. "Let go," Harriet ordered her. "Let go, goddamn it, let go." Like a scrubwoman pummeling at stairs, Mary pulled at Harriet's feet. "Stop it," Harriet wanted to kick out. "Go back to your room." Backing off, Mary began to crawl toward the door. She's a toad,

147

Harriet shuddered. She's left toad flesh on me. Then she remembered Mary's father, her mother. "Go away," she said, forcing herself toward charity. "Sloan's okay."

And I wish she were dead, she cried out to herself as she slammed the door on Mary.

In Gould Hall, in every Harwyn Hall, seniors were anxious, sweaty, intimates through panic. Even students like Harriet, who feared drugs, took tabs of dexedrine to stay awake. She wrote fifty pages of her senior thesis in twenty-four hours, letters leaping from her typewriter to the page as if they were shards of a manic rainbow. The night before her first comprehensive exam, Harriet was cramming. She had eight hours in which to read and underline *Paradise Regained* and *Samson Agonistes*. Though the Smoker windows were open, spring was too frail to penetrate through the smells of cigarettes, sweat, dirty shirts, bare feet, and the coffee Amarillo brewed, breaking a dorm rule. Amarillo sat across from her, dressed only in pink, sheer pajamas, breasts slumped near the waistband, straw-blond hair pulled back. She was whispering the titles of constitutional law cases to herself in order to memorize them.

"I can't do it." she said abruptly.

"Sure you can," Harriet answered automatically. She was concentrating on Delilah's speech to Samson. "Everyone passes their comps. If anyone flunks, it'll be me."

"I don't give a shit about the comps," Amarillo said. Her voice was violent but trembling. "I don't want to get married."

Harriet looked up. Amarillo's book had slipped to the floor; her right hand was yanking at the diamond ring Eddie Jacobs had given her in April. "I don't love him," she said. "I'm marrying him because he wants to marry me and because my father wants me to marry him."

She's nothing but pink and yellow, Harriet thought. Her eyes and hair and skin and nails and pajamas are all the same colors. And now she's going to sit here and slobber. She tried to smother her disgust.

"Isn't Eddie going into your father's business?" she asked. She was still holding her Milton book.

"That's why my father wants me to marry him." Amarillo's voice was floating on a sludge of panic.

"You can't worry about it now," Harriet said firmly. "You've got to study for your comps. You can think about Eddie later."

"You don't understand. Tonight may be the last time in my life that I'll be tired enough and frightened enough and single enough to say what I feel."

"You'll be fine," Harriet said.

"But I don't want to get married." Then Amarillo began to cry, hulking, hacking sobs.

Since the engagement, Harriet had wondered why Amarillo was going to marry little Eddie and return to Texas; why she had decided to break the glasses of wine, to spread the buffet, and to assume her place as Mrs. Eddie Jacobs among rich Texas Jews. But now she wanted Amarillo to stop so that she could finish Milton and sleep before her comp. "Here," she said. As gently as she could, she handed Amarillo the box of Kleenex they kept in the Smoker. "It'll be all right." Then she stood up. Ostensibly she was stretching and touching her toes, but she had to avoid looking at the huddling, penned Amarillo.

"No," Amarillo said, "it won't. It won't ever be all right." She stared at Harriet defiantly. But then, to Harriet's relief, she forced herself to stop crying. "I can't do a goddamned thing about it, can I?" she said. She sounded as defiant, but now she seemed to be arguing against her own rebellious misery. "So I might as well take my last goddamned exam." She picked up the fat, blue book of law. As she read, she tapped the page with the edge of her diamond ring. "I'm sorry," she muttered two hours later, when Harriet left for bed. "That's all right," Harriet said.

The next morning Harriet walked across the campus. Blossoms from the Japanese cherry trees floated across the walk. As her shoes crushed them, they whitened the dark gravel and gray concrete. Worrying about the exam, she reviewed the structure of the Miltonic epic. When she saw her mimeographed questions, she knew the old test-taker could handle them. Parker pen filled, she began to outline her response to Virginia Woolf's theory that only an age of gusto produced great tragedy. "Define an age of gusto," she wrote briskly. "Define great tragedy. Athens of Aeschylus and Sophocles. England of Elizabeth."

Ten days later she stood in her dismantled suite, in black cap and gown. She was tired. At the Parents Dinner the night before, the Springers, the Weissbergs, and the Reichs had shared a table.

149

At every silence Harriet felt it necessary to ask a leading question. Then she and her father had packed her trunks: one for New York, where she would share an apartment with Naomi, which Mr. Weissberg had leased for them; one for Northville.

"You sure left your old dad a lot to do," he said, sleeves rolled up. Harriet had wondered if he was the only father who wore striped suspenders.

"I don't think Mrs. Lacey liked me," her mother said anxiously from her place on the window seat. "When we met at the graduation tea, she looked right through me."

"The Laceys are fine, Mommy," her father had said.

"I thought the Weissbergs and the Reichs were very strange, didn't you? They seemed a little vulgar."

"You think I know too many Jews."

"Darling, that's not what I meant at all. I don't have those prejudices. I did everything I could to raise you without them."

Now Harriet was seeing Sloan alone. A junior marshal, Sloan was arranging cables of gold braid over her shoulders.

"Good-bye," Harriet said, hoping to provoke a response, even the proposition that they had been ships that passed in the night.

"I'm going to be at the ceremony," Sloan reminded her.

Harriet opened a desk drawer. Except for a wrapped package, an edition of *The Songs of Innocence and the Songs of Experience*, a rubber band, and some dust, it was empty. "Here," she gave Sloan the package. "I got you this."

"Thanks." Sloan put it on the mattress of her stripped bed. "I'll open it later."

"Why don't you come see Naomi and me in New York?"

"Maybe." Then Sloan left for the last time. She stopped at the door to pose, one hand on the door jamb, eyes drooping playfully. "Bye for now," she said, a parody of the parody farewell she had done in the Smoker, in the gym, in their Harwyn rooms.

"So this is how I'm leaving," Harriet thought. She put on her black cap and gown. On her way to the procession, she picked up a letter, postmarked Camp Pendleton in Southern California. Inside was a card with a bright picture of a fluffy-haired girl in a white cap and gown waving a rolled diploma. CONGRATULATIONS, GRADUATE was printed in bold, cursive script. Covering all the available white space was a runny, ball-point ink:

150

"Dear Harriet:

I suppose you wonder whatever became *of me* after our graduation from high school. Well, I wondered too for a long time. I had three things I could do. I could become a nun and join the Catholic faith. I went to their services all summer. I could become a lady Marine. Or I could kill myself. I decided I should join the Marines. It seemed the best way of the three. I'm pretty happy. The only trouble is that my hair sticks out from my cap too much. I have met a sergeant. He's a twenty-year man. We may get married soon. I think of you a lot and I hope you have been happy in your school in the East.

Your sincere friend,
Betty Dowsey, U.S.M.C."

Christ, Harriet thought, Mom will make me send her a wedding present. She returned the card to her box. Thirty minutes later she was filing down the aisle of Woolbrith Auditorium. As she passed her mother, she noticed that she was trying not to cry. "I'm so proud of you," her mother mouthed at her. On the stage were the president, the chairman of the Trustees, and the speaker, a delegate to the United Nations. At the head of the aisle were Sloan and another junior marshal, holding beribboned batons. Harriet was about to become a B.A. *cum laude* from a distinguished liberal arts college for women. Exhaustion and misery were weighing down her eyelids and the inside of her mouth, as if they were made of the heavy black material of her academic gown. "The feminine, the precious feminine, has a special place in world politics," the United Nations delegate was telling her. "If not on the stage of history itself, then in the rooms in which history is also made." She fell asleep.

151

PART 3

I looked for work for several weeks. The rules baffled me. My degree mattered, but not my mind. Neither earnestness nor flippancy was enough. I wore trim suits and carried gloves, but I was not stuck-up. During an interview at an adventure magazine, a man put his feet in a desk drawer and told me he wanted someone who could swing. The magazine was trash, but I compromised and said, "Oh, sure." He said, "No." Slogging on was the only response I knew. I slogged on.

Dr. Rufus Hill dangled Harriet's one-page resume before him. He leaned back in a swivel chair in his corner cubicle of the offices of Project: The Brightest Lamp. Behind him were the tall, graceful skyscrapers in which *Time* and *Life* were created. "Harwyn," he said, "Harwyn. Why, gosh, that's a good school. A Harwyn degree spiffies up an office. I'm a Yale Divinity man myself."

"Yale Divinity has a wonderful reputation," Harriet said. "My brother graduated from Yale." She was enthusiastic. She wanted this job: researcher for the Religion, Philosophy, and Other Humanities Division of Project: the Brightest Lamp, an encyclopedia that Knowledge, Inc., was planning for the mass market. Dr. Hill—graying, balding, bespectacled, about fifty—was more like a professor than any man she had met so far.

"I need a researcher who values scholarship," he went on.

"Harwyn really taught me that."

"But gosh darn it, I want to warn you about something. I don't mean to complain. This is a wonderful outfit. Knowledge, Inc., is one of the fastest-growing companies in America, and the head

155

of Project Tibble—that's what I call Project: The Brightest Lamp, TBL, Tibble, you understand, of course, you would, you're a Harwyn girl—the head of Tibble used to work for the Encyclopaedia Britannica. But darn it, they won't let us offend the three-year-old mentality. That's what they want us to write for. But I want a researcher who won't throw scholarship out of the window."

"I couldn't agree more, Dr. Hill."

"Why don't you come back tomorrow morning at ten and meet the Hill Climbers? That's my little joke. It's what I call the people who work for me in my division."

"I'd love to. I'm very grateful to you for giving me this opportunity."

That evening, in the kitchen of the apartment on East Seventy-ninth Street and York Avenue that she shared with Naomi, she was hopeful. "I have another interview tomorrow morning. That's a good sign, don't you think?"

"I hope it is a more moral office than mine," said Naomi. She had been working for a month, since mid-June, as a receptionist for a public relations firm.

"What happened with Miss Lawson today?"

"Miss McNally left three messages while Miss Lawson was out having lunch with Miss Schwartz. I had to tell Miss McNally that Miss Lawson was interviewing somebody for the gossip column that she ghostwrites, but then that bitch Miss McNally said that she didn't believe me. I had to play dumb, especially when it got to be four o'clock and Miss Lawson still hadn't come back from lunch with Miss Schwartz. Ugh, Harriet, I think they're all Lesbians." Naomi slashed her polish brush across a thumbnail.

"Really?" said Harriet, quartering a tomato. "How do you know a thing like that?"

"Well, you should hear how mad Miss McNally gets when she calls on the days that Miss Lawson is having lunch with Miss Schwartz. And besides, Miss Lawson never lets me tell Miss McNally where she really is when she's having lunch with Miss Schwartz. I always have to lie." In a fervor of moral rectitude, Naomi blew on her fingernail.

"Naomi, do you think I'll get that job?"

"It would be about time."

The next morning, dress: shirtwaist. She took the bus downtown. Three people were sitting in straight chairs in front of Dr. Hill's desk. In the next cubicle, separated by a five-foot wallboard partition, someone was typing.

"Ah, Harriet, ah, Harriet," Dr. Hill rubbed his hands. "I wanted you here at ten so that you could get a little notion of how the Hill Climbers and I work. Every morning at ten we get our coffee, and then we sit together in my office and chat about current affairs. It gives us a sense of perspective on the past. Isn't that right, Jarvis?"

"Right, Dr. Hill."

"Harriet, this is Jarvis Kellogg, the anthropology editor. Next to him is Carla Storm, who does archaeology and classics. And next to her is Jacquelyn Lindstrom, who is in charge of religion and philosophy. Her husband teaches at New York University."

"How do you do?" Harriet said and took the empty chair Dr. Hill offered her.

"What I do now," said Dr. Hill, "is to read something from the *Herald Tribune*. That starts the conversation off." From the briefcase behind him he took the paper and carefully unfolded it. "Let's keep those keys going, Joanne," he called to the typist before he began. As Harriet listened to an article about Russia, she inspected the three editors, whom she would have to please. Jarvis was huge, shambling, glum. He, too, was balding, but the blond hair that was left tumbled over his scalp. Dark, frail Carla was wearing a sleeveless white blouse, flared flowered skirt, printed silk scarf, and sandals. Jacquelyn was tall and emaciated. Her blond hair, to her shoulders, and her features, thin and elegant, might have belonged to a *Life* cover girl, but she had yellowish teeth with gaps between them.

"Reading about Russia," Dr. Hill said, folding the paper up, "reminds me of the genius of Dostoevski. The genius of Dostoevski is in his presentation of death. In contrast, the genius of Tolstoy is in his presentation of life."

"Unless you happen to be reading the end of *Anna Karenina*," Jacquelyn murmured, bending to adjust the strap of her slingback pump.

"Don't you agree about Tolstoy, Harriet?" Dr. Hill asked.

"I like *War and Peace* very much." She was conscious of the fact that the four of them were staring at her, and a job was at stake.

157

"You see," Dr. Hill leaned back, hands now folded over his vest, "even though the intellectual standards of Tibble may not be those we would choose to emulate in our own life, there's no reason why our little crowd of Hill Climbers has to be dull." He smiled benevolently. "I don't hear those keys, Joanne," he called, high voice becoming louder. "Let's hear those keys." A furious rattle battered back at them.

"Dr. Hill," Jarvis mumbled, "I think I've got a contributor for the essay on American Indian schools."

"Ah, good, Jarvis, very good. Harriet, if you become a Hill Climber, you'll take that article and then you'll check it to make darn sure everything's accurate."

"It sounds like a good chance to learn," Harriet said.

"You could track down a copy of *Handbook of South American Indians* for me, too," Jarvis told her.

"Some of our articles are truly dull," Carla blurted out. Her right foot shook nervously.

"If Harriet comes to Tibble, she'll learn the ins and outs for herself," Dr. Hill said. "Now it's back to work for us Hill Climbers. Harriet, I'll call you."

Interrogating each detail of the interview, she came out of the lobby into the heat of West Forty-seventh Street. She thought she had done well, been all right, but self-appraisal did not dissolve doubt. A young Negro in a business suit was loping down the block. With desperate conviction he was saying to himself, "My old woman's there, and my little boy is dead." At home, waiting for the call, Harriet wrote her mother that being a New Yorker thrilled her. She never knew what she would meet around the corner.

Dr. Hill phoned that afternoon. "I like the possibility of having a Harwyn girl with us," he said.

"I'll do my best," she exulted.

"The bottom of an office is a good place to use to climb to the top," he advised benignly.

"That's what my father says," she told him. After she hung up she ran around the apartment gleefully. She had a job, a respectable, dignified job. Then she phoned her mother.

Naomi had a boy friend. Five years older than she, he was the heir to shoe factories in Massachusetts and Maine. His body and his speech were soft, slurring, a bland Army pink. Together they worried about Harriet's social life. She had been in New York for two months and no one had asked her for cocktails or to the movies or for an evening with a comic named Lenny Bruce in the Duane Lounge. Occasionally she went to dinner with girls from her office.

"Sit still; you're wriggling like a baby," Naomi ordered. She was putting makeup on Harriet in their bathroom. Joe was reading *The New York Post* on the green couch in the living room. They were taking Harriet to a party.

"Why can't I just look natural?" Harriet complained. "Why do I have to have all this gook over me?"

"Because it will make you more presentable."

"Joe doesn't want to have to drag me along."

"Don't be silly. He likes to do what I tell him to do." She spoke as if she were Madame Curie rebuking a lab assistant who whined about the sullying quality of pitchblende.

At the party Harriet stood in her yellow-and-white brocade jacket dress by the piano. She figured that if anyone started to play, she could sing. "Know many of the good folks here?" a man asked her. He was swarthy, thin, sharp. His eyes were a metallic gray, like a vending machine coin slot.

"Just the people who brought me."

"I know the guy who's giving it. We work for the same insurance company."

"Are you an actuary?"

"Hell, no, I'm in their counsel's office."

She asked him about his work; he offered to fix her drink. She was safe for the evening. When he took her home, he began to neck with her outside the apartment door. Kissing him was like being part of a collision of two ironing boards. She stopped his hand from going inside her skirt. "Oh, shit," he said, "another frigid New York career girl." She was glad he left immediately. In the bathroom she wiped off the futile pancake base, powder, lipstick, eyeshadow and mascara. She lay in her twin bed waiting for Naomi to come home. Outside the metal fire escape glinted in the moonlight of the air shaft.

Naomi arrived around five. She showered, and then, in a cotton bathrobe from Harwyn, she sat on Harriet's bed.

"Did you like that guy you left with?" she asked.

"Not much," Harriet said.

"Guess what happened to me?" Naomi said. She was giggling, as if she were high, though she never drank.

"What?"

"I'm not a virgin any more. My daddy will be furious."

Harriet was unsure if Naomi wanted praise or censure.

"Were you careful?" she asked.

"Joe used a little rubber thing. It was so little I didn't think it could go around his great big peenie. It's not so much, is it, not being a virgin?"

"It depends."

"But I was tired of being a virgin. It was worse not to do it than to do it."

"Does Joe want to marry you?"

"He says so. And my daddy knows his daddy. We're visiting his house next weekend."

"Well, congratulations." Unsure if she was sincere.

"Thank you." Giggling again, Naomi went to bed. The next day she slept late. In the afternoon, wearing pajamas and pearls, she answered the telephone.

"No," Harriet heard her say, "I can't. I'm seeing one person now. Why don't you ask my roomie? She was Sloan's roomie at Harwyn." She gave the receiver to Harriet. Edward DeVore, the Crip, Sloan's Branson beau, was having a party on Friday and invited her to his place.

She spent the week wondering what Edward DeVore was like now. In the Forty-second Street library she also worked dutifully to check entries on Roman religion, on haruspices, fulgurators, and gut-gazers. She envied the Romans their Lupercalian rites. There malign spirits were exorcised, benign spirits celebrated. She wanted to wield the skin of goats, to lash out at evil, to whip the good. Whack, Richard Nixon would choke on his slanders of Alger Hiss. Whack, Martin Luther King would be Attorney General. Whack, Dr. Hill would fall eleven stories to the ground. She wanted Dr. Hill to promote her, but she seemed to irritate him at their morning coffee hours. Once he had been praising Norman Vincent Peale. "He's so banal," she had said impulsively. He had gazed out toward the invisible Hudson River. "You don't know how hard it is to write a sermon every week," he had said. His voice had been as edged with warning as hers with discontent.

160

On Friday Naomi again took Harriet into the bathroom and began another bout with glamour. "Your horrible eyebrows," she said clinically. "I am going to pluck them with my little tweezers. Sit still."

"It hurts," said Harriet. She was writhing on the toilet seat. "Behave like a grown-up, would you."

She loaned Harriet some jewelry. Then she took her into the living room to have Joe inspect her.

"You look sharp," he said. He was sipping the Wild Turkey he brought to their apartment.

"Joey," Naomi pouted, "don't you think it's funny that Harriet has to go to a dinner party all the way in Brooklyn?"

"Every man and woman for themselves," Joe said comfortably.

Harriet liked walking to the East Side subway, even in the heat. Above her, New York buildings. The white squares of light that broke their walls were both merciless and promising. Edward DeVore lived in a six-story red-brick walk-up without a doorman. Across the street a billboard asked for funds to fight cystic fibrosis. He met her on the third floor. He was Sloan's height but heavier, dressed formally in a summer suit, a red weskit, a tie. "Hi, there," he said, "I didn't think I'd ever see you again."

He showed her to a seat on a couch under the windows at one end of his living room and prepared them drinks at the pullman kitchen at the other. "He does all right for a guy with a withered arm," Harriet thought. Between them was a table with a white paper cloth, napkins, wine glasses and a Chianti bottle, candles. However, there were only two places. Harriet wondered what had happened to the other guests.

"Heard anything from your old roommate?" he asked, lounging down beside her.

"Not much." Neither she nor Naomi had heard anything.

"I wanted to marry her," he said grimly. "But I lost out to Charles or to that boy friend she had down south. I never knew which one beat me out. Who was it, anyway?"

"She didn't confide much in anyone, not even me." She smiled at him more confidently than she felt.

"Really? I'm sorry to hear that. I thought maybe you or Naomi Weissburg could fill me in on some particulars. Oh, well, here we are. Let's eat, drink, and be merry."

He shrugged and lifted his Scotch. She clinked the rim of his glass with hers.

Even if he had wanted her information more than her, he had made an effort with the dinner. He had put fresh mushrooms in the beef Bourguignon; garlic on the bread. But as Harriet ate, his image across the table circled and blurred. "It's the candles," she warned herself, "Or the Scotch and wine. I never should have mixed them." To pull herself together, she asked him more about his job as an international division trainee at the Chase Manhattan Bank.

"America's too committed to the U.N.," he said. He jabbed his spoon angrily into his beige mound of butter pecan ice cream. "It's as soft as this stuff here. I know the Rockefellers practically capitalized the whole U.N., and I work for the Rockefellers, but there's going to be trouble for the U.S. if we stick around."

"But there must be an idealistic institution somewhere."

"You Harwyn girls are too soft." He opened another bottle of wine. "I have to say that for Sloan. She was tough. She knew the world was a jungle."

"I'm not soft. I just think there's more to politics than Thomas Hobbes."

"That's enough politics. It's Friday night. Let's dance," he suggested suddenly. He turned the lights down, removed his jacket, and put Frank Sinatra on the phonograph.

Now images of Sloan and her father, who had tied Sloan to him with ropes of top-secret microfilm, were revolving around Harriet. I'm getting drunk, she thought. Edward's belt buckle and fly were next to her head. She stood up, grateful that the room became more stable. At least, Sloan and her father disappeared. Edward's right arm was around her waist. His left dangled from his side as his necktie did from his collar. Unsure what to do with her arms, she put them woozily around his shoulders.

"Fly Me to the Moon" began. Edward clamped her to him and squared her off in a fox-trot, no less insistent for being languid. In the dark his skin was caramel colored. He began to kiss her face and hair. Between kisses his tongue caressed the inside of his lips. She wanted to float into his skin. Her period was so close that she was safe. One dinner, she denounced herself, and you're ready to go to bed with this man. The swiftness of her calculations upset her.

162

Edward's right hand went for her zipper.

"Let's just dance," she murmured.

"Let's play."

"Let's dance." Her mollifying mouth touched his eyelids.

"If you won't play, don't stay."

Was this a joke?

"At least Sloan was never a tease. I thought you might be more like her."

The bastard. What gave him the right to believe that because he had cooked a cruddy casserole and served cheap Chianti, empty bottles of which hung in every college room on the eastern littoral, her body was his; her timing was his; her Sloan was his with which to insult her. Particularly after she had taken the subway to Brooklyn, ostensibly for a dinner party. Violating the historical trend, inner impulse rode over outer direction. She plunged into his bedroom as if it were a thicket of poison ivy, tree stumps, and bull briar to get her coat. Branson boys. Thirty percent of all Harwyn girls married them, reported on them in the alumnae magazine class notes. If Edward DeVore symbolized them, she was lucky that none of them had ever called her for a date during her Harwyn years.

The next morning she wrote Jean Maurin at Yale. At least he had been gallant. "I'm living in New York now," she said, "working for a publisher. If you're ever in the Big City, I'll give you a tour."

Harriet wanted to do more with her life. She needed to feed a moral appetite. Walking home from the subway after work, she had often noticed a storefront between a dry cleaner's and a delicatessen. GOTHAM DEMOCRATIC REFORM CLUB blocked out in black letters on the plate glass window. She had read about the Reform movement in *The New York Times*. It was going to challange, purge, and change the ruling Democrats in the city. Its method was to elect new party leaders in each assembly district, the building block of local politics. Curious, attracted, Harriet went in.

Several women were writing at unvarnished trestle tables. At the rear of the room a dark-haired man was talking, harshly, secretively, on the telephone. Behind him a large map of Manhattan was erratically divided into numbered sections. On the walls were framed photographs of Eleanor Roosevelt and two liberal governors of New York State. Telephone books weighted down stacks of paper and protected them from the wind of a large standing fan. The messy, slovenly, purposeful room reminded Harriet of a bigger smoker, with men in it.

Then an alert, slight, feral man approached her. His graying hair was cut neatly. He was wearing immaculate clothes, gold jewelry, a seal ring. "Hello, honey," he said eagerly, "are you interested in Reform?"

"I think so," she said.

"Well, you've come to the right place. We're the best club in Manhattan." His name, he said, was Harvey Draper. Perched on a tin chair, he told her about Paul J. Flynn, the leader of the Paul J. Flynn Club, the regular Democrats in the district. "We've got to defeat Flynn this time out," Harvey said passionately. "Maybe you've seen his club."

"I haven't. I'm pretty new to New York."

"Well, it's over a Ukrainian dance hall three blocks away. The Primary is in October. That's not very far away. We're running two wonderful candidates—a man for district leader male, of course; a girl for district leader female. That's another thing that makes Reformers better than the Regulars. We let the women have a say. The Regulars hide them away in a separate room."

"Like the Arabs," said an older woman, in a cotton dress, at the next table.

"Like the Jews," said a thin woman in pants across from her.

"Don't pay any attention to her," Harvey said. "She's Jewish, too. So am I. What did you say your name was?"

"Harriet, Harriet Springer."

"Oh, that's a good, nice name. Honey, if you join us, you've got to watch out for the Regulars. They're nasty. Just before the last Primary, two years ago, they put glue in our keyhole and slashed Bryant's tires. He's our candidate for district leader male. He's a lawyer. I wish I were a lawyer, but I had to run my family's clothing store."

"I'd like to join," Harriet said.

"Pete," Harvey shouted to the dark man at the back of the room. "Pete, we've got a volunteer. Her name is Harriet."

"Well," said Pete, "tell her to sit down and help Marie and Carolyn with the envelopes."

Harvey found her a pen and a list from which to copy voters' names and addresses. "Don't pay any attention to Pete either," he whispered. "He's the president and the campaign manager. He thinks he's such a big political *mensch,* but I think he's just a bossy boy."

Harriet wrote with quiet diligence. One of her Harwyn recommendations had said, "She's not afraid of being a beaver for work." She listened to the other women gossip. "That Pete," the thin one said, wiping her neck, "he forgets that we're a *reform* club. We're supposed to run on democratic principles."

Then Pete sat on the table by her. "Have you ever been an election district captain?" he asked. His voice was intense, nasal, drawling.

"No," she answered.

"You could do it," Harvey hovered near them.

"Every assembly district is divided into election districts." Pete spoke as if even rote information were liturgical. "Every election district has a captain. The captain is the link between the club and the voters."

"It's a big job," Harvey added. Pete waved him away. "We need someone for the 49th," he said. "It's a hard nut to crack. In the last primary, it went against us, two to one."

"I'd like to try," she said.

"Fine," Pete got up. "Here's your registered voter list. There's a stack of brochures in the corner." He stalked back to the telephone.

"Don't worry," the thin woman said to her, "he never thanks anyone."

Harriet hardly cared. She was happy. She had a cause. She would convert her voters from the ignorance of being a Regular, through a limbo of indifference, to the judicious clarities of Reform. With twigs of persistence, and sticks of principle, she would transform the swamps of the 49th Election District into a sturdy dam. "Don't forget, honey," Harvey said, "we have a general membership meeting tomorrow night. We used to have them here, in the club, but then we got too big. Isn't that wonderful?"

The meeting was in the basement recreation room of the Mother Theresa Home for the Aged. On the walls were mezzotints of Jesus, Mary, some saints, and Pope John. Harvey beckoned to Harriet to sit next to him. He offered her some of his Coke and introduced her to a tanned woman, with short, dark, glossy hair, in a lime-green culotte dress. Her name was Marcia Gold. She was drinking an imported beer. In the front of the room Pete was instructing two people. "That's Bryant and Mary," Harvey said approvingly, "Our candidates for district leader."

"Bryant's a horse's ass," Marcia said.

"Come on, honey," Harvey said, "you can't always be so cynical."

Bryant Ochshorn seemed too well dressed for the room. His bunched, muscular body was in a seersucker suit, white shirt, loafers. His hair was cut to seem as thick in the middle as on the sides. Mary O'Fay was a lean, bony, redhead. She was wearing a cotton shirt and wraparound skirt. "She's always so damned cheerful," Marcia said.

"That's why she's a good candidate," Harvey reminded her. Harriet envied them for whispering together like old friends.

"All right, club," Pete said to the sixty people in front of him. "We're going to decide the issue of the ice cream party tonight. I'm damned tired of having it hang over the campaign. When we win the Primary in October, we're going to be the Democrats in this Assembly District. We'll have a say in the 1960 presidential fight. I'm not going to have us look like a lot of sloppy amateurs."

"I support the ice cream party," Mary said enthusiastically. "But the membership must choose. That's what the Reform Movement is all about."

"An ice cream party?" sneered a chubby, gray-haired man. "Do our esteemed leaders want to have us play pin-the-tail-on-the-donkey, too?"

"Pipe down, Lew," Pete said. "I didn't recognize you."

"Lew's a dentist," Harvey instructed Harriet. "He has a lot of celebrities. I think he even capped Milton Berle."

Harriet could not understand why the debate about whether or not the Gotham Club should give a free ice cream party for the children of the Assembly District in Locust Park at the end of August was so provocative. Club members were throwing procedural points from *Roberts Rules of Order* back and forth as if they were temper tantrums. She wanted the club to be a family, a just community. Her performing self, which the city had subdued, began to rise and tug at her. She stood up. Pete recognized her. "I don't think we should argue like this," she said passsionately. "We have to reach the district. Mothers will bring their children and see that Reform can be a part of their everyday life. I'm just a new member, but I'd like to work on this, with everybody pulling together, not apart."

"My store will pay for some of the ice cream," Harvey shouted. The club voted for the party.

"You're crazy," Marcia Gold muttered to Harriet. "Do you know what it's going to be like to distribute free ice cream to three hundred kids in late August in New York?" But she offered Harriet some of her beer anyway.

Now, at night, Harriet canvassed her voters. She carried club literature and index cards, legs aching from climbing tenement stairs. She phoned her voters during the day. She listened to their problems and consulted Pete and the club lawyers about solutions. Each Wednesday she called Mrs. Ruby Butz, who needed comfort more than most. Mrs. Butz believed that Paul J. Flynn, and others, were jumping out at her from her television set and trying to take her ears and mouth away. "But Mrs. Butz," Harriet would cajole her, "if you're talking to me, Paul Flynn can't possibly have your ears and mouth." She wanted to help Mrs. Butz.

One morning she was talking to the sales office of the Good Humor Company, trying to arrange a discount on ice cream bars for the club party. Passing her cubicle on the way to the Hill Climbers' coffee break, Carla mouthed, "Get off the phone." At the meeting, Dr. Hill was more sprightly than usual. "Gosh, people," he said, "we have a new assignment from Mr. Potter, the Executive Editor himself. A good man, a very good man. He used to be with Britannica." Harriet was convinced that Mr. Potter's body was composed of gray straws. He wanted the endpapers of each volume of *The Brightest Lamp* to be a chart that would trace a vital development in the history of civilization. If someone, with thrift and shopping coupons bought all forty volumes of *The Brightest Lamp*, he or she would have flow charts of the full rise of human culture: architecture, water transport, food, marriage, armaments. "We can show Mr. Potter how good the Hill Climbers are," their leader enthused. "There's no reason why religion and philosophy and classics and ancient history and anthropology have to lag behind the social sciences and the natural sciences."

167

"I guess not," Jarvis said. He rubbed his left cheek and jowl as if galvanizing of one section of his skin might animate his whole body.

"There's certainly not." Carla's right foot jiggled toward him.

Coffee over, Dr. Hill beckoned Harriet to stay. Did he want to congratulate her on her report on Celtic mythology? Or offer her the job of coordinating their division's plans for endpapers? "Yes, sir," she said, with goodwill.

"Harriet," he began, "I'm a loyal Republican, but it doesn't matter to me if you have some doubts about the Grand Old Party. This is America, and it's one man, one opinion."

"Of course, Dr. Hill."

"But I must warn you that I am concerned about the time you spend on your Reform political business on the office telephone."

"But Dr. Hill," she as a monument of genteel puzzlement, "I'm hardly ever on the phone."

"Now, Harriet, that's not my impression, and I am your chief. Anyone is entitled to one or two personal calls when it involves a personal emergency, but you're asking Tibble to support your extracurricular activities. You could have a real future at Knowledge, Inc., if you applied yourself. Look at Carla and Jarvis and Jacquelyn. They've applied themselves, and now they're subject editors.

"Dr. Hill," she said nervily, "I know I've only been here a little while, but I'd like to be an editor. I'd be glad to start by coordinating our division's plans for Mr. Potter's endpapers."

He frowned, an emotional eruption. "I'm surprised at you," he said. "I'm telling you you're taking advantage of Project: Tibble, and you're asking to be an editor?"

"I'm sorry, sir," she said, subdued.

"Be careful, Harriet."

"Yes, sir." She could not get in trouble on the job. Not a Springer. Not a Harwyn girl.

Back in their cubicle Joanne lifted a hand from her typewriter long enough to give Dr. Hill the finger. At lunch Harriet retreated to Harvey's clothing store on Third Avenue. Like the Gotham Club itself, Harvey had become a compatriot. "The Compleat Gentleman" was only ten feet wide. In the display window were male mannequins, trousers, and bikini bathing suits cut tightly around their wire/fabric/plastic loins. Along both walls were stacks of sweaters, socks, shirts, slacks. Harvey's assistant, tanned and suave, was tidying shelves. "The Old Bitch isn't here today," he said. "Thank God." The Old Bitch was Harvey's mother. Co-owner of the store, she appeared, from Queens, two or three times a week to sit behind the cash register and watch. Now Harvey was alone at the register.

"Hello," he called cheerfully. "Come sit by me. Business is just terrible."

"Harvey," Harriet confessed, "my boss warned me about making phone calls for the club."

"The club comes first, honey. Lie low for a few days, but then you've got to do your duty. You could always get another job, a smart girl with an education like you. I'll help. That's what friends are for."

Harriet was dubious. Harvey treated her as generously as anyone she had ever known, but the owner of The Compleat Gentleman, who had never been to college, might not have the right contacts for a Harwyn graduate.

"Come on," Harvey said, "I'll buy you lunch."

They were eating pastrami and French fries when Marcia Gold sat down in the booth beside Harvey. "Hi," she said, "want to buy me lunch, too?" She was wearing a rose-colored silk dress.

"My, my," Harvey said, "it's the Jewish princess. Where's the outfit from? Bolton's or Bergdorf's?"

"Bergdorf's. Mother's charge account."

"You're too old to need that."

"I can't help it. I only have my salary as an art gallery assistant. It's not enough to dress for the marriage market."

"Some market," Harvey said.

Marcia was muscular but limber, a tennis player, a skier. She lacked the shivering aestheticism of Harwyn, but her tough urbanity appealed to Harriet. She wanted Marcia to notice her. During lunch they talked about the club's campaign. After lunch, in her office, Harriet admonished the Jesuit author of the entry about Peter Abelard, even if he was a friend of Dr. Hill's. "I find it passing strange," she wrote, "that Father McGraw mentions neither scholasticism; nor *sic et non*, Abelard's most famous book; nor conceptualism, Abelard's philosophical synthesis of nominalism and realism." Yet, as the stern pencil marked her yellow pad, she dreamt of Heloise, lying on an altar, while Abelard made love to her, before they rode through fields of flowers and the dark green leaves of wild strawberries, before Abelard screamed as the knives of the wicked cut through his body as he lay alone on a cot in his cold, stone monastery.

A few days later Marcia phoned her at the office.

"Where did you get this number?" Harriet asked. She was surprised.

"From Harvey. Listen, if it's sunny tomorrow, take the day off and drive to Jones Beach with me."

Harriet hesitated. She was caught between fear of having Marcia think her a stick-in-the-mud and Dr. Hill think her a goof-off.

"Tell your boss you're doing research outside the office," Marcia said.

"Okay," Harriet agreed boldly. Then, to placate Dr. Hill, she personally gave him her latest research report. On Abraham Ibn David, commonly known as Abraham Ben David.

"Was that you on the phone, Harriet?" he asked.

"I was talking to someone who works for an art gallery. She's promised to show me some Byzantine icons. I thought it would help me in my work on the medieval philosophers here."

"Keep buckling down, Harriet."

"Of course, Dr. Hill." Old fool, she thought.

The next morning the phone rang at six thirty. "For you," Naomi said, sleepy, incredulous.

"Who's your social secretary?" Marcia asked.

"My roommate."

"I didn't know you had one." Cautious voice.

"It's an old friend from college."

"Oh." More relaxed. They arranged to meet in an hour. "You're going to the beach, on a workday, with a woman?" Naomi asked, as if Harriet were proposing child molestation.

"She's just a friend from the club," Harriet explained defensively.

Marcia was driving an air-conditioned, pearl-gray Lincoln. It belonged to her father, a doctor who specialized in prostate surgery. "I canceled my shrink to get some sun," she said.

"You see a psychiatrist?" Harriet had believed it to be a sign of weakness, but so many people seemed to go that she wondered if she were wrong.

"My father pays. It's his fault, after all."

"What did he do?"

"What didn't he do?" Marcia answered.

At the beach, Harriet inspected the green waves, the long expanse of blue-green water fading into a white mist. She was unaccustomed to civilized beaches: parking lots; tiled restrooms; beer concessions; papers among the rose bushes. Yet, as they walked three hundred yards to sand where they could lie without hearing a portable radio, she began to feel her body loosen into the sun. Marcia showed her how to dive through waves. A wave that loomed powerful enough to slap a body against the beach would become nothing more than air and spray if the body catapulted beneath the breaking crest.

"Do me a favor," Marcia said as they were on their towels again. Harriet turned her head, as if the muscles were part of a languid flow. "Get the zinc oxide from my duffle bag and rub a little on my nose? I don't want to move."

Harriet rummaged among Marcia's sweater, car keys, Omega watch, thermos of vodka and pineapple juice. The white strip of zinc oxide, spurting from the tube, was cool against the inside of her finger. Slowly, carefully, she painted it down the straight bridge of the woman's nose, over the wings. The woman's forehead was broad, her cheeks too heavy and long for the bones that supported them. Her eyes were closed. She had several freckles. Concealing three of them, Harriet traced the rest of the oxide across the cheekbones. The woman's breath was as warm against Harriet's face as the sun was against her back and neck and legs and shoulders. My God, Harriet thought, what's happening to me? For she wanted to spread her hand over the woman's face, her neck, her breasts. She wanted to soothe the woman's skin until her hand itself became the skin. She wanted them to breath as closely together as their skin would be. She caught her breath. Her body was in anguish. To restrain it, she lay flat on her stomach. Her hands stretched out and dug into the sand until she could leash and pull herself together.

Harriet and Naomi took turns cleaning the apartment. Harriet did her share on Sundays. Because it was hot, despite the thumping air conditioner, she defrosted the refrigerator. She rubbed the old ice over her skin. It streaked the dust and soot that lingered

171

there. She was Windexing the glass coffee table when the phone rang.

"Harriet, I reached you," Jean Maurin said. His voice was the same—soft, insistent, accent curling around the words.

"Where are you?" She was startled, excited.

"In New York, in the Waldorf Astoria hotel, with air conditioning. Come see me."

"But I'm cleaning the apartment. I'm a filthy mess."

"That doesn't matter. You can have a shower here. You must come. I am leaving for France tonight. I cannot go without saying good-bye to you."

She was persuaded. She bathed and put on a checked skirt and sleeveless blouse. She took part of the *Sunday Times* to read on the bus. She carried it gingerly so that the print, in the humid air, would not inkily tattoo her hand and arm and clothes. When he opened the door of his room, Jean looked as he had that afternoon in Minnesota two years before: plump but at ease, as if he enjoyed his flesh; black hair combed back; sleeves of his open white shirt rolled up; gray trousers. He held her face and kissed it. The smoke from his cigarette drifted past her cheek and through her hair.

"We have a ritual," he said. "We see each other every other summer. Come in." She felt welcome and came in, but the room dismayed her. She thought the Waldorf Astoria would be more glamorous. She sat in a yellow armchair. Maurin, on the edge of the bed, was a handbreadth away. He smiled, as if he basked in their reunion.

"You're well?" he asked. "Of course you are. American girls are always well, always healthy, always on the go."

"It sounds like you don't think very much of us." She smiled. It was sophisticated to be bantering with the man who had taken your virginity, two years later, in a hotel.

"I think very much of you," he said. Gently he was spreading her legs apart. His fingers were exploring the soft caverns behind her knees. His nails were stroking, teasing, scratching the inside of her thighs.

"Did you miss me?" he asked.

"Should I have?"

"Do not be difficult," he said. "Has there been anyone but me?"

172

His hands had stopped, as if the answer mattered, but he was smiling and humming tunelessly.

"Should there have been?" she answered. As she spoke, she knew she was evading what would happen. Her body responded to him, to his humming, as her will might have to a hypnotist.

"I hope for your sake there has been," he said. "But that you still want me. Do you want me?"

More strongly now, his hands were circling inside her thighs. They reached up to touch and flick at the band of the bikini pants Naomi had had her buy. Yet he talked as if they were sitting in a public room. "I am going to France to see my sister and to do some work. Yale has given me a leave. American schools treat poor Europeans very well."

She wanted him to touch her breasts, to go inside her clothes. "What will you be studying?" she asked. Her voice was strained.

"The usual. Political history. Power. Everything but this." Then he pulled her toward him on the bed. "Come, Harriet," he said, "don't waste time. I need you now."

She kicked off her shoes as she collapsed toward him. He undressed her, taking off his clothes as he stripped her, efficiently, as if his hands were a labor-saving device.

"Are you all right?" he muttered. His body was next to her, over her, rubbing into her, his mouth opening down on her. "Yes," she said. Then, as if his whole being were concentrated into his body, into his erection, he was fucking her. She wrapped her legs around him. "No," he said. "Wait. Lie still." She was aware that he was aware of her, yet he was focusing, not on her, but on some point ahead of him, toward which his need was driving him. Again, as his excitement strained and grew, hers reached after, to fall, dissolve, spend itself. He held himself aloft for a moment, and then he came. Her body felt flat but oozy, warm, wet from his sweat and sperm. He lay on her before he held and kissed her and stroked her back. He panted, sighed, "Harriet, sweet girl. Sweet girl. Touch me, would you."

His soft penis shocked her. It was inhuman, smooth, like a fish belly and crumpled velveteen. "You see," he smiled, "how kind you are." He had some Scotch in a bedside table drawer. They lay on the bed, his arm around her, while they drank from a bathroom glass. Raw liquor still made her wince, but she sipped valiantly. She inspected their bodies. His flabbiness disarmed him, helped to defuse whatever threat his power over her might have ignited. He was so much hairier than she that she felt relaxed and ordinary.

"You are a funny girl," he said. "I want you again." To experiment, as if innovations might grant some autonomy, she leaned over him and tried to lick his penis. She wanted to see if she could bring him up, but he pulled her under him again. "No," he told her, "I am still your teacher. We'll do first things first." Still again, the more he was aroused and gratified, the more he lost her. She did not make the mistake of clasping him with her legs. She knew him better now. The satisfaction of being more experienced balanced out the flattening of her ecstasy.

As they had more Scotch, she became constricted, anxious. The room seemed to be bearing down on her, as Maurin had before he came, before his spasm, sigh, and thanks. "I've got to go," she said.

"Oh, no," he protested. "My plane doesn't leave until nine. Have a shower. Stay. I'll order food."

"No," she said. "I have plans. I've got to go."

She dressed. He watched and hummed some more. "We have a tradition," he said. "I'll be back. I will send you a picture of Venus from the Louvre."

He kissed her at the door. Her legs felt sticky. On the street she did not know if it was Jean or the heat. In the shower, in the clean bathroom at home, she brooded over the afternoon. If she was having a drink with Marcia Gold, after a meeting at the club, she did not want things to end, though they did. If she was talking to Harvey, she did not much care if things went on or not, but she was always glad to see him again. She trusted him. With Jean she had suddenly longed for the afternoon to end. She remembered it pleasantly. She hoped he would write from France. But he gave her less than she thought he promised, though she wanted what he gave her, for a while.

Harriet now plotted her phone calls for the Gotham Club around Dr. Hill's absences from the office. He would return whistling Stephen Foster tunes. "Way Down Upon the Swanee River" caught her as she was talking to a voter, a retired schoolteacher. Dr. Hill summoned her as soon as she hung up. His Venetian

174

blinds were closed, so that white metal or wallboard surrounded him on three sides. His face was flushed. He looked like a rosy-gray, packaged egg.

"Harriet," he said, "it's not every researcher that gets the chance to be on such good terms with the senior editors and the project director."

She understood that.

"But you have apparently chosen not to take advantage of your opportunities. I warned you before about your phone calls."

Was she about to be fired, she wondered, in disbelief and panic. She was. "It was your first real job, Harriet," Dr. Hill said. "Because of that, and because you're a Harwyn girl, I'm going to give you a month's notice and a good reference. I hope you learn from this experience."

"Thank you, sir," she said and slunk back to her desk. Joanne typed her a note, "Don't get me wrong, but I think you're lucky." Clammy with shame, Harriet looked out at the Time-Life building. There good people, successful people, could still gather facts and research aspects of reality. Pretending to go to the library, she phoned Harvey.

"I've been fired," she said. Her voice was shaking.

"Don't worry," his breathy, energetic voice leaped out at her. "I'm going to make some calls for you. You remember that I'm your friend."

Back in the office she typed up a report about the Roman Coliseum mechanically. Titus may have dedicated the Amphitheatrum Flavium in A.D. 80, but after Labor Day she would be unemployed. She left the office early. When she reached the apartment, Naomi was there.

"I've been fired," she said.

"I've got something called the crabs," Naomi answered.

"I said, I've been fired."

"I don't care." Naomi was distraught. "I've just come from the doctor. I have this awful itching, down there, where all these awful little animals are living in my hairs. I have to paint myself blue with a medicine the doctor gave me."

"Where did you get them?"

"From Joe. How can I marry him now? How can I marry someone who gives me crabs? And what will my daddy say if the doctor tells him?"

"Joe's not good enough for you anyway," Harriet said. Then, undressing for a shower, she burst into tears.

To her surprise Harriet learned that people often got fired and survived. Women at the club cut out *Times* help-wanted ads for her. Harvey reminded her that he was making calls. Marcia bought her a drink. Still, she slept badly. The night before the ice cream party, she dreamt that fat bald policemen in summer uniforms were going to take her into an alley. When she woke up the insides of her eyelids were prickly, her limbs like thickening asphalt. That afternoon she picked up Harvey's V.W. at his garage. She was to chauffeur Bryant Ochshorn to the party. Driving in New York shackled her to a carnival ride of terror. Stomach jolting, she stayed close to the curb.

"Do you like being a candidate?" she asked.

He pulled at the French cuffs of his white shirt and lifted his chin as if it were the bowsprit of the ship of state. "It's hard work," he said. "And it interferes with my private life, but when people like you are putting everything they have into me and my campaign, I have to work as hard as I can too. Be careful of that bus there."

"I will. What got you interested in Reform politics?"

"I've always found the idea of government service fascinating, even when I was a little boy, living on the West Side, listening to Franklin D. Roosevelt and Fiorello LaGuardia on the radio."

"Then it's really important to you that Mrs. Roosevelt is a sponsor of the Reform Movement."

"Oh, yes, she's a wonderful woman. I've met her, of course."

Harriet wondered why the taxi behind her was honking so belligerently. Bryant's body bulked beyond his seat. Shifting down, at a red light, she hit his leg. "Sorry," she said.

"Don't mention it." He leaned closer to his door. "Would you mind if I rehearsed a speech I have to give to a community group after the ice cream party?"

"Not at all," she affirmed falsely as the car motor died.

Locust Park was a shaded, pretty block near the East River. When they arrived, children with mothers or nurses were standing in front of a Good Humor ice cream truck for their treat. Women from the club, in white straw hats with ribbons on the crown that read VOTE GOTHAM REFORM, were handing out bro-

176

chures and balloons. Harriet joined them. Bryant found Mary O'Fay and began to work the benches.

Harriet was helping an old woman get in line for her ice cream when Harvey approached her. He was waving as if he had a gift so marvelous that the world would be incomplete until she opened it. His tie clasp, ring, belt buckle, and blazer buttons glittered in the sun. He was escorting a woman about the age and height of Eleanor Springer. However, she was far more polished. Her makeup was as much as an extension of her flesh as skin is of the fruit it covers. Her champagne-colored hair was a subtle bouffant. Her apricot-colored dress matched her shoes and bag. Harriet felt lumpish in her black cotton dress and white straw boater.

"I want you to meet a very special voter and a very special person," Harvey said as if in awe. "Harriet, this is Phyllis Hendricks, Mrs. Phyllis Hendricks. I know you've read her advice column in the papers."

"How do you do?" Harriet said. At Harwyn they had often read the personal advice column out loud and laughed at it.

"Harvey tells me you're job hunting," Phyllis Hendricks said. Her voice was warm but carefully pitched, as if she had trained herself to be charming but prudent.

"That's right. I'm on the market."

"I'm looking for a secretary who might double as a researcher if she has to. Could you come to my office around ten tomorrow and bring your resume to talk about it?"

To hell with the Hill Climbers coffee hour, Harriet thought. "Of course," she said.

Phyllis gave Harriet an apricot-colored business card. "Just ring the bell," she said. "My personal assistant will let you in."

She smiled and walked away, Harvey carefully touching her elbow. "Can I have my ice cream now?" The woman whom Harriet had been escorting was talking to her. "I don't know what's so special about that lady. She wears fancy clothes, but I'm over eighty years old, and I'll bet I've lived in the neighborhood longer than any of you." Quickly, apologetically, Harriet plucked her a Strawberry Surprise bar.

Harvey returned a few minutes later. "Did you like her, honey?" he asked eagerly.

177

"Did she like me? That's more to the point."

"She didn't say. She's very famous, you know. Her column is syndicated everywhere."

"But Harvey," she fanned herself with her boater, "I don't know anything at all about that watered-down psychology she hands out in her column."

"You're a smart girl. You'll learn. This is a real opportunity. Phyllis is my voter, you know. That's how I met her. She won't give you any problems about the club. Just brush your hair and be yourself, a smart girl like you."

Harriet thanked Harvey. Watered-down psychology aside, she needed a job. The next morning, Phyllis Hendricks' office surprised her. She had not realized that people could work amid such private elegance. HENDRICKS ENTERPRISE FOR HUMAN DEVELOPMENT was stamped on a bronze plaque beside the white door of the brick building on East Fifty-fifth Street. Phyllis ran her business on the first floor. She lived with her husband in a duplex overhead. A willowy woman, streaked hair tumbling neatly to her shoulders, met Harriet. "I'm Elizabeth Light," she said with overbearing clarity. "I supervise whatever other staff Phyllis has." She then led Harriet through a trim outer office to a spacious back room.

Phyllis was standing at her desk: a leather-topped table with slender, curving legs. To her left was a marble fireplace. Behind her were potted trees and a sterling silver watering can. Beyond them, through the long windows, was a real garden. To her right was a wrought-iron wheelbarrow. It held Phyllis' books in leather bindings. On the walls were photographs of Phyllis with people who had scrawled their names across the prints.

Phyllis was wearing a tailored skirt and blouse. She greeted Harriet and asked her to sit in an antique Windsor chair by the fireplace. Both her dress and speech seemed more direct, more businesslike, than they had in Locust Park. Harriet's heart was thumping as if she were about to take an exam.

"I'm not looking for flash," she told Harriet. "I want someone who's reliable, who won't mind dirty work, who'll type and file and do it right. And I've got to have someone who won't look down on the people who read my column and buy my books. My staff has to respect my audience."

"I went to a public high school," Harriet said quickly. "And

178

I'm a captain for the Gotham Reform Club in an election district that's full of Regulars."

Phyllis rummaged through a wicker basket next to her. "Here are some of the letters that came in today," she said briskly. "The ones that were left after Elizabeth sorted through them." She gave Harriet a white envelope. "Here's something easy. A woman's written to me because she thinks she's ugly. She's scared. She wants me to make her feel better. If you were writing my column, what would you say to her?"

She summoned Elizabeth and told her to give Harriet some paper and a typewriter. In the outer office, Harriet sat on a leather-and-steel typing chair. An ugly, fearful girl, she thought. What ugly, fearful girls do I know? What solace can I offer? But an adrenaline frenzy pushed her on to meet Phyllis Hendricks' test. She would write to Betty Dowsey. She would act as if Betty had petitioned Phyllis Hendricks. She would counsel Northville once again. She checked the name of the woman who had actually called out to Phyllis, and then wrote:

Dear Maribelle:

Do you know about the Greek goddess Aphrodite? The most beautiful of the goddesses, she was the spirit of love. Unhappily, you and I are only mortals, but we can try to be goddesses here on Earth. We can try to be a Human Aphrodite and bring the spirit of beauty to ourselves and to mortal men. Some of us, so falsely, may think of ourselves as the discards of Aphrodite, but we can be, if we want, her handmaidens. I have found a wonderful book that will help us shed the light we may have been hiding beneath the bushel of self-doubt.

Eager, apprehensive, she stood in front of Phyllis and waited for her response. "It's rotund," Phyllis said. "You overwrite. But it's all right. I'll call you soon. I want to check your Harwyn references." Then she glanced at Harriet as if she were amused. "Don't worry about Dr. Hill," she said. "I'll take Harvey Draper's word for what happened there."

"I guess I had the wrong attitude," Harriet said. She grinned, apologetic, shy.

On Monday Elizabeth Light phoned Harriet at Knowledge, Inc. Phyllis Hendricks was prepared to match her salary of $85

179

a week and her medical insurance benefits. Harriet was to start after Labor Day. Harriet crowed her acceptance, shook Joanne's hand, and marched on Dr. Hill. "I've got another job," she said.

"Gosh, Harriet," he looked at her over his rimless glasses. "That's wonderful, that's fine and dandy. You'll come to appreciate the favor I did you when I encouraged you to branch away from Project Tibble." In her cubicle again, Harriet openly phoned Harvey. He was jubilant. She called Naomi, too. She was glad that Harriet could now keep on with the rent. So was Harriet.

Dr. Hill gathered his entire staff for a farewell party for Harriet at the Century Club. "My heavens," Carla said to Harriet and Joanne as the group struggled down the street, "I didn't know he cared so much. The Century Club matters more to him than anything else in the world."

"I'm surprised he asked me," said Joanne, the typist. Harriet was, too.

Inside the disappointing, blank facade of the club, they took brown leather chairs in an upstairs room. "You're lucky to be here, girls," Dr. Hill said. "The Club doesn't have women members."

"That doesn't seem fair," Harriet pointed out.

"You see," Dr. Hill winked at Jarvis, "I've got her all riled up about that old horse chestnut, women's rights. Now what are we going to order? Is it too hot for Martinis?"

He urged them all to have one, but Joanne ordered a Coke. Her parents had forbidden her to drink. "It's a rare family that has old-fashioned standards," Dr. Hill said approvingly. Then he proposed a toast, "To the Hill Climbers and to the one who is descending from us today." Harriet gagged. To change the taste of the vermouth-heavy yellowish drink, she chewed her olive.

Before the silence could be too prolonged, Carla asked Dr. Hill who the nineteenth-century gentlemen in the grave, austere oil portraits that hung about them on paneled walls might be.

"I only know five of them," he said ruefully, "but it would be a peach of an idea for me to learn about them all. The gentleman to your right, Carla, in the middle of the top row, was a fine Biblical scholar."

Harriet sat back. Better to hear Dr. Hill ramble on, to watch

Joanne crook her little finger, Jarvis and Jacquelyn examine their feet, and Carla puff cigarettes than to have nothing at all happen. Dr. Hill was beginning the story of a third portrait when Jacquelyn banged down her drink. "Oh, I'm sorry," she gasped, "but I didn't know a Martini glass could make so much noise. I'm really terribly sorry, but I have to break up the party first. My husband and I are going away for the weekend." She slung her bag over her shoulder, shook Harriet's hand, and fled. Her long disheveled hair grazed her neck and shoulders. "Well," said Jarvis, "look who's left."

"Need another glass?" Dr. Hill asked. "Can't let Friday pass with only one Martini." He summoned a Negro waiter with a little bell.

Harriet discovered that if she ate peanuts between each sip, they would, like salty communion wafers, make the drink less warmly rancid. Jarvis asked what her new job was. "Interesting," he said. Harriet thought his morose face and dissolving body more attractive than she had before. The flesh no longer resembled a series of collapsing landscape terraces but a body's natural, soft contours.

"I'll miss you all," she said.

"Oh, yeah?" Jarvis managed a smile.

"You'll never come back," Joanne said. "Especially as long as *he's* around." She tilted her glass at Dr. Hill.

"What's that, Joanne?" he asked.

"Nothing, nothing at all. I'm just telling Harriet good-bye." She left next. When she was gone, Dr. Hill beamed at them bleakly. "She's a nice girl," he said, "but I feel that the Hill Climbers can have a real discussion more successfully when it's just us. It's a pity what schools do to young people today. They don't teach a darn thing."

Harriet wondered if she ought not to defend Joanne, to say that she was too bright to be a typist, but Harriet was feeling too congenial. "Another round before it's time to bid farewell to Harriet for the last time?" Dr. Hill asked.

"You're very good to do this," Harriet told him oozily.

"I'll have another," Jarvis shrugged. "I've got nothing else to do. The wife and kids are off at the wife's family in Vermont."

"Martinis and I aren't such good friends after one or two of them," Carla giggled, "but I'll try."

After another toast, this time to the truth, Dr. Hill winked again at Harriet. "I wonder if that new employer of yours will give you and your Reform Democrats as much free telephone time as Project Tibble did. I like to josh you about your wild-eyed politics." Then he sighed. "My, my but time does fly. I've got to be moseying along, but I don't want to disturb the fun. I'll just sign this chit, and you can sit here and drink up." He and Harriet shook hands.

"We'll miss you," he said. "Now I must fly." The figure, with its scurrying walk, passed down the marble stairs.

"These glasses aren't very big, are they?" Harriet held hers up to the ceiling fixture, watching them both change shape.

Jarvis slurrily looked at her and Carla. "I've got an idea," he said. "Why don't the two of you come on up to Tarrytown with me. I know it sounds nuts, but the house is empty, and I've got a lot of food. You can take the train back. The house is only a block from the station."

"Oh, Jarvis, I don't know." Carla was wary. "Is it really wise?"

"It's Friday night."

"Let's go," urged spontaneous, reckless Harriet.

"Jarvis," Carla said, "Are you sure you want to do this? We can have dinner here in town."

"No," he sounded challenged. "I want you two to see my house. I don't care what the neighbors say."

He led them east to Grand Central Station. Ducking inside a liquor store to buy gin. Inside the station Harriet managed to snag a schedule from the rack at the Information Booth. She was afraid of being too dependent on Jarvis, despite his unexpected energy. Once on the train, they tried to slump on the prickly wicker seats. "Good stuff, gang," Jarvis drank from the bottle in the bag. "Better straight than with that vermouth chaser." He grinned at them, the sweet rakishness of the depressive, surprised at having emerged from his painful torpor.

For the first time since graduation, Harriet was riding through Harlem, on the line that went to Harwyn, deploring poverty. Then the Hudson appeared on her left. She thought the river ugly, brown, sluggish. She preferred the turbulent green-and-white waters of the Cascade Mountains east of Northville. Ignorant easterners romanticized rivers that were nothing more than monster bathtubs, draining dirty waters into sludgy seas.

"I know something about Dr. Hill I bet the two of you don't know," Carla said, teasingly, smugly.

"What?" Jarvis spoke over the noise of the train.

"I said I know something about Dr. Hill the two of you don't know. He used to be a minister."

"I know that," Jarvis said. "That's old stuff."

"But I bet you don't know that he fell in love with a Miss Finland when she visited his parish once. He divorced his wife and married her, and then, just six months later, she ran away with an Arab diplomat. The parish fired Dr. Hill."

"No kidding," Jarvis said. "How did you find all this out?"

"He told me one night. He took me to the movies and held my hand."

Jarvis and Harriet both stared at her. Harriet's imagination utterly balked at seeing Carla and Dr. Hill, fingers meshed with fingers, thigh by thigh. "But that's all he tried to do," Carla said quickly. "I felt sorry for him."

"I don't see why," Jarvis said. Until their stop he looked out the window. They walked up a hill from the toy station of Tarrytown to his house. The air seemed to restore his demonic humor. He settled them in his basement playroom. "There's the family," he said, pointing to a colored photograph on the top of a piano, "Just introduce yourselves. I'll get some stuff for us."

"When Jarvis gets back," Carla said, as if she and Harriet were conspirators, "let's ask him to play his Dixieland records. He has a fabulous collection."

When Jarvis returned, carrying a tray, he was wearing a bright yellow sports shirt. He seemed happy to show off his old 78s. "Here we go," he whooped. "This is a good one."

The raucous clarinets and trumpets raged toward Harriet. She tore off great bites of ham and cheese and bolted a gin and tonic to beat back her thirst. When she stood up to go to the bathroom, she hoped that Jarvis and Carla would not notice how much she wobbled. She had to grab the back of the rattan-and-chintz sofa for a moment. However, Jarvis was at the piano, accompanying the record, body bouncing up and down in rhythm on the wooden seat. Behind him Carla was swaying in time. When Harriet returned, she joined in. "Oh, when the saints," she wailed and danced, "oh, when the saints come marching in."

183

"My, oh my," Carla said. Jarvis sent a final chord into the last scratch of the record. "I'm hot."

"Let's go for a swim," the transformed Jarvis said. "In the Hudson. Right over there." He waved toward it with the glasses he had taken off to wipe his face on the hem of Carla's peasant skirt.

"But it's filthy," Harriet objected.

"We don't have any suits," Carla said.

"Forget it." Jarvis' blond locks were falling over his head as if diabolic keys were turning them. "I'll wear my suit, and the two of you girls can swim in your underwear. I won't look."

"But we'll be wet when we get out," Carla again.

"We'll dry you out in the clothes dryer. All the comforts of a suburban home are right here."

Harriet and Carla looked at each other for permission. Swimming in her underwear upset Harriet, but it was worse to think of herself as incapable of daring. "Let's go," she said. "I just have to go to the bathroom again first." There she tried a trick Marcia had told her about at a bar: if you feel drunk, run cold water over both wrists.

Jarvis drove a Rambler. The streets were empty, but Harriet was sure that a police car was lurking near the river. Its spotlight would flash yellow and red and pluck them out of the notorious obscurity of a midnight swim. They bumped over the train tracks near the station to stop on a flat, deserted piece of littered dirt. Soft clouds scudded across the moon and went on to extinguish random stars.

The river was darker than the sky. A tree dominated the bank. Roots, as thick as the trunks of lesser trees, pronged out into the water. Jarvis wandered up toward them. Opening the car doors, Harriet formed two small cabanas in which she and Carla could undress. She wrapped herself in a towel, walked to the water, and dove. The cool water sobered and refreshed her. Reminding herself not to swallow any of it, she swam out. She submerged and emerged, submerged and emerged, moonlight catching the tips of her hands and feet. Her eyes were freeing themselves from the film that had begun to cover them. Then she saw against the tree a white mound, then a white streak, then a new heap of white, as soft as mayonnaise.

"My god," she thought. "It's Jarvis and Carla. They're neck-

184

ing. They're actually screwing around." She had to escape, to tell someone who would see the joke about this unexpected vision of lust. But first she had to figure out what to do. If she told Carla and Jarvis she was vanishing, she would interrupt their bizarre happiness. Carla's shame would make her leave with Harriet. If she did not tell them, they might worry and think she had gone under, that her corpse was floating downstream like a polluted shad.

What the hell, she thought. I can't stay here. I'll leave a note. As surreptitiously as a cautious water sprite, she swam to the bank, crept to the car, dressed, and disappeared. Damp but free, she caught a late train at the station three blocks away. Once safely there, a sense of not wanting to go home seized her like a cramp. If Naomi were in the apartment, she would be suspicious. She had begun to interrogate Harriet about phone calls from "that silly club" or "tough-sounding women." If Naomi were not there, Harriet would have no one. But Marcia Gold had told Harriet that she was an insomniac. She liked distraction and did not mind if people called her late at night. Go there, Harriet told herself. I can't, she argued back. It's too late. It isn't done. Oh, go on, the first Harriet said. Call Marcia. If it's too late, she'll tell you. Harriet dialed from Grand Central Station. "You're right," Marcia said. "It's crazy, but come on over."

Near Marcia's building Harriet was glad she had a skirt on, no matter how bedraggled it might seem. An Oriental driveway curved through a garden of rock chips; of bark; of stunted bonsai evergreens. A doorman in white tie and swallow-tailed coat gave her a security clearance. An elevator man in white gloves pressed the button of the automatic elevator for the eighteenth floor.

"You look like a pack rat," Marcia said.

"I've just escaped from a midnight swim in the Hudson after my office farewell party," Harriet said.

"Congratulations," Marcia said and closed the door.

Inside, Harriet stood agape at Marcia's apartment. She had thought that only married people or the rich lived so comfortably. Marcia had one bedroom, but two bathrooms; a mirrored wall in the living room; wall-to-wall carpeting; a long sofa trimmed in gold cords; a spinet piano; works of art. Harriet recognized some of the artists' names from *The New York Times*. Marcia pointed to a large beige abstract painting that had blue, fishlike creatures floating in the middle. "I got that at the artist's studio," she said. "It's new." Harriet saw few books. For a moment her Harwyn training rebuked Marcia, but she reminded herself that Marcia was a figure in the art world.

"Stop prowling around," Marcia said. An abrupt, cheerful brutality was common to her. "Sit down and have a drink. That's what you're here for, isn't it?"

Harriet sprawled in a corner of the sofa. She crossed her legs. She might behave with bravura unconventionality, but she could not be a slob. "I couldn't have bought this co-op on my own," Marcia said. She brought them vodka and tonics and sat next to her. "My parents paid for it. It was a tax break for my father. It's also part of their campaign to marry me off to a nice Jewish boy. Since I'm nearing thirty, they're getting pretty desperate."

"What do they think of Harvey?"

"Harvey? Don't you know that Harvey is, well, unacceptable to them. He sells men's socks on Third Avenue."

"But he's a nice guy," Harriet protested.

Instead of answering, Marcia looked at her. "Why are you really here?" she said. "For this?" And then she bluntly kissed her. Astonished, Harriet sat up. She felt as blank, as stiff, as a shut door.

"What's the matter?" Marcia kept her arm around Harriet's shoulder. She seemed quizzical. "Didn't you know what you were coming for?"

"Not this," Harriet blurted.

"But you're not a virgin. I can spot them a mile off."

"Of course I'm not a virgin, but I don't sleep with women, and you're a woman."

"I can't deny that."

"But that's not right." Harriet stared at her. Marcia looked back enigmatically. She had not moved. Harriet's body felt as if the water of the river, once cleansing, was now choking her. To fight against the suffocation, she got up as quickly as she could. "Where's my purse?" she asked. "I've got to go."

"You put it down," Marcia said quietly.

Harriet saw her purse, on a polished table, reflected in the wall mirror. She could not look at her own image as she walked toward it. "Don't run," she warned herself. "Calm down." Clutching her purse, without turning back to Marcia, she left the apartment and the tall building with corridors of gold-flecked wallpaper.

At home, Naomi was somnolent in the other twin bed. Harriet showered and tried to sleep, but she felt as if an assassin were circling her. If this was the meaning of the exhilaration she had experienced with Marcia, or with Sloan, or with other women, it was a sin, no less contagious because it could not be visited upon the children it could not breed. To have a willfully erotic Marcia touch her? Harriet shuddered. She was hardly in thrall to every stricture of her culture. She no longer wholly believed that she had to be a dewy-eyed Elizabeth Taylor, walking down the aisle on the paternal arm of Spencer Tracy, being given in marriage to a sleek, sweet Don Taylor. She sensed that men and women could twist and shatter each other; live in mutual derision, division, delusion, and deceit. Had not Elizabeth Taylor divorced Nicky Hilton? But Elizabeth had still been right to hand over her body to a man.

When she did sleep, she had one of her old dreams about Gary Cooper. He was wearing a khaki shirt and pants. He put a needle in her arm. It passed beneath the elbow and forearm. When he pulled it out, there was no pain. But when he stood over her, her body hurt as if a steam shovel had scooped it out. She woke up, restless, with a headache, her mouth dry. She was alone. Naomi had gone to work. She twisted anxiously in bed until the phone rang. Though her body was acting sluggishly, she cupped the receiver eagerly.

"Hi," Marcia said. "Can you have a drink later? I want to explain about last night." She sounded affable but edgy.

"I guess so," Harriet said slowly. "I guess I ought to know."

Marcia told her to meet her at a midtown hotel. When they hung up, a sudden surge of energy exhilarated and bothered Harriet. She instructed herself that the only reason she was seeing Marcia was to be fair.

In the hotel bar, they sat across from each other at a wooden table. Marcia ordered a double Scotch, Harriet a Bloody Mary. "Look," Marcia said, "I don't usually do things like I did last night, but I'm a part of the art world. Almost anything goes there, and sometimes I do things that belong to that world. I wish you'd forget it happened."

"That's all right," said Harriet tolerantly.

"No, it's not. I want you to understand that I'm not what I seemed last night. I don't know what I would have done if you hadn't walked out. I don't want you to spread the wrong idea of me around."

"I won't. I believe you."

"Fine," Marcia smiled. "That's settled then. I've got a date at an opening downtown. Can I drop you someplace in a cab?"

Marcia insisted on paying the check. They left together, but Marcia found a taxi quickly. "I'll see you around the club," she said as she got in. Harriet began to walk home. Sweat was staining the underarms and back of her dress. She suspected that Marcia was not telling her the truth, but she had no logical basis for her doubt. Nor was there any logical explanation for the heavy sense of disappointment that clung to her as she walked ten blocks north, then one block east, until she was home. Naomi was out having dinner with the businessman who was Joe's replacement. Harriet turned on the TV, ate part of a chicken leg, and drank some orange juice. She fell asleep on the floor in front of the TV and woke up cramped, thirsty, skin raking. She struggled up, showered, and went to bed, administering to her loneliness with habit's rectitude.

For the first few weeks with Phyllis, Harriet was nervously on guard. When Phyllis said good morning, her body constricted and her response scorched her throat. She disliked Elizabeth Light. Elizabeth lived with her parents in a large apartment on the West Side. She arrived each morning a few minutes late, immaculately clad in flowing dresses or suits with ruffly blouses. She was deferential to Phyllis, domineering toward Harriet. To please Phyllis, to defend herself against Elizabeth, Harriet toiled scrupulously. She organized the coffee. She filed. She addressed the form letters that Phyllis used to answer many people seeking help and all requests for money. She transcribed from the dictaphone. Plugs in her ears, pedal beneath her foot, hands poised over the typewriter, she was kept from being as dull as the machine only by a whiff of claustrophobia. By five o'clock her back ached, but she had done her job.

Then, on the first of October, Phyllis appeared in the outer office Elizabeth and Harriet shared. "Elizabeth," she said, her voice crisp, modulated, "don't you think that Harriet ought to start doing the monthly magazine analysis?" Each month Phyllis wanted a breakdown of the advice people were getting from *Vogue, Women's Home Companion, True Confessions,* and seventeen other competitors,

"Harriet is very busy doing things for me," Elizabeth said, her voice rising plaintively. Harriet listened, apparently impassive.

"I think she can manage one more thing," Phyllis said. "How about it, Harriet?"

"It's fine with me." She was delighted at the prospect of going beyond drudgery.

Phyllis lingered at the door. "Do either of you have any idea about what I might tell a sixty-five-year-old woman whose seventy-five-year-old husband tells her he wants a younger girl friend who lives in the trailer next to theirs?" she asked, at once serious and bemused.

"I'm sure you'll think of something," Elizabeth said.

"Tell her to tell him to get lost," Harriet said with surprising effrontery.

Phyllis looked as if she were reappraising her. Then she laughed. "Not a bad idea," she said, "but I'm not sure Phyllis Hendricks wants to lead a social revolution." She turned back into her own office.

"Doll," Elizabeth Light said, her manicured nails tapping at her blotter. "Go to the post office and buy some stamps, would you? I need them right away. I have to pay some household bills."

"Okay, Elizabeth," Harriet said. "I wanted to get some air anyway." Her resistance was barely perceptible, but she savored it.

A few days later Harriet entered Phyllis' office to ask if she could take Primary Day off the following week to get her voters to the polls for the club. Phyllis was writing. She used an old Royal, set on a battered typing table, as if they were talismans of a past she had defeated.

"Just ask Elizabeth if you should make the time up," Phyllis said. She was distracted, but as Harriet left, she looked up. "Get rid of Paul J. Flynn," she said. "The old bastard."

Elizabeth stared at Harriet suspiciously as she sat down. You shouldn't have bothered Phyllis. You should have asked me first."

"I'm sorry," Harriet lied.

"You're going to have to work an extra Saturday, doll," Elizabeth decided. "Phyllis doesn't like it if the office gets behind." Harriet gazed at her thin face, the expensively done hair, the blouse, the strings of pearls. "Don't worry about it," she said and began to type the current draft of a talk Phyllis was going to give to a women's group on "You, Your Child, and Love."

"Doll," Elizabeth's voice rose again, "do you have to type so loud? I have a terrible headache." Glancing around, Harriet saw her stroking her temples, chiffon ruffles swaying from her wrists like tiny curtains in the wind. "Can't you sort some letters? That's quiet work."

"All right, Elizabeth," Harriet said, resolutely calm.

Harriet left her apartment at six on the morning of Primary Day. She had been up until one the night before stuffing personal notes into voters' mailboxes, but she felt exhilarated. She was carrying a Saks Fifth Avenue shopping bag she had borrowed from a skeptical Naomi filled with her materials: a poll watcher's certificate; a list of eligible voters; her own index cards. Pete had told her what to do if Flynn tried any tricks. The depravity of the opposition enraged Harriet, but she was prepared to embody the Gotham Reform tactics of cool courtesy and meticulous legality.

The voting machine she was to guard was one of six in the basement of a Catholic youth club. Grudgingly the inspectors, Flynn appointees, acknowledged her poll watcher's certificate. "Nothing we can do," one shrugged. "Last election some of the girls tried to stop one of you, but the cop had to back your friend up, even though the cop was a boy who'd been in the Service with my youngest boy." Harriet brought a chair to the end of the table holding the voter registration books. When the first voter went through the line, Harriet politely, firmly, asked his name. "O'Hara, James P.," another inspector told her aggressively. "He's registered and he's one of us." James P. O'Hara seemed not to mind the irregularity of having an inspector claim his vote. "Got one of the Reds watching us, have we?" he asked as he shut the curtain of the voting booth. Harriet told herself to indulge and ignore him. Flynn followers thought the Reformers were Communists, but only because their leader misled them. She smiled at the inspectors as her father might have at a loan applicant he was going to reject, but with his customary bluff affability.

She watched for several hours, more and more impatiently. There were no irregularities, and she wanted to go check her

190

own district. She had watched over it like a tender Fury, a smiling Eumenides. When her replacement arrived, she ran two blocks to the elementary school where her district would be voting. She began to collect her harvest for Bryant and Mary, for the club, for Reform, for herself. By eight thirty that evening most of her reliable voters had appeared; to greet her, if she were there and not on the phone; to receive her thanks. But Ruby Butz, poor hallucinatory Ruby Butz, was missing. Her line was busy. Harriet pounded to her worn apartment building. "Mrs. Butz," she called through the door, "it's Harriet, Harriet Springer, from the Gotham Reform Club. I need your help at the polls right now."

"What?"

"I need your help at the polls." Beneath a naked hall light bulb, Harriet's watch showed twenty minutes before they closed.

"How do you know that I'm not Mrs. Batz, Mrs. Betz, Mrs. Better, or Mrs. Best?"

"Because every Wednesday on the phone, and lots of nights, through the door, you've told me you're Mrs. Butz."

The door was pulled open, to stop abruptly at the end of a chain. In the six-inch crack she saw a swatch of body. Blowsy, graying hair, like an old plant in a worn-out field. Shabby dress. Bandaged legs. Carpet slippers.

"Hello, Mrs. Butz," she said. "It's safe. I've turned off the voice in the set."

The chain dropped. Behind Mrs. Butz was a bathtub, an old gas stove, a table. A paring knife dangled from each rabbit ear on a television set in the middle of the floor. "Come to the polls," Harriet said as gently as she could. "We'll take a taxi. I'll bring you right back. We'll be safe and you'll be glad you've voted. Reform will make the neighborhood a better place for you."

"They're waiting for me to slip," Mrs. Butz told her.

"I'll hold them back." Then, as if Harriet's desire had absorbed and dissipated even her paralytic fears, Mrs. Butz said yes. Harriet rattled them both down the brown linoleum stairs, into a taxi, to the polling place. As Harriet watched over her, Mrs. Butz signed in. Reform palm card in hand, she entered the booth, to emerge to Harriet's smiles and praise. On the street Harriet put her back into the waiting taxi. She was handing the driver some money when Mrs. Butz leaned toward her.

"Girlie," she said, voice urgent, low, "I didn't pull any of those little handles inside the thing. If I did, the voices said they would hurt you."

Oh shit, Harriet swore. "That's all right, Mrs. Butz," she said. "Go on home." Her desire to get her final tallies spun her away from her disappointment, from such irrationality, back to the polling place, but she hoped desperately that Bryant and Mary would not lose by one vote. She stood by the back of the voting machine. The inspectors unlocked it slowly, gingerly. "Flynn and McCush," one called out, "104." Come on, come on, whispered Harriet. "Ochshorn and O'Fay," she called, "119." She had done it. She had won. Never before had Reform triumphed among these six-story tenements, these stores, these red-brick apartments; these streets in transition from stooped houses to lobbied buildings. Jubilant, she thanked the inspectors and taxied to the Mother Theresa basement. The club was spending Primary Night there.

"How'd you do, honey?" Harvey asked. He was in a three-piece, pinstripe suit, as if tallying votes were a formal event, but he was twisting with excitement. "I brought my district in."

"Me too," she said, more modestly than she felt. "Let me tell Pete." He was waiting at the front of the room by a blackboard. "49th E.D. in," she reported neatly, "119 to 104. For us."

"Oh, great," said Mary O'Fay, "Oh, great. Just greatsky." Unable to control herself any longer Harriet hugged Harvey. They stood toasting each other with waxed cups of Coca-Cola.

Then, in slacks and a tunic, Marcia Gold walked into the room. She gave her tally to Pete. She, too, had won. Grinning, she ambled toward Harvey and Harriet. Harriet's poise dropped like the pressed lever of a voting booth. Though she had seen Marcia at the club, they had managed not to speak.

Together they watched the board. Their vigil was strong and pliable enough to absorb the tension between Marcia and Harriet. Harriet no longer prayed, but with the ardor of belief she longed for her tally to set the pattern for the other districts. But, like a skin disease, the Flynn votes were spreading over those for the club. "That fucking Flynn," Marcia swore.

The room was quiet, as if silence might prove a stimulus to victory. But Flynn, promising patronage, not principle, was surviving their assault. They had liberated his outlying lands and set up a democratic government. They had drained his moat and

192

chopped great holes in his castle walls. Yet he was still alive, still the lord. At ten thirty Bryant waved both hands to get the club's attention. "I'm sorry, I'm so sorry," he announced, "but Mary and I have decided to concede."

"But only for this year," Mary cried out, as sincere as a flame. "You've all been wonderful. Just wonderful. Stay with us, and next time we'll win."

Like a zipper torn abruptly open, tough Pete wept into a handkerchief. The members of the Gotham Reform Democratic Club applauded their leadership and their hopes. The hollow retorts of their devotion collided against the framed religious mezzotints. "Let's get a drink," Marcia suggested.

"Nonalcoholic for me," Harvey said.

"I should go home," Harriet tested them to see if she were really wanted.

"Oh, come on," Harvey said. "You can't go home right away after what we've all been through."

They found a neighborhood bar. In a booth they told stories about the past campaign as if history might stoke them for a future struggle.

Then, abruptly, over her third Scotch, Marcia invited Harriet to come with her to the Gold country place that weekend. "Don't take it personally," she warned. "I'm just looking for protection against my parents."

"I'd be glad to," Harriet said. She was surprised, but she wanted to go away. She was also pleased to think that she had not wholly lost Marcia. She would rather be with her than most people she knew in New York, and she knew too few anyway.

Harvey was looking at Marcia as if she both amused and worried him. "Don't worry, Harvey," Marcia said, "Harriet will be just fine."

"To the next election," Harriet raised her glass defiantly.

On Friday afternoon Harriet told Elizabeth she would be unable to make up her lost time that Saturday. "I'm spending the weekend in Connecticut," she said.

"That's nice, doll," Elizabeth responded with rare respect.

On Friday night Marcia left a key for Harriet with the doorman. She let herself in and sat on the bedroom floor watching T.V. The bedroom was at the end of a corridor hung with pictures.

Two large twin beds, pushed together, formed a lavish sleeping space. An avocado tree dominated a corner.

Harriet felt highly-strung. Harwyn had cured her of her fears of sleeping away from home, but she was listening too solicitously for Marcia's key. Marcia was out on a date. Since that was the regular order of things, Harriet ought not to have felt so anxious, so helpless. But she did, as irrepressibly as nausea. Then, at midnight, she finally heard the apartment door open, a man's voice, a woman's voice, the door being bolted, and then Marcia, alone, walking across the living room. Harriet's body relaxed.

Marcia sauntered into the bedroom. "God, what a bore that guy is," she said. "I wonder why I put up with it. Why aren't you asleep?"

"No particular reason. I was having a cigarette and watching an old musical on TV."

"We have to start early. We're expected for lunch." Marcia grimaced. She went into the kitchen for a drink; into the bathroom for a shower. In the left bed, Harriet pulled the sheet up around her shoulders. She felt watchful. Yet, as she had waited, she had—unsystematically, unconsciously—been letting go of the Harriet who had righteously walked out of this apartment some weeks before. That Harriet had been real enough. Particularly when they first attracted her, that Harriet did respond to men. That Harriet did abhor the notion of women having sex together. Sophia's maneuvers had scared her. Poetry, fear, and ignorance had ecstatically mystified her love for Sloan beyond carnality.

But, by revealing herself so clearly, that Harriet had also mapped out her limitations. If that Harriet were to be Harriet, she would rule out possibility. Care would become constriction, constriction cowardice. That Harriet would rein in and regulate those impulses that were urging another Harriet to explore the world of the body and the self, to transform for herself those drives that had compelled her ancestors to march and struggle across a continent.

Wearing a white bathrobe, Marcia sat next to her. She surveyed Harriet affectionately, as if she were an interesting pet. Harriet stared back, as if Marcia were a guide to a new order of things she might now be strong enough to recognize.

"Still afraid of me?" Marcia asked. She was smiling, more

sweetly than she ever had, as if to show that she, too had another self.

"I never was."

"You're lying. But then, I lied to you that day that we had drinks. I do want to go to bed with you."

"But I don't know anything about this," Harriet confessed. She had to forestall accusations of ineptitude, to cling for one last time to the familiar.

"You'll learn," Marcia said patiently. "It's not hard if you don't want it to be."

She sloughed the sheet and the pajama top from Harriet's body. "Lie down," she said gently. "Lie down. It's going to be all right." She knelt over Harriet to touch her breasts, her stomach, her thighs. Harriet felt as if she were a tree and Marcia, intently, intelligently, were taking a branch there, a leaf there. Then Marcia traced the boundaries of her pubic hair and moved through it to stroke her clitoris. Harriet's body obdurately hardened. "That's enough for now," Marcia said. She lay beside Harriet, holding her, offering her some of her Scotch. To her surprise, Harriet wanted Marcia to go on, but she was too shy to ask. She took the drink instead.

During that first night Harriet would reach out and almost caress the naked body next to her. She wanted to remind herself that she could violate the space between them, if timidly. Marcia woke up once, coughing badly. She cursed cigarettes, said hello to Harriet, fell back asleep. "I'm in bed with a woman," Harriet said to herself, over and over. She wanted to see if the phrase would end wonder, would provoke cramps of guilt, but, miraculously, it did not. The reality of Marcia's body blocked the fear that the idea of its being there had once released. Flesh negated the words that had forbidden it.

Harriet thought of other women she had known—Olivia, Sloan. She tried to picture being in bed with them. It was impossible. The rules and the reasons that had enforced their chastity still controlled her imagination. It hardly mattered. She was here, in the present. Experience, less strange than it ought to have been, as if some subconscious memory were nurturing it, took her in.

The next morning Marcia kissed her face, her neck, her shoulders. She made them Chemex coffee and fresh orange juice.

195

They took the elevator down to the garage to pick up the new Peugeot Marcia's father had given her. Harriet's ease, a sense of being close to home, even when Marcia was teasing her, amazed her.

"You've got a lot to learn," Marcia said. "I'll bet you don't even know that Harvey's gay."

"Harvey's homosexual?" Harriet could still not bring herself to follow Marcia and use the word "gay."

"He's been living with a man named Stephie for years."

"Is anybody else in the club that way?"

"Not that Harvey and I know of. We wondered about you for a long time, but we decided that you weren't. Then, when I told Harvey I'd made a pass at you, he was horrified. He told me I was taking too big a risk. He also said I wouldn't be nice enough to you after I brought you out."

"Brought me out?" Harriet asked, experimenting with the new idiom.

"Initiated you."

"Oh." Harriet wondered if Harvey and Marcia had rejected her as a breathing homosexual because they thought she seemed too ordinary, but she asked Marcia who had brought her out.

"A woman who worked at a museum with me six years ago. I was almost exactly your age. I wonder if I should tell my shrink that detail." That possibility snuffed out her jaunty mood. "I'll never get married and fill my parents' sunset years with grandchildren," she said. "At least they're consistent in what they want."

"You're a marvelous driver," Harriet said, to deflect Marcia from her unhappiness.

"An old boy friend of mine, named Stan, taught me how. He used to do a lot of racing."

Harriet braked her accelerating jealousy and lit cigarettes for the two of them. "Do you really want me to meet your parents?"

"They're the price of a weekend in the country. Don't worry. We'll drive around this afternoon and go antiquing. My shrink says I have to think of myself and of what I want to do."

Built on the top of a hill, the Gold country home was gussied up in a refined ranch style. An unturning wagon wheel rested on the front lawn. Varnished pine paneled the walls. A Negro woman in a white uniform was in the kitchen. Harriet was in-

196

troduced to Dr. and Mrs. Gold in the living room. He was short, paunchy, fussy; she slimmer and more elegant. Harriet did not see them again until dinner. Do as the Romans do, she warned herself and asked the Golds about their latest cruise to the Caribbean. After dinner, she was the fourth for bridge. The Golds treated each other like distant cousins. Beyond the plate-glass windows of the living room the moon transformed the lawns into pale, gray stubble, which bore the plump shadows of Scotch pines.

At ten the Golds went to bed. Marcia poured herself another Scotch. "How did you like the family?" she asked.

"It seemed to go pretty well," Harriet observed. She thought the Golds were as boring as anyone she had ever known in Northville, but could hardly say so.

"Did you notice the scarf my mother was wearing? Didn't you think it was awfully big?" Marcia sat down across from Harriet and looked at her pointedly.

"I didn't really notice," Harriet confessed.

"Well, you should have. My father can only have sex with my mother if he ties her up with scarves. It turns him on if she wears one at dinner first. And they want me to be straight." Marcia slammed her glass down on the card table. "What would you think if your father could only screw your mother if they practiced bondage?"

"How do you know about this?" Harriet was horrified.

"My mother told me. I saw her packing once for one of their cruises. This time they were going to Brazil. I asked her why she was taking so many scarves."

"Your poor mother," Harriet was aghast with sympathy.

"I guess so. Well, it's their problem. Let's play Scrabble."

At midnight, Marcia left her in the guest room. Reading in bed, Harriet felt exhausted. Then she saw the black, cast-iron, imitation colonial door latch lift. Christ, she anguished, it's Dr. Gold. His other game is screw the guest. It was Marcia. "Move over," she whispered.

"Your parents will hear." Harriet's body was as rigid as a cut board. She wished the door were locked. Waving scarves as strong as whips, the Golds could fling it open and lacerate them.

"Don't worry," Marcia said lying next to her. "They can't hear. I'm not that self-destructive. Now tell me, if you could touch me in just one place, just one, where would it be?"

197

This seemed manageable. "Your mouth?" Harriet said.

"It's a start. Now try doing it, but sit on me. It's all right. You won't hurt me."

If she did as Marcia suggested, Harriet discovered that it was easier to touch, to be touched. Her sense of power permitted her to relinquish muscle, bone, and nerve more freely. "My God," she said, "my whole body feels funny, like there's an electric current going through it."

Resting herself on her elbows, Marcia looked as if she were pleased. "I'm going then," she said. "I don't want too much to go on here." Too curious to feel guilt, too aroused to feel dread, Harriet fell asleep. The next morning, at breakfast, she asked Dr. Gold about the high cost of practicing medicine in New York. She noticed that Mrs. Gold was wearing a blouse and necklace. She and Marcia carried the *Sunday Times* outside, Covertly, Harriet examined Marcia. In black slacks, blue sneakers, one of her brother's shirts, she looked tough, butch, a word Harriet had learned on the ride to Connecticut. But, Harriet thought, she's sophisticated; she likes art; and if I stop her I will be stranded in a desert again. She unfolded the "News of the Week in Review" to read.

That night she went to her apartment, but only to pick up some clothes to wear to work the next day. Naomi was with her father. Later, in bed with Marcia, Harriet had an orgasm. It was brief, a gasp, not a grand climax, but not even suave Jean had given her as much. This, she thought, is what people are talking about in love poems. I never really understood John Donne. The next morning, at work, she told Elizabeth cheerfully that Connecticut, with the leaves turning, had been beautiful. Later in the week she walked into the Compleat Gentleman. Harvey kissed her. He was as protective as usual, but he treated her less as a vulnerable ally than as a vulnerable coconspirator. "Your roommate doesn't know anything, does she?" he asked.

"Nothing at all," she said. Her delight in secrecy, and the fierceness of the apparent need to be secret, surprised her.

"You should get your own apartment," he urged, attending to her and yet scanning the door for customers. "I've got a friend, just a private friend. Stephie doesn't know anything about him. You'll have to meet Stephie now. My friend has a friend who's subletting an apartment. It's in the district. You won't have to leave the club."

She saw the apartment: two little rooms over a bar on Second Avenue. Marcia urged her to take it. The rent was the acceptable 25 percent of her salary. She moved in. She had a pullman kitchen, a bathroom tiled in pink, a Victorian sofa, her own name in the Manhattan telephone book. Naomi was angry. "You're a bitch and a faithless friend," she wailed. "Now I have to find someone to pick up the other half of the rent." Harriet assured her she would find someone easily. She felt culpable, but less than she would have if Naomi had not made a capital crime out of a misdemeanor and if her newer, better friends, Marcia and Harvey, had not helped her move.

Without a conscious decision, Harriet stopped sending a weekly letter to her mother. Her mother wrote more and more beseechingly to her:

Hello, darling:
    You haven't written us for a while, but that's no reason why I can't write to you. I suppose it's the curse of parents to feel more for their children than their children do for them. Autumn is really here, in Northville. Today the sky is clear blue, and Daddy and I could see the mountains from the dining room window while we were having breakfast. The big news is that your Uncle Charles may actually have sold that property of his, to an oil company, to build a refinery. They say the water of the bay is deep enough to let tankers come in, and the land running back from the shore is flat enough for a refinery. He's very pleased with himself, that his gamble may have paid off, and he may be rich. Daddy and I are sick. They say there's a constant smell around these refineries and, of course, the big ships will ruin the bay, but Daddy says that some jobs will come into the area because of it, which will be good for the bank, of course. Anne's sorority at the university is planning to run her for Homecoming Queen, a big honor, isn't it?
    Please write. We don't understand why you don't, or why it has been so hard to get you on the phone.

Much, much love,
Mommy

199

Harriet felt harassed. She folded the letter to the size of a playing card and threw it into a litter basket on her way to work. She was too busy there as well to pay much attention to her mother. Phyllis was thinking of sponsoring a series of seminars for businessmen. To be called the Phyllis Hendricks Career Workshops for Men, they would offer lessons in public speaking and other skills necessary for polished mobility. Privately Harriet thought it was dopey, but she trusted Phyllis' instincts too much to comment. Helping Phyllis plan the new project, Elizabeth had given Harriet most of her old jobs.

However, Marcia Gold, not her job, was shaping Harriet's world. After both chastity and violations of chastity that made it seem preferable, the regularity of an affair was gratifying. Harriet enjoyed the security of domesticity. When she gave Marcia an orgasm for the first time, she felt competent, generous, successful. Marcia could be erratic, but her unpredictability also compelled and tantalized Harriet. In private favor, she was happy. Out of private favor, she longed to regain it. That was more powerful than the knowledge that her intimacy would not claim much public approbation.

On Thursday Marcia gave Harriet a key to her apartment. "You'll have to let yourself in tomorrow," she said. "I've got a date."

"Who with?" Harriet tried to keep her voice steady.

"Just an old friend," Marcia told her. "'Nobody you know."

Waiting for Marcia to come home on Friday night, Harriet could not rid herself of a picture that forced itself upon her, a blurred transformation of an old scene. A man was bending Marcia back, kissing her. She was submitting. His penis was swelling to enter her. As she welcomed it, both wiped Harriet out of consciousness. She was as trivial to them as a sperm, lost in an ejaculation, drying to death in a towel on a motel floor.

Marcia returned late. "Maybe I'll see him again," she said and passed out on the bed. Harriet undressed her, each gesture a reclamation of Marcia's body. On Saturday Marcia woke up groggily. "Jesus," she moaned, "I've got a hell of a hangover. That'll teach me to go out with men I don't like."

"Last night you said you wanted to see him again," Harriet reminded her tensely.

"I must have been drunk." Marcia was sitting on the edge of

the bed, coughing. "I'll take you out tonight to make up for it."

They went to a girls' bar on West Fourteenth Street, a windowless building between a motorcycle shop and a parking lot. A burly man stared impassively at them before he let them in. "The Mafia runs this place," Marcia whispered to Harriet as they waited for their drinks. "And get a look at those bull dykes behind the bar."

At first the novelty of the bar, the chill sense of peripheral evil, intrigued Harriet. Then, as she and Marcia sat on a fake plush bench, she grew depressed. She wondered if being queer entailed a lifetime of paying too much at illegal bars; of sloshing over wet concrete floors to go to a bathroom scrawled with dull, blunt love calls; of watching heavy women court girls with teased hair.

"Is it all like this?" she asked Marcia.

"What's the matter?" Marcia answered. "You can always have fun in dumps like this."

"Maybe," Harriet said, "but I couldn't live my life with people like this."

"You'll get used to it," Marcia told her roughly, as if she wanted to push Harriet's fear away from herself.

The next week, as if to console her, Marcia took Harriet to a party in a penthouse. A tree-thick terrace surrounded it. Though it was cold, men were dancing with each other outside. A man in a tweed jacket and turtleneck asked Harriet to dance. She had never managed the hula hoop or the twist. When she tried to coordinate hips and shoulders, her body was like an animated square with its corners veering off in separate directions. But now, being invited so quickly elated her and gave her a new debonair fluidity. This, she thought, is how girls can feel at parties. She flung her ice cubes over the terrace railing. "Olé," she shouted jauntily and went off to find Marcia. But they were the only women at the party, and the sight of nothing but men, the symmetry and similarity of them, began to provoke the same dull sense the bar had the week before.

Then Marcia was touching her. "Hi," she said lovingly, "I've missed you. I want you to meet our host." He was tall, lean, his graying hair brushed as smoothly as the bowl of a silver spoon. He was dressed in slacks, a blazer, a silk scarf.

"That's a nice scarf," Harriet said.

"I've had it ever since college," the man said. "You must know Arthur Rosenberg's, the shop in New Haven. I got it there."

"I had a brother who went to Yale." Harriet hoped her signal of belonging to a respectable world would be received.

"Then you know what a small town New Haven can be." Her host took her elbow. He introduced her to a playwright. Her pleasure expanded until she felt she was in a charmed aviary. Her fellow creatures would neither ignore her nor beat at her with the peremptory, willful beak of desire. Devlin Mason, who owned a penthouse, who had money, who had gone to Yale, was homosexual. If he had not betrayed Yale, how could she betray Harwyn? He assured her of homosexual propriety and reassured her of her own.

One late November Sunday, Harriet was lying in Marcia's bed. Alone, naked, she was lifting her legs one at a time, admiring them. In the living room Marcia was tinkering with the glass-cutting machine that resembled a small guillotine. Stretching, relishing the novelty of being naked with another person, Harriet walked toward her.

"How's it coming?" she asked casually.

Marcia stared at the machine. "I think we'd better break things off," she said.

Harriet felt as if she were a glass bottle, drained, then broken.

"I can't handle being queer," Marcia added.

"But I'm happy," Harriet told her.

"That's not my worry," Marcia said. "I'm not." Then she looked up at Harriet, who felt heavy, gauche. "Have some coffee, and then get dressed and go home, would you? I can't handle this anymore."

"But why did you start?" Harriet said, willing herself not to cry.

"I didn't think it would turn into anything. I didn't think you'd be so serious."

"But I don't want to go away," Harriet said, slowly, so her voice would not crumple.

"You haven't got a choice." Marcia held a bottle up to see how it might refract the Sunday light. "I don't want to be a homosexual. If I'm with you, I am. I don't want to discuss it anymore. Just go, would you?"

Don't break, Harriet told herself. Don't break. "All right," she said. She went into the bedroom to dress. She lingered at every door, giving Marcia a chance to tell her to stop. She heard nothing but the shimmering crunch of the glass cutter. On the street, she still refused to carry the full weight of rejection. Marcia had not asked her for her key, she told herself. If she had meant it, she would have asked Harriet for her key. She stopped at a phone booth. Marcia's line was busy. At the fifth phone booth Harriet tried, the line was free, but then there was no answer.

In her apartment her body seemed numb, without the luxury of painlessness. Cursing herself for being weak, she phoned Harvey at his country place. She was jovial for a few sentences before she said, "Marcia told me everything was over. Just a few minutes ago."

"She wasn't good enough for you, honey," Harvey consoled her. "Come have lunch with me tomorrow, and you'll feel better. This happens all the time."

"I don't know why she did it," Harriet said, again wanting to cry.

"I'm going to give you a little piece of advice that's seen me through some hard days," Harvey said, as if his voice alone could shake her out of misery. "It's a slogan that goes, 'God give me the courage to change the things I can, the strength to bear the things I can't, and the wisdom to know the difference.' "

How corny, Harriet thought. "Thanks, Harvey," she said. She did not want to offend him. "I'll see you tomorrow."

After she hung up, she did cry. When she was through, she showered. She hated herself for the tears. When she was dressed, she walked to East Eighty-sixth Street to buy the Sunday paper. There, coming out of a bakery, was Bryant Ochshorn. He was wearing slacks, an open shirt, a sweater, a tweed jacket. He looked confident, handsome.

"It's Harriet, from the club, isn't it?" he said.

"What are you doing here?" she asked.

"I like to buy my mother something at this bakery."

"That's nice," she said. She wanted to distract and hold him. "It's cold out here. I live a block away. Why don't you come up and have a Bloody Mary."

He looked at his massive gold wristwatch. "You've got time

for one," she urged. "I've always wanted to get to know you better."

"Maybe one," he agreed.

"Marvelous," she said. The presence of Bryant Ochshorn beside her pulled her attention away from her sick loneliness. For a moment she was even glad that Marcia was not there. Bryant might have preferred to be with her.

"I'm sorry to say that my landlord is a Regular Democrat," she told him as she unlocked the street door.

"There were too many people like him in September," Bryant recalled bitterly.

"Their loss," she said. Miss Supportive of Second Avenue, she rebuked herself.

In the apartment he sat in a corner of the Victorian sofa. "Your place is charming," he said. After she made the drinks, she sat next to him. "Did you like running for district leader?" she wanted to know. Her voice was concerned enough to have been asking about famine. "You certainly worked hard enough."

"It was hard to lose, especially after I got the endorsement of the *Times* and the *Post*. I guess people, like your landlord, are still so brainwashed by the machine that they don't realize what the good government the club could have brought them would have meant."

"You're *so* right." I sound like Mary O'Fay, she thought.

"Sometimes I wondered if it was worth it. There I would be, a rented hall, talking to a Ukrainian club about the need to preserve neighborhood values, when I could have been home, or in Westhampton, cooking a steak for a lovely girl."

She peeped over her glass as if it were a nose veil. She had slugged the drinks, inexpertly. "I didn't know men liked to cook," she said, flirting blatantly.

"It's much more fun than going out. I get a big steak, and put a little salt and pepper on it. Then I broil it. The girl and I have a couple of Martinis beforehand, very dry, very cold, and then we have the steak, with some really good wine."

"It sounds like fun."

"I barely know you," he said. "Tell me about yourself. You have good muscles." He squeezed her thigh above the knee as if she were a racket handle. "You're not a prude, are you?" he asked. "When I saw you at the club, I hoped you were one of those people, like me, who believe in direct action."

"No," she said, thinking of Marcia, "I'm not a prude."

"Good," he said. His hand reached out to touch her sweater. "I'm sorry," she blurted, "'I have little breasts."

"I like small breasts," he said. He traced the outline of her bra, then of her underpants. She kissed the palm of his strolling hand. "You like to lick, do you?" he murmured. "Wait a minute."

He's banal, she thought, but things were too far gone for her to stop because of mere banality.

He stood up, closed the Venetian blinds, and then went behind her red easy chair. When he emerged he was wearing only his shirt and socks. His penis was thrusting through the panels of the monogrammed shirt as if it were an exhaust pipe of an expensive car. "I want to watch you take your clothes off," he said. "Start with your sweater." Pulling the soft wool over her head, she smelled her own sweat. She had forgotten to put shields in, but if she had, he would have seen them. "Go slower," he asked. "I like watching this." Then, through the cloth, she heard the buzz of an alarm. It could not be her clock. Sweater off, she saw Bryant pushing at his watch.

"What's that?"

"Nothing." Walking toward her. "I have a wristwatch alarm. It accidentally went off."

He's lying, she intuited. He set his alarm to remind him how much time he had given himself to put the make on me. However, his body began to block out her desolate suspicions. Pushing her down on the sofa, he pulled off her slacks.

"Bryant," her speech was spurting over tongue and out through her teeth. "I've slept with a woman."

"I find that exciting," he said. Then he lowered his body over her as if her torso were a saddle. His penis rested on her chin as if it were thick, purplish reins. Then it was inside her mouth, slapping and growing and domineering. I'm going to throw up, she thought, I'm going to gag. But she also wanted to suck and pull on it, to thank Bryant for being there, for praising her pleasurable shame, for blocking in her empty time. As she finally choked on the flooding bit of his semen, he sat back and sighed. As if he had gone over a leap and landed, in flowers.

"Ah," he said. "That's not a bad way to spend an hour." She was exhausted, still involuntarily swallowing. "I've got to go," he said. She watched him, snapping the elastic waist of his monogrammed boxer shorts. He kissed her battered mouth. "We'll stay in touch," he promised. "I'll cook you that steak." Then he let himself out.

He had not taken her phone number. Though he could get it through the club, one mark against him in the sincerity-about-calling column. She lit a cigarette, wondering what the smell might be if she held the tip to the vertical line of dark hair running between her navel and her pubic hair. The taste of the smoke began to burn away the taste of Bryant. She pulled her knees up so that she might no longer be tempted to see what might happen if she did hold the cigarette to her body. The idea of the rest of the afternoon and evening closed around her, as if it were baling wire. You only have to get through one night, she told herself, before you can go to the office; before you can see Harvey. She longed for Marcia to call, to say she had made a terrible mistake. As the silence in her apartment lengthened, she was bleakly pleased to think that she had fought back; that she had fucked a man; that Marcia had not forced a premature foreclosure on the mortgage of her flesh.

Yet, during the next days, she lived as if anesthetized. At lunch Harvey instructed her not to call Marcia; to remember that lightning strikes more than once; to work hard.

"But Harvey," she protested. "I didn't do anything wrong. Why did she treat me like that?"

"'Because she's just a silly girl," Harvey said decisively, unhelpfully. "Don't you worry. There'll be others."

"We'll see," Harriet was too numb to believe him. "But if there are, I wouldn't know how to find them."

"It's a big town."

"We'll see," Harriet repeated. Harvey's confidence seemed too inane for her to offer him her doubts. Marcia had taken the initial risks in their affair. She had revealed herself to Harriet. Harriet had not learned that she could begin the process of exposing her sexuality to a stranger and survive. Then, when Harriet had succumbed to Marcia, Marcia had broken her. Harriet had learned that she could begin the process of exposing her sexuality to a lover, and get hurt. She wondered if the bitter second lesson would prevent her forever learning the first. But if she did not learn it, she would probably never again have the original pleasure she had had in Marcia's company and Marcia's bed.

"You'll be all right, honey," Harvey said. "Just keep working."

On Friday Phyllis summoned Harriet to her private office. "I wonder why she wants to see you," Elizabeth brooded. "She didn't mention anything to me when we discussed the day's appointments earlier."

Harriet straightened her Harwyn wool skirt and sweater. As she walked into Phyllis' room, she hoped her old high heels would not catch in the scattered, shag rugs. Phyllis, in a dress and polished pumps, was sitting next to the fireplace, massaging her temples. When Harriet sat down she stopped, leaned back, and folded her hands. She seemed tired but reluctant to admit it.

"Do you like it here?" she asked.

"Very much," Harriet said quickly to mask her surprise.

"I wasn't sure it was going to work out as well as it has," Phyllis told her. "I was afraid you weren't going to be able to appreciate my work or my audience."

"I've always respected it." Harriet repressed the memory of the times when she had not.

"The seminars for men are going to go," Phyllis continued. She seemed to be speaking both to Harriet and herself. "I'm going to make money on them, but I can't run the risk of seeming to forget my responsibilities to women. I've got to write a book for women, about women."

"Do you mean a whole new book, not just columns?" Harriet asked. Pleased by Phyllis' confidence, she wanted to be helpful.

"Yes, for what's it's worth," Phyllis said wryly. "But I need a peg, something to hang the book on. I haven't got it yet."

"Mrs. Hendricks," Harriet began cautiously, "I know you've told me that we have to be careful about religious subjects, but people used to compare women to goddesses and to angels all the time. They don't so much anymore. Why don't you tell women that each of them has something divine inside of her that she can cultivate? That every woman could be an Aphrodite, or a Demeter, or an Athena, or a Diana?"

"Those names you just mentioned, they're not Christians or Jews are they?" Phyllis asked. She seemed interested.

"No, they're Greek, classical Greek." Harriet was growing more excited. "We could remind women that they don't have to be ordinary people. They can be like divinities. Every chapter could be about a different kind of goddess that women could resemble and imitate."

"The Greek goddesses all had something to do with feminine love, didn't they?" Phyllis probed.

"Athena, the goddess of wisdom, and Diana, the goddess of the hunt, were virgins." Harriet was delighted to be able to tell Phyllis what she knew, to bring Harwyn to this job. "But the Greeks thought that virgins had some special power."

"Like the nuns," Phyllis said. "But nuns aren't really my natural audience." She paused, then laughed, as if Harriet had pleased her. "Oh well, it's as good an idea as any I've had. We can say that Athena and Diana were like career girls who might get married any day."

"We could," Harriet said. She savored the "we."

"All right," Phyllis said, standing up. "Bring me some more research on those goddesses, would you? I need about five pages on each of the important ones. But Harriet, tell me things about them that our readers will want to know. Remember that most of our readers have never heard of Harwyn. It doesn't have that much to do with the real world."

"That's what it praises itself for," Harriet said, proudly, rue-fully.

"I put myself through Hunter at night," Phyllis told her, tone matching Harriet's. "And I hire Harwyn graduates. It's interest-ing, isn't it?"

"You've worked very hard, haven't you?" Harriet asked. She had never spoken so boldly to Phyllis.

"I suppose so," she said dispassionately. "It's late. Go enjoy your weekend." Harriet felt dismissed but not despised. She left, happier than she had been that week.

In the outer office Elizabeth asked her what Phyllis wanted. "Just some help on a new book," Harriet said.

"Don't forget you're going to have to do your usual jobs, too," Elizabeth pointed out.

"I won't," Harriet brushed her off cheerfully. At last she had a real responsibility. Over the weekend she investigated current books to see if goddesses were already on the market. In *Dear Teen-Ager,* Abigail Van Buren used literary names—Griselda, Romeo, Mr. Chuzzlewit, Brunhilde, Frankenstein—but the pagan pantheon seemed to be waiting, patient in its antiquity, for her updating. She bought a newly published guide to Greek mythology. It was hard to translate some of the raucous, tough, independent goddesses and legendary figures into believable modern terms. Even Leda, who was relatively conventional, had literally laid the eggs from which some of her children were born. Nevertheless, on Monday morning, at her office typewriter, she began typing the index cards that would be the base for her reports to Phyllis.

"Please, doll," Elizabeth complained. "I have another one of my terrible headaches. Do you have to type like that?"

"Sorry," Harriet said. "These memos for Phyllis have a high priority."

"So do the seminars for men," Elizabeth told her. "I've got to compile the cost estimates for them right now."

To Harriet's surprise Elizabeth, who seemed so whining and vapid, was very competent. "I'll be quieter," she promised. She believed in respecting the rules of office etiquette.

When the phone rang, Elizabeth answered it. "It's for you," she said, looking at Harriet with some disbelief. Inside her skin, Harriet's body flared in apprehension and hope. She still wanted every call to be Marcia. It was Bryant Ochshorn, inviting her for that dinner, but not until the New Year. He had a busy schedule over the holidays. "I understand," Harriet said. "I'd love to see you in January." But writing the date down, she shrank a little. Seeing Bryant would mean sex with him again, and the memory of that half manacled her pleasure in the invitation.

A few days later Harriet's father called to order her home for Christmas. Her Grandfather Springer was sick. "I'll pick up the tab for your ticket," Big George said. "The family's got to be together for a while."

"But what about my job?" Harriet asked sullenly. Phyllis might reprove her if she returned to the plundered, fertile lands of Northville while research memos on *The Goddesses and You* were incomplete.

209

"You tell your boss it's a family emergency," Big George said. "You tell your boss it may be the last chance you have to see your grandfather."

Phyllis' understanding surprised Harriet. "I know you'll have a lot on your mind," she said carefully. "But listen to people while you're out there, too. Try to figure out what we might say that they might like to hear."

Harriet wondered why, when people were trying to tell her something, they often seemed so simple. Had the well of Phyllis' wisdom, or Harvey's, evaporated to a shallow pool? Or was Harriet a snob, who confused wisdom with the esoteric?

"I'll try," she promised Phyllis.

Two days before Christmas the plane to Seattle was crowded. At Idlewild airport she had mailed Bryant a Victorian postcard, asking to postpone their date. She had been afraid to phone him. He might have been angry with her. Despite everything, she was glad to be going home. She had had no other Christmas plans. Shopping bag of presents crowded between her knees, she tried to sleep. Circling the mountains and hills before landing, she noticed, with drowsy shock, how many of the slopes were stripped, the trees ravaged by bulldozer and chainsaw.

Her brother Georgie was waiting for her. They kissed unenthusiastically. "You've lost weight," he said. "I was afraid you were going to be fat. Anne looks terrific, really thin."

"It's none of your damn business if I'm fat or not."

"Maybe not, but you look awful when you are, Hairy."

Twilight was ending as they drove toward Northville. The hills and low clouds were like the humpy, misty landscape of an Oriental wall hanging. "How's your love life?" Georgie asked.

"Could be better, could be worse. How's the bank? Glad you're there?" She was not crude enough to ask Georgie if he had lost his virginity.

"It's okay. Mom's still bitching about Charles having sold his land to the oil company."

"What's really wrong with Granddad?"

"Nearly everything."

"Merry Christmas to all, and to all a good night."

"You don't have to be so damn cynical. It's hard enough without that."

Don't fight, Harriet reminded herself. "I don't suppose Mom

and Dad have anything to drink," she said. Maybe she and Georgie could share the battle to overcome their parents' resistance to having liquor in their house or in their children. "Do you have anything in your apartment?"

"We can get one on the road," Georgie said. At least he was willing to reveal that much humanity to her. "There's a raunchy place this side of town." Younger members of the town's managerial class enjoyed crummy bars, the closer to the Nookagillish Reservation the better. Georgie parked before the Little Log Inn. Built to resemble a large log cabin, it was cut into the side of the hill. Inside, a hostess, in peasant costume but wearing a gardenia corsage, escorted them to a round table with a red-checked cloth. The salt and pepper shakers were little imitation tree stumps.

" 'Tis the season to be rustic," Harriet said.

"There you go again," Georgie sat down. "What do you want? Bourbon?"

"Scotch. Just because I'm in Northville, I don't have to drink Northville."

"Are you going to help the rest of us get through this Christmas, or are you going to make cracks all the time?"

"Irony has never been your strong suit, has it, despite your Yale education?"

"Oh, for God's sake, grow up."

She wondered, wistfully, what it might be like to have a brother who enjoyed her, to have a brother to enjoy, but events on a small stage to their right distracted her.

"I forgot to tell you," Georgie said, as if he might want to apologize, "'that this stage show here starts early." He ordered doubles.

A beige curtain opened. A man, in a tuxedo as shiny as futuristic metal, pranced out. "Welcome, welcome, welcome to the Little Log Inn. We hope you're all going to have a Merry, Merry Christmas and a Happy New Year. 'Tis the season to be jolly. 'Tis the season have the little log in."

For a moment Harriet wondered why the five other customers were guffawing. "And now, ladies and gentlemen, our most unusual and unique attraction: Myrtle and Her Girls."

"My god, Georgie," Harriet said, "you've really hit the jackpot this time." Four gray-haired women, in plain dresses, beige stockings, and Red Cross shoes, came on stage. Carrying their chairs and instruments: trumpet, trombone, set of drums. Acknowledging the drips of applause with an indifferent salute, Myrtle took the upright piano on stage right. "Happy Holiday," she said. Then the four lifted their heads and broached, "Roll Out the Barrel." Harriet was going to ask Georgie if he wanted to polka, but the stiff energy of the music made her sarcasm seem cheap. For Myrtle and Her Girls were musicians: ferocious, skillful, alive in their community. "They're too good for this place," she said. "They're dogs," Georgie said. "Where else would they get a chance?"

Myrtle cleverly modulated some bridge chords. The group began, "Deck the Halls with Boughs of Holly," trombone and drums growling together to parody, "Tra la la la la la la la la." As they played, laced shoes firm on the ground, their bodies were oddly beautiful. For they were alert to the brassy, cheerful world of sound, to the world they were shaping from their mocked desire for art. They swung into "Oh, Come All Ye Faithful" as if the worshipers they summoned could dance through palm boughs to adore the radiant king of angels.

"I want to talk to them," Harriet said.

"What do you have to say?"

"It's not what I have to say. It's what they have to say."

"Don't be a phony. You don't give a damn about what they have to say."

"My boss tells me," Harriet knew that Georgie would have to accept this, "that I should interview the kind of people who read her column while I'm home out here in the boondocks."

"Well, do it later. Mom's keeping dinner for us. Besides, some of the people here might know us, or do business with the bank. You've got to behave like a Springer."

They left. She was lighting a cigarette in the car when he asked if she remembered Jean Maurin.

"More or less," she said cautiously. The creep had not sent her a postcard from the Louvre.

"I got a Christmas card from him," George said. "He's gotten himself engaged to some rich woman he's been seeing for years in New Haven. She's going to inherit ten million dollars worth of stock in some cold cereal company."

"No kidding," she said dully. "Lucky Jean Maurin." Don't react, she told herself. Don't give anything away.

"Typical Frenchman," her brother said enviously.

She said nothing. She smoked. At least her brother did not expect any response from her, be it good wishes, or dismay, or the flattening sense of betrayal she was now experiencing. Forget it, she told herself brutally. These things happen.

Colored lights framed the windows of the Springer house. A holly wreath hung on the back door. Her mother and sister were waiting in the kitchen. Her mother embraced her fiercely. "Darling," her voice choked, "I'm so glad you've come. It's been so hard around here." Harriet found being touched by her mother, for the first time since Marcia had seduced her, asphyxiating. More abruptly than she wanted, she was forced to confront the possibility that while her mother had been central to her life, a subterranean current of eroticism had borne them along, to emerge in Marcia's bed. If so, how could she embrace her mother now? How could she consciously love her mother and act, no matter how remotely, as a lover, too? "I'm here," she muttered, and pulled away.

Her grandfather was in the first-floor bedroom next to their childhood playroom. He was sitting in a chair, the white sticks of his legs showing beneath his purple bathrobe, splintery studs in a breaking house. The cheeks of his round face were hollows; his hair and moustache as wispy as tattered curtains; his teeth chattered as he breathed. Big George sat next to him, reading an interview with the Secretary of the Treasury in *U.S. News and World Report* out loud.

"Hello there, girl," her grandfather said. She kissed him, then her father. "Been tying one on?" he asked. "Not really," she said. Next time, she noted to herself, chew some Sen-sen before the domestic scene.

She and her father escorted the older, ailing man into the dining room before she helped Anne and her mother in the kitchen. "Usually," her mother was angry and miserable, "he's got to have a tray in his room. Dad won't let him go into a nursing home, of course, but then Dad doesn't have to do most of the work around here."

Anne had covered the polished oak table with a white cloth. Five tall red candles were burning in each of two silver candelabra. The reflection in the dining room window flicked glassy darts and dashes of flame between the world of evergreens, soil, industry, and bay outside and the family within: the fragile grandfather; the father, carving, an edge of gold filling glittering between canine and molar teeth as he smiled; the mother, dispensing vegetables; the son and heir, drinking milk to soothe the bites at his stomach from an incipient ulcer his double bourbon had inflamed; the first daughter, Girl Friday to a New York columnist; the second daughter, university homecoming princess. Harriet guessed what they would think if they knew she had slept with a woman. They would see her as aberrant, her sexuality their excuse for severing all ties except those of strict legality and guilt. They could take courage and comfort from their own normality. For a moment she despised and envied them.

"Good food, good meat, good God, let's eat," Big George said. "Need any help cutting up your roast, Dad?"

"I'm not dead yet." The old man's voice creaked like a warped drawer.

"I wonder if Kennedy has a chance in the Democratic convention," Harriet said. Her safety lay in keeping the conversation as impersonal as possible. "Who's Henry Jackson going to support?"

"Scoop wouldn't be so bad himself," Georgie said. The Springer men knew both senators from the state.

"Remember 1952?" Harriet continued. "Remember how we fought over whether the Republican candidate should be Eisenhower or Taft?"

"Agnes wanted Taft," Big George remembered grimly. He had never liked his stepmother. She had died, unaccompanied by her husband's family's grief, during Harriet's senior year at Harwyn.

"You only supported Eisenhower because you served under him during World War II," Harriet reminded him.

"Since it's Christmas, I don't see why we can't have something to drink around here," Georgie said.

"Now that you kids are grown-up, we're going to start serving cocktails," Eleanor soothed.

"Bankers can't afford to be drunks. Don't let that bank go down the drain in a bottle," Grandfather Springer spoke. His energy and authority startled them all. "Of course not, Granddad," Georgie said.

The old man subsided. He could no longer worry if the grandchildren, whom he loved, were softer than he. The boy lacked his character. He had never had to get up at four in the morning.

214

The girls lacked his first wife's character. They never had to feed a fire with one hand and chop the ice on a bucket of water with the other. Their educations were too fancy for girls. He had told his daughter-in-law that, without much effect. It was, he supposed charitably, hardly the grandchildren's fault if they had merely inherited the land he had conquered; that they would merely inherit the money he had accumulated and earned, though in trust funds as tight as the bank's lawyer could devise. Had he not worked; hardened his heart during the Depression, taking back mortgages from defaulting friends; endowed his church; buried two wives; had he not done all this for them? Better family than the government as his legatees.

Doing it had made him as tough as the rocks he had dynamited as a boy on a railroad construction crew; as scrappy as second growth on logged-over land; as agile as the salmon purse seiners wanted to trawl and net, can and pack. But his family was less tough, less scrappy, less agile than he. Though the girl Harriet seemed after a life of her own. But had not his success deprived them of the challenges on which he had flourished? If they were less than he, was it not because of what he had done for them? Before such questions, he waited stoically for death.

Christmas Day was foggy. Harriet gave her grandfather an auto-bridge set she had bought at Macy's. "Remember how you taught me to play rummy during the war?" she asked.

"You were always good with figures. If you'd been a boy, you could have been the banker."

"I'm doing all right now."

"You're going to inherit some money from me, you know. Not much, but some."

"I know, but you've got it so tied up that I couldn't get at the principal even if I wanted to."

"You should never spend capital." He regarded her warily, as if deciding how much of his breath he should invest in her. "Spend income. Never touch your capital. Does this job of yours pay enough to support you?"

"Barely, but I got sort of a promotion. My boss thinks I don't know enough about real life."

"You don't have to spend your capital to learn," he told her.

After dinner he took off the suit he had worn for Christmas. Big George hung up his clothes. While the grandfather slept, the rest of the family drove to have holiday eggnog with Uncle Charles, his wife, and their two children in the old mansion they were having renovated on the other side of town. Eleanor fretted as they passed Penney's, the 5 and 10, Ray's Foto Shop, the drugstore, the bank building. "It's Christmas; he'll put on all his charm," she said. "But he'll have to brag about having sold his land, about the killing he's made. I know he laughs at me for keeping Daddy from investing in that land with him."

"Where did he get all the money?" Harriet asked. "Georgie, now that you're at the bank, you can check the books to see if he really got it all from his wife."

"Don't ruffle the waters," her father warned. "What's past is past."

Silver bells and red ribbon bows hung from every lamppost. "I wish to hell, Daddy," Harriet complained, "that you would use your position on the Board of the Chamber of Commerce to get better decorations in this town."

"You're over twenty-one, and on your own," her father said, "but I don't like to hear girls swear."

Her uncle was heavier, grayer. She patted his red velvet vest. "You're looking wonderful," he told her. She kissed Alice, his nervous, pleasant wife. Her cousins, a boy and a girl, hung back. Charles served the eggnog from a crystal bowl on a table near the living room fire. Beyond French doors was a patio; beyond it a lawn that ended in a cliff overlooking the fog-sheeted bay. Carols by the Salt Lake City Tabernacle Choir pealed forth from the German-made stereo.

"Let me show you something great," Charles said cheerfully. Harriet, Big George, and Georgie went with him into the den. Supporting the burning logs in the fire were huge, black andirons, each of which ended in the head of an Oriental man, mouth distorted and agape as the flames devoured him.

Expansively Charles presided over a three-dimensional model. "This is what the refinery's going to look like. I got this when I closed the deal. The refinery is going to be a tip-top operation." L-shaped jetties thrust out from what had been his beach into the water, on which the modelmaker had painted impotent white caps which would never surge to shore. Model boats were moored to the jetties. On land were squat, white, cylindrical tanks. From a series of long buildings rose high tubes, curving at the top,

216

knobs jutting from the sides. Around the entire model was a barbed-wire fence. Harriet touched it. The barbs, built to scale, were no bigger than an infant's hangnail, but they hurt.

"You sold the whole property, Charles?" she asked.

"I sure did. Construction begins this spring. I paid off my mortgage on the place and invested in the oil company's stock."

Her father stared down at the model, hands in the pocket of his three-piece gray suit. He smiled, more gently, more sadly, than she had seen even when he had caressed them all before going off to war seventeen years before. "I'll miss the beach roses," he said.

"Dad, the whole area's changing," Georgie said.

"I know," he answered. "I'm not a banker for nothing."

As Harriet inspected the model, she remembered a summer Sunday on the beach. Charles, recently married, was looking the property over. The whole family had come for a picnic: her Grandfather Springer and Aunt Agnes; her Grandmother Yates; her parents; her brother and sister. Her mother had not wanted to come, because she was fighting with Charles. Harriet's ego was lurking, guilty and shy, because of her memory of the hayride to this beach, of the kissing record she and Terry Neilsen had set.

The beach had been littered with driftwood, seagrass, bushes of beach roses. She and Anne, though too old to do so, wanted to play boat with a log in the water. Dark bark still clung to the salt-bleaching wood. They had swum out, but when they tried to pull themselves up on the log, it had rolled under them, too heavy to stop. Then Charles had come out to them, the water on his arms and shoulders shining in the sun. "You girls are too beautiful to be alone," he had said. The three of them had then managed to straddle the log, Charles between them, behind Harriet. He paddled them into shore. "Here's the captain and his crew of lovely maidens," he had shouted. Harriet had been enchanted, as if she were married to a Charles who was magical enough to transform her into desirable beauty. When they had landed, the stones beneath her feet seemed painless.

"We had some good times there, didn't we?" Charles said.

Harriet wondered which of the three men would say, "But progress is progress." None did. She did not know if each thought it unnecessary, or if, like her father, all were, for a moment, mourning the past, its rugged pastorality close enough to have been their responsibility, too close to have generated a consoling myth.

"If my dad had known how much I was going to make, he would have wanted me to make the deal. He would have been proud of me," Charles said.

"Maybe," Big George answered. "You can't speak for the dead."

"He hung himself in '32 because there wasn't enough money to support his family. I know that Eleanor and I have had our troubles, but she did a hell of a job in bringing Mother and me through the rest of the Depression."

"Hung himself?" Harriet's appalled question echoed Georgie's.

"The kids don't know," Big George explained softly. "Eleanor could never bring herself to say."

Charles touched the model. Then he shrugged, as if his gestures could, for them all, push pain back into the strongbox of silence. "No reason for Eleanor to know about my slip, is there?" he asked.

"None," Big George answered.

"I always wondered how he died," Harriet said.

"Don't cry over spilt milk," her brother told her roughly. "I'm going to get us all another drink."

During the next days the knowledge about her Grandfather Yates titillated rather than shocked her. It gave her life drama. A family suicide carried an element of dark poetry. She was able to keep the pact of silence before her mother. Dying before she was born, her Grandfather Yates had not been memorialized in the conversation of her mother or of her Grandmather Yates. Harriet could neither be released from an old burden of ignorance nor weighed down with a new burden of secrecy.

Other tensions were more severe. She had to help with her Grandfather Springer. Emptying a bedpan made her gag. She had to listen to her mother, try to sympathize with her. She feared and resented the demand to do so. Her mother's body had carried her. Harriet had burrowed into it, seeking comfort, love, food. But now, after Marcia, her mother's body was repellent. It threatened annihilation or engulfment. As she had always done, Harriet fled from one anxiety to another. She wondered how she was to obey Phyllis and get out into the world.

A few days after Christmas she and her mother were in the

kitchen, cleaning up after breakfast. Her mother was telling her about a woman whom she admired. The woman was trying to start a weaving project on the Nookagillish Indian Reservation. She was using native labor and designs. "She's going to share all the profits," Eleanor said. "She's got an uphill fight, but she's really trying to put her ideals into practice."

"Maybe I should go see her," Harriet said. "Phyllis wanted me to go talk to people around here."

"If it's for your job, dear, you really should," her mother said. "Maybe you could even tell your New York friends about the project. They could do with some publicity."

My New York friends, Harriet thought guiltily, but she agreed to try. She drove her mother's car the twenty miles to the reservation. The drizzling fog and rainclouds were as low as the tops of the Douglas firs. She crossed the narrow bridge fording the Nookagillish River. A boundary of the reservation, it was the color of corrugated boxes. In the village, she stopped at a grocery store with a glass gas pump in front of it. However, the proprietor was mute when she mentioned a weaving project. So was the Indian in the white house trailer next door with tin covering the window openings. Arbitrarily she turned left and stopped at a brown, shingled shack. An old icebox sat in the yard. Neither flowers nor bushes grew in front of the shack's sagging veranda, but a broad stand of light green bracken fern caught what light there was, which shattered the drops of water on its crenellated leaves into blue and pink and orange and purple beams.

I wonder if this is what Phyllis really wanted me to do, she thought dubiously. She was annoyed that she had not worn boots. Mud slurped over her spike heels before they punched on the soft timber of the front steps and verandah. After she knocked, the windowless front door opened. Standing there was a young woman, in blue cotton dress and brown loafers. Her black hair was parted in the middle and bunned in back. Her face was flat, plump, with a broad nose like a soft hillock in the reddish-brown skin. A child, in torn overalls, clung to her leg. Behind her another child was crawling.

"I'm sorry to bother you," Harriet said, "but I was looking for the weaving project. Do you know anything about it?"

"A weaving project?" The Indian woman shook her head.

Oh, hell, Harriet thought. Clearly, the weaving project was a wild-goose chase. Still, she hated not to do something while she was here. "It's all right if you don't know," she improvised, I'd like to talk to you anyway. I'm conducting a public opinion survey for a New York firm, and I'd like to get your ideas about some things."

"Are you from the government?" the woman asked.

"No," Harriet reassured her genially, "I'm from a private company, Hendricks Enterprises. First I just want to ask you some questions about what kind of cosmetics or other beauty aids you might use."

"Cosmetics?"

"Powder, lipstick; nail polish, that sort of thing."

The woman shook her head. "Things like this," Harriet said. She reached into her Peck & Peck leather bag and found a tube of Elizabeth Arden red lipstick. A mirror rolled out of the case.

"Wait," the woman said. Harriet stood on the porch, trying to peer through the screen, until she returned, holding a scratched tube of lipstick.

"One lipstick," Harriet wrote. "How did you learn to put it on?" she asked. "Did you read about it? Did your mother or a girl friend help you?"

"I don't read," the woman said, "but I want my children to go into town for school. The school here isn't good."

"That's wonderful," Harriet said. She admired the woman's concern. "Do you have anything else? Shampoo? Deodorant?"

The woman shook her head. "But what do you keep in your bathroom?"

"A bathroom? I carry water from the faucet by the store."

"You don't have any water of your own?"

"No. I carry it from the faucet by the store."

Suddenly Harriet was ashamed: of her fraudulence, of her impertinence in asking questions about cosmetics in the face of such daily toil. Phyllis was right. She had much to learn but not this way. "Here," she took the Elizabeth Arden tube, "maybe the children would like to play with this. You've been very helpful. Thank you for your time." She stumbled from the verandah, through the mud, to her mother's car. No running water, no good schools; no transportation—she drove home in a frenzy. "It's not fair," she exploded to her mother in the kitchen. "Something's got to be done about it." Her anger, which her mother

220

had taught her, cultivated in her, wiped away the space between them.

"I know," her mother said. "A lot of people around here think they're shiftless and drunk and lazy, but I've never agreed with that." Then she turned from Harriet back to the stove. "But you're in New York," she said, her voice low. "You don't really care about things around here any more. You don't even care about us."

"That's not true," Harriet cried out. "Just because I live in New York, it doesn't mean I'm a brute."

As if she were avenging Harriet's rejections, her mother had pushed her away, had hurt her dreadfully. But the pain purged even as it punished. Scourged, scoured, Harriet saw the paucity, the emptiness of *The Goddesses and You*. It was not enough to tell women that they might embody and animate some ancient archetypes. They had to do more; to be good as well. Whatever divinity might ultimately mean, surely it demanded altruism, some humanitarian decency, here on earth.

"I'm going to ask Phyllis to write more than just some ordinary beauty book," she told her mother, her voice breaking, offering them both a promise. "I'm not working in some second-rate place."

"I hope so, dear," her mother said. "I didn't send you east to college so you'd end up in some Northville office." Then, as if she wished to make amends, she went on, "I wish you'd tell me more about your friends. I want to know more about your New York life."

My New York life, Harriet again thought guiltily. "I have a date after Christmas, with the guy who ran for district leader male in the Reform campaign," she answered. She hated the way her voice and body tightened. "He's a lawyer."

"That sounds nice," her mother said. "I'm glad you're a Democrat. I would have been if I hadn't had to live as Daddy's wife in this narrow-minded town."

Harriet knew that her mother wanted her to stay with her in the kitchen, ritualistically helping with the food, but actually talking, coping, dreaming. Despite their truce, it was too dangerous. "I'm going upstairs," she said. "I've got to write my boss." She could not look at her mother as she left.

Two days later the family celebrated New Year's Eve. Anne

221

and Georgie dutifully declined invitations to other parties. Georgie bought a bottle of champagne. Eleanor had prepared the traditional feast: ham festooned with pineapple and maraschino cherries; salads; scalloped potatoes; cakes. Even if Grandfather Springer could not eat the vivid food, he could see it.

At 9 P.M. they watched the New Year's Eve midnight celebration in Times Square in New York on television. "Dad," Big George asked, "you going to be able to last until midnight our time?" Grandfather Springer, in his purple robe and slippers, a blanket wrapped around his legs, in his usual chair, nodded. For the next hours he dozed sporadically. The others played games; Ping-Pong, rummy, bridge. Harriet read. They ate. At eleven-fifty, Georgie went into the kitchen for champagne and fruit punch.

"Time for the countdown," Big George said.

"Daddy," Harriet protested, "we're too old for this ritual."

"Not in this house," he said and gave each of them a bell. They stood around the old man's chair, reflected in the big window, Big George inspecting his watch as if he were a doctor taking the pulse of time. "Ten seconds to go," he incanted, "nine, eight, seven, six, five, four, three, two, one, HAPPY NEW YEAR."

Then, in passion or in shame, they shook and rang their bells. Even the old man, gallant, decrepit, mouth in a wry twist, as if he were the victim of a smile or a stroke. "Happy New Year," they shouted out. Eleanor Springer went to the piano at the other end of the room. "Should auld acquaintance be forgot," they sang, "and never brought to mind, Let's drink a cup of kindness, now, For the sake of auld lang syne." Still singing, Big George went to his wife, put his hand on her shoulder as she played. Anne and Georgie, arms around each other, laughed at each other's bellowing. The old man was no longer singing. Gently, Harriet took the bell from his hand. "Happy New Year, girl," he said. "Save your capital. Be more careful than we were of the land." As if she were a child again, she wanted to sit on the arm of his chair, but he, pushing at the blanket, asked her to help him to bed. "Enough music for the night," he said.

As she was walking with him through the old playroom to his bedroom, Anne interrupted her. "Phone for you, it's long distance, a man. I'll help Granddad." A man? Her family would be pleased. It was Harvey, in the country with Stephie. They had

222

stayed up to call to wish her a Happy New Year. He could meet her plane if she was coming in on January 3. Grateful, she gave him the flight number. "Honey," he said, "I also have a message from that bitch, Marcia. I saw her at a party. She said to tell you Happy New Year." Harriet, voice low and rasping, in case the family was listening, asked if Marcia had been alone. "No," Harvey said, "she was with a new girl friend of hers. She said to tell you that she had made a mistake about herself."

"What am I supposed to do about that?" she asked.

"Forget it, honey. Have a Happy New Year. I'll see you at Idlewild."

When she hung up, she thought she would be sick. She ran into the bathroom her grandfather now used. She momentarily hated women: the stomach, the thighs, inert like wet clay, which still moved to influence, cover, suffocate, flay, seduce her. There were times, when her mother kissed her, when she wanted to scream; when the insistent arms and body, when the insistent mouth and tongue of affection, threatened to destroy her. Yet that same body could also threaten to destroy through abandonment. Her mother, once, had sat naked on the toilet. The taut bulge of her stomach rested on her legs. The coils of flesh of the navel were stretched apart, as if two hands had tried to pull them open. Her eyes were flaring as if the same hands had pulled one lid toward her damp hair, the other toward her cheekbone. "Is the baby coming?" Harriet asked. "Yes," her mother gasped. And she, Harriet, had run over the mottled bathroom floor, to cudgel her fist into the belly that held the baby that was to replace her, to scream, "Old hag, old hag, old hag."

But what was she to do now with her own flesh? That careless gift, that casual splash in the evolutionary pool. Flesh without deformity but without the grace of the great dance. Men had touched it, left. Women had touched it, left. Men and women alike were finally indifferent to her body, as they eagerly attended to their own. Who then wanted her? Who then approached as she waited, with the passivity of those who need to be desired? Harvey Draper, the proprietor of a men's clothing store, for whom her body was as much an erotic concern as meat to a vegetarian.

Her mother was summoning her, to learn who was on the phone. "A friend of mine from New York who wants to meet my plane," Harriet said, to mislead them, to protect herself. To avoid

223

more subterfuge, she went upstairs. Next to her bed were outworn books: a biography of brave Florence Nightingale; the detective stories of Nancy Drew; a tale about a chipmunk, Nibbles, that Elizabeth Taylor was said to have written by herself. In the book was the old autographed picture of Elizabeth Taylor—the delicate smile; the ringlets that spilled around the perfect oval of the face. Harriet wanted to rip off her own skin; to jaw away at the flesh of her own thighs; to yank at the mat of her scalp; to reach through her heart to release blood sufficient to smear against the mirror, over the image of the unwanted, disconcerting flesh.

She pulled at her hair. It hurt. She pulled again. "Springers avoid nonsense." Whose voice was that? Her grandfather's? "So do Yates." Whose voice was that? Her grandmother's? It barely mattered. Looking at herself she knew, as she had with the Indian woman, a present fraudulence. She saw twenty miles away the Indian woman with her children. Or twenty-seven years before, her own mother, with the discovery of the corpse of her father. There, a sparse, sensible voice told her, was real anguish.

"Fuck it," she said, conscious of the minor blasphemy in her father's house. Clearly, she had to act—more bravely, in larger ways. The job with Phyllis was a chance. She would begin to infiltrate morality into Phyllis' column, into the new book. Through Phyllis she would start to reach out, to nourish beauty with idealism, conscience with charm. She could not talk to Phyllis about her sexuality. Phyllis preferred discreet employees. Harriet would have to leave this room, this house, and alone decree that sexuality. If a man, or a woman, said that she grazed beauty, she grazed charm, she would try to believe it. She would no longer envy Elizabeth Taylor or languish for Gary Cooper. Things were simpler, and more difficult.

She could no longer submit so easily to the matrix of another's will. She need not want a Jean, or a Bryant, because they wanted her. And if a Marcia did not want her, she could still want a Marcia, or a reincarnated Sloan. Despite taboos, despite the pain the taboos nurtured, despite the bite of her mind against itself as it sought a reunion with the body, she was happier with women than with men. She did not seek a divorce from men, but if her private world were to be stripped to one terrible choice between a woman and a man, there could be little choice. She could not deny the body and its desires. Others would haunt her. When she slept with a woman, the imprint of her mother would impress her still. So, too, would the harsh, contradictory judgment of that same mother, of her family, of the world they signified. This would trouble her, but she would remember that there were more pressing worries. She would not denude the world to the flesh.

As if his soul were already scattering, each bit a cryptic message, she heard her Grandfather Springer. "I knew all this without a fancy college degree." And, she answering, "But you had to die to tell me."